COMPANY OF THREE

Jennifer MacCann is from Monaghan and worked in Dublin in publishing and bookselling before moving to Glasgow. She is currently working on a PhD on Jane Austen and on her second novel.

JENNIFER MACCANN

COMPANY OF THREE

TIVOLI

For my parents

Tivoli
An imprint of Gill & Macmillan Ltd
Hume Avenue
Park West
Dublin 12
with associated companies throughout the world
www.gillmacmillan.ie

© Jennifer MacCann 2005
07171 3818 6

Print origination by Carole Lynch
Printed and bound by Nørhaven Paperback A/S, Denmark

*The paper used in this book is made from the wood pulp of
managed forests. For every tree felled, at least one is planted,
thereby renewing natural resources.*

A catalogue record is available for this book
from the British Library.

This book is a work of fiction. Names, characters, places
and incidents are either the product of the author's imagination
or are used fictitiously. Any resemblance to actual events or
locales or persons, living or dead, is entirely coincidental.

1 3 5 4 2

Chapter One

Linda crossed and uncrossed her ridiculously long legs and drummed her finely manicured nails on the desk as she studied me with a mixture of disdain, pity and irritation. It really was amazing how many expressions she could fit onto one face.

'Olivia is not happy, Anna.'

'Olivia is *never* happy, Linda.' I don't know what came over me, the words just popped out before I could stop them. The fact that they were accompanied by a fat sigh didn't help. Linda opened her mouth to speak but then paused. She continued to stare glacially at me. Persecuting me was Linda's favourite hobby and I had learned the hard way not to interrupt these ghastly silences.

'Anna, *dear*, Olivia is the writer. *You*,' she heaved an enormous martyred sigh, 'are the junior editor. It is your *job* to make her happy, and it is not *my* job to mop up the aftermath of your attempts to do that job. I don't want to have to deal with any more upset writers—'

'What other writers have I—?'

'Don't interrupt me. I don't want to have to deal with any more upset writers so I suggest that you go back downstairs and take stock of the fact that you are very lucky to have a publishing job in this country. I would also suggest that you start to think about how you might go about doing that job properly. That's all I need to say, you can go now.'

I was just about to open my mouth and bravely defend myself from these groundless accusations when James, the senior editor, stuck his ugly mug around the door.

'Everyone for tea?' he beamed.

'Ooh, lovely, thank you James.' She was suddenly all sprightly and giggly. 'I could really do with one at the moment,' she said as she cast another icy glance at me, the guilty cause of this dire need for tea and jammy dodgers. 'You know how I like mine, don't you James?'

'Indeed I do, Linda.' I think he might have winked but I couldn't be sure. The sun was shining too brightly on his rimless glasses so I couldn't quite see.

Welcome to my world.

I joined O'Sullivan & Hackett as an enthusiastic junior editor in 2001 and by 2004 I was a jaded, battered and scarred junior editor. You could say that my projected fast-track career in publishing ground to a halt the day I joined the company. However, because listening to someone else's work woes is notoriously dull, I will summarise – I hated my boss and she hated me.

For some bizarre reason Linda had always insisted that we all take our morning tea together. I think this may have had something to do with the spare personalities she carried around in her handbag. She was the queen of mood swings, which I suppose had the dubious consolation of bringing a kind of variety into my life. I really wanted to take my tea and dodgers back to my desk where I could play a nice soothing game of mah-jong on the computer. Linda, however, had apparently dived into her handbag and pulled out her jolly head so we had to stand in the dark little staff room and indulge her in this temporary spell of niceness. James, of course, was more than willing to do this because he was a lick-arse.

'So what exciting things will you be up to *this* weekend, Linda?'

'Oh, James, you always make it seem as though I have some sort of hectic social life.'

'Oh, but you *do*, Linda.' He said all this with a straight face, but I knew what he was up to.

'Oh, that is *so* not true.' *Oh just tell us and be done with it, God damn you.* 'Well, Mark is taking me to Guilbaud's on Saturday. It's our anniversary,' she added with a girlish simper.

'Oh, your anniversary?' I squealed delightedly. 'How long has it been now, Linda, with you and Mark?' Ha! Got her.

'Two months,' she said a little tersely, but I thought I detected a slight note of deflation in her tone.

'Oh, *really*? God, that is quite long, isn't it? I'm not surprised you're celebrating . . . must be pretty serious. Do you think he could be *the one*?' All this was said with an expression of concerned delight so she couldn't possibly haul my insubordinate ass over any coals. I had long ago discovered Linda's Achilles heel and I never failed to attack it when necessary. She could well have pulled and shagged for Ireland, but underneath it all she longed to be settled in a relationship that would last from Christmas through to Valentine's Day.

'Have you ever been to Guilbaud's, Anna? You really should, you know, it's wonderful.'

'I'm sure it is, Linda, but unless you're about to spring a surprise pay rise on us I won't be going any time soon, ha, ha, ha.' James graced this quip with a slight chuckle and Linda seemed to think it was the funniest thing she had ever heard because she practically went into hysterics. Then her mood played musical chairs again.

'Well, I wouldn't know anything about the cost as any time I've been there someone has paid for me,' she said a little repressively. Linda didn't like to talk about money, she thought it vulgar, particularly any mention of the word 'salary'. I think that was why she didn't give me enough of it. She couldn't bear to think about it. Bless her.

For a few minutes she and James chatted about how wonderful she was, then out of the blue, she turned to me.

'What time is Olivia coming at?'

'Eleven,' I hissed through gritted teeth.

'Best go and prepare yourself then.' She thought this was highly amusing. James seemed to agree and offered a sycophantic chuckle of appreciation.

'You'd want to watch yourself James,' I said when we were back in our office, 'you might get used to laughter, then you might start experimenting with other emotions and before you know it, you'll turn into a human.' No reaction.

James was a pain in the ass, but in fairness he took a lot of abuse from me. He was the most emotionless person I had ever met. I suppose that accounted for him never being offended at anything I threw at him. He was thirty-eight, still single and apparently quite happy with this state of affairs — freak. To be honest I don't know what woman would have had him. It's not that he was hideously ugly or anything, but he was icy cold. Nothing moved him to excitement of any kind, except perhaps Linda's jokes. He lived for all things academic. His favourite TV show was the *Late Review*, he revered Mark Lawson as a god and he only ever read books with subtitles. The highest praise he could bestow on anything was that it was 'very interesting'. I suppose he never found a sufficiently interesting woman with whom he could have interesting intellectual conversation. Out of curiosity one day I asked him to describe his ideal woman.

'Blonde, quiet, a good cook . . . someone who likes to read so I wouldn't have to entertain her all the time.' I suggested to him that people in love often like to spend as much time as possible in each other's company and that a day spent apart could seem like an eternity, blah, blah, blah. He replied that he didn't think that was a 'healthy state of affairs'. Nothing would ever change this man. I sometimes thought that I was working with a plank of wood that could talk.

At eleven o'clock exactly the buzzer went and my stomach lurched. Olivia Henderson was the author of a particularly awful novel about a priest and a nun who have an affair, but then the priest decides that he's actually gay and falls for the nun's brother, who is an artist, and then the nun finds out, threatens to go to the Pope and tell the whole story, blah-de-blah. What made dealing with Olivia even more difficult was the fact that she was, inexplicably,

Linda's best mate. Meetings with her left me feeling as though I had just undergone some of the SAS's more extreme methods of psychological toughening.

'Olivia, how are you?' I smiled my biggest 'I'm not scared of you, you old boot' smiles as Olivia stormed into the office.

Olivia did not look how you would expect the author of hysterical, risqué fiction to look. She looked like Miss Marple. She was small and had a nice, sensible hairdo and wore nice, sensible navy suits. I could see why Linda hung around with her; she was the perfect foil to Linda's glamour, the ugly bridesmaid to Linda's bride. How wrong can appearances be?

'Anna.' No smile. She knew mine was hypocritical so didn't bother offering any in return. 'Anna, I'm not happy.'

When are you ever happy, you miserable cow?

'Oh dear, let's go through the changes then, Olivia, and see which ones you have problems with.'

'Get me a coffee like a good girl, I'm afraid we could be here some time.'

Certainly, and how many spoons of arsenic would you like?

'Milk and two sugars, isn't it?'

'You ought to know by now. You drag me in here often enough.'

I decided to pretend that the accompanying withering look on her hatchet face was ironic and tittered nervously in response. She glared at me balefully.

'Anna, I wasn't attempting to be amusing. When I *am* joking one is clearly aware of it.'

'I can imagine,' I said with a broad smile. She looked at me over the rim of her glasses for a few seconds, clearly debating whether or not she would respond. However, she magnanimously let it go.

'Now,' she continued, 'I really am tired of all these ludicrous changes. My characters are dead now, I simply cannot keep resurrecting them. Do you understand?' She threw me another of those evil glares and muttered, 'No, I can't imagine that you would.'

After a little more therapeutic sighing and casting of eyes heavenward, she continued. 'Do you usually treat authors with this kind of disrespect? I spent many months crafting this work and that, Anna, is what writing is about. I had no idea when I signed the contract with O'Sullivan and Hackett that I would have to endure the humiliation of being lectured by someone only barely out of college . . . where did you go, by the way?'

Barely out of college? I felt a momentary rush of liking for the woman.

'Er, Trinity.'

'Well, that is something, I suppose, but as I was saying, being told by someone like yourself what is wrong with my work is more than I can tolerate. Do you write?'

'Er, no.'

'I suppose that's why you became an editor then. Let me see. You graduated with a degree in English and literary aspirations, tried to write, failed and turned to editing as a second best? Am I right?'

Yes, you twisted old witch.

'No, Olivia, I never aspired to being an author.'

'Just as well, as I can see from your suggested changes that you may not have made the grade.'

Metaphorically I was banging my head off the table at this stage. I wasn't sure if I most wanted to cry or beat her to death with her own manuscript. Now was my chance to take things in hand and tell her that I was in charge and she just had to get on with that. But no! What did Anna do? She took the road of least resistance and tried to placate her, sooth her artistic feathers, suggested that we would go through the changes one by one until she was happy – which would, of course, be never.

I began by trying to tactfully explain why some readers might find it difficult to believe that a nun doubtful of her vocation and of her sexuality would go shopping for glamorous underwear in Roches Stores.

'And what is wrong with Roches?' she asked, clearly annoyed by my scepticism.

I had to tread carefully here, as Olivia could take my comments as a personal affront. Looking at things from her point of view, it was bad enough that I was criticising her work, but a woman's choice of underwear is sacred.

'There's absolutely nothing wrong with Roches, Olivia, if she was looking for serviceable cotton underwear. But she's supposed to be exploring her wicked side. Wouldn't she go somewhere a bit more . . . glamorous, and for something a bit more risqué?' I couldn't even begin to tell her how cringe-worthy I found the very idea of a nun shopping for underwear in order to seduce a deacon in the vestry after mass.

'So where do you suggest, then? Ann Summers?'

'Well, no. You've mentioned on page five that Mary was, and I quote, *someone who, in her past life, had always shown exquisite taste in the way she dressed. She had loved the feeling of soft, sensual fabrics next to her peachy skin. She had particularly enjoyed the feeling of cashmere against her naked breasts . . .* "and so on and so forth. I don't think that Ann Summers would be quite the shop for her.'

'Well where on earth do you suggest that I send her?' Olivia demanded and I realised that I had no idea where to send a potentially nymphomaniac nun for glamorous but tasteful underwear. It was with something very like depression that I realised that Mary, the fictional Ursuline nun, was having more fun than I was. It had been a very long time since I had needed any unserviceable underwear.

After three hours of intense debate and discussion, Olivia agreed to five of the fifteen suggested changes.

OK, Olivia, if you want your book to be an even

bigger pile of embarrassing shite than it already is, that's your problem.

'Great, Olivia, I'll go ahead with these and if you could get that rewrite of the last five chapters to me ASAP that would be great.'

'You will have those chapters when they're ready. Inspiration does not come on tap, it doesn't work to deadlines.'

Maybe not, but you have to.

'Of course, of course, I understand.' I was such a wimp.

'You'll get them when they're ready and not before,' she repeated sternly, and with that she stomped out of the room, colliding with a bent-over Linda as she opened the door. Her presence there didn't surprise me, I had got used to the fact that listening at doors was her third favourite hobby – tormenting me and sex being the first and second, respectively.

'Linda! How lovely to see you!' Air kiss!

'Olivia, how are you? Coffee?'

'I could do with something stronger,' she said with a huge sigh.

Judas sniggered conspiratorially and commiserated with her. She even threw a threatening glance my way before going off to bend each other's ears, Linda about Mark, Olivia about having to put up with a second-rate editor. A second-rate editor for a second-rate novelist, I would have said had I been there. Which you know by now is a lie.

Mondays were usually relieved by a visit from Trish, our sales rep, and we often went out for lunch and a moan and by two o'clock my stomach had unknotted itself just enough for me to contemplate lunch.

'Hello you two. How is the queen bee?' Trish asked as she flopped into the chair by my desk. 'Good mood I hope, sales figures are appalling, but what am I supposed to do if she insists on publishing drivel like . . . *The Nun, the Priest, the Artist and His Lover* . . . what the hell?' she asked, eyebrows raised, pulling the manuscript from my in tray.

'Working title,' I assured her.

'Well thank God for that, a title like that would be enough to force any rep with a conscience to hand in their notice.'

'Is there such a thing as a rep with a conscience?' This was James's idea of a witty quip. We ignored him.

'Let's have a little read then,' Trish said and she began to read from the stunning opening chapter.

Owen could feel the heat from Mary's eyes burning a hole in his back. He turned and there, just as he suspected, she stood.

'Owen,' she said in her low, sultry whisper. The way she said his name filled him with so much unwanted pleasure. He was filled with agitated anticipation as he waited to hear what she would say next.

'Owen,' she repeated slowly, lingering over his name, 'Father Dempsey asked me to come and find you. He needs to speak to you urgently.' But Owen could tell from her voice that the only real urgency was in her desire for him . . . .

'Oh holy mother of *God*,' Trish moaned.

'I think Owen says something similar on page sixty-three.'

'It's like some horrific cross between *Father Ted* and Jackie Collins. I need lunch, let's go.'

Leaving James behind, we went to a pub over the road and ordered rubber fish and cardboard chips. Trish ordered a vodka. I looked slightly shocked. 'Dutch courage,' she said. 'Figures are really, really, really bad and she won't smell vodka on my breath.' She downed it in one and pulled a face.

'She might suspect something though when you fall off your chair and under the table,' I suggested as she ordered a second.

'To be honest I don't care. Sometimes even *I* cannot handle Linda, especially when I've just had a blazing row with Julie. I have to explain to her that not even my charm can convince bookshops to take the shite she insists on publishing and I hate the way she continually tries to let me know that she is *really* okay with my being gay by not being afraid to touch my hand or stroke my arm a million times a minute.'

'Maybe she's closet and she fancies you?'

'Oh Jesus, that would be enough to make me run out and sleep with the nearest man. Would I be insane to have another?' she asked, swizzling the ice around in the bottom of her glass.

'Very definitely.'

'Okay, I'll settle for a coffee,' she mumbled as she crunched up the last of the ice, making sure to extract the very last dribble of vodka.

'So what did you and Julie row about, or am I being too inquisitive?'

'Oh, what do couples ever row about?'

'Wouldn't know, do tell.'

Trish smiled at me. She was one of the few people who could give sympathetic smiles without making you want to punch them. She actually meant them.

'It was really stupid. It started off with me grumbling about her slightly obsessive-compulsive need to straighten all the bottles in the bathroom and before I knew where I was she was screaming at me that we should probably never have moved in together and that we clearly aren't suited and maybe we should call the whole thing off.'

I laughed.

'It's great having such a sympathetic friend.'

I'd heard this kind of thing before. Trish and Julie had been together for three years and had what you might call a tempestuous relationship. However, despite the tantrums and the rows they were devoted to each other and the idea of them not being suited was the part that I found amusing.

'You are like two peas in a pod and you know that by the time you get home tonight the whole thing will have blown over. Anyway, you're not allowed to break up as you two are my living proof that true love exists.'

'I think I'm going to vomit,' she said, but I think she was secretly pleased.

'So is the crisis sorted then?'

'Mmm, we'll see.' In other words, she knew I was right but wasn't going to admit it.

All pleasant thoughts of Julie vanished, she buried her head in her hands and groaned. 'God, I cannot face the Gorgon with these figures.'

'That bad?'

'Worse. I can't convince her that this glut of novels she's taken on board is not the answer to all her problems. If they were good that would be one thing, but she has no eye, she rejects the good stuff in favour of what she thinks are going to be best-sellers. But I would get further talking to this chip here,' she said, waving one in my face.

Trish had worked as a rep for ten years and she was fairly successful. She had even managed to screw a halfway decent salary from the tight gits, but why she wasn't on the board of directors was anyone's guess. Everyone knew that Trish was the one with the good ideas. She, rather than Linda, should have run the show, but unless Linda dropped dead that was not going to happen.

'Now I must go and face the wrath of the Great One. Wish I'd had that other vodka.'

As I sat in the George's Street gridlock that evening for what seemed like a thousand years I fell into one of my increasingly frequent fits of dissatisfaction. I used to quite like being stuck in traffic because I did most of my reading and sometimes even a little scribbling on the bus, but on this occasion I couldn't concentrate on anything and so I fell to staring listlessly out the window. Olivia must have disconcerted me even more than I had realised.

I had been getting stuck in this same jam for three years and it had gone beyond being another mildly comforting part of my routine to being frustrating, and all of a sudden I felt a rush of claustrophobic panic. Dublin was changing while I stood still and watched. With my pathetic salary and my lack of a mortgage, car and fabulous wardrobe I felt out of kilter with a city I had once loved. I noted with a feeling of glum vindication that even the students milling outside Trinity that day seemed to be better dressed than I was. All relationships change and sometimes we just can't keep up with things we once thought we knew so well. Was my refusal to catch up the result of laziness or inability? Whatever the answer, it was going to frighten me. I was pushing thirty and no longer had all the time in the world to put things right again. I pushed these unpleasant thoughts to the back of my head, however, and concentrated instead on the fact that *ER* was on that night so life wasn't all bad.

But that evening, thanks to my housemate's mother, I experienced an epiphany of sorts.

My housemate's mother had been making increasingly frequent and lengthy visits to the house. Now I have no objection to mothers (apart from my own), but I felt I was too young to be subjected to daily doses of *Emmerdale* at levels I didn't know a television was actually capable of. When she told me that evening that she had left my dinner in the oven but that it was a bit dried out because I was late home, I realised in a panic that I had to get out of there and get something like a life.

Of course, if I had been living in a movie the director would have chosen that moment to cut to scenes of me circling many, many adverts, jumping on buses to various parts of town, getting lost and tired and despairing but finally finding somewhere utterly fabulous. Unfortunately I was not living in a movie and the big director in the sky decided for some reason best known to Himself that what I really needed just then was a phone call from Mother. I would have ignored the phone as I recognised her ring but my housemate's mother got to the phone before I did and there was no way one mammy was going to lie to another mammy and tell her I was out.

Phone calls from my mother usually followed the same pattern of me listening to her telling me about my many wonderful cousins who were all lovely and partnered and sprouting babies. They never got drunk, headaches, bad moods, hangnails or any of the usual symptoms of being human. As for my brothers, well, they were different; they were bloody men so they could do no wrong in Mother's eyes. One of them was currently living in a squat in Zurich while supposedly attempting to pursue an acting career. No point trying to tell my mother that Zurich was not where most aspiring actors made their way. The other was on holidays with his wife in outer Mongolia or somewhere like that. Lovely, I was happy for them. But why couldn't she just leave me to be the dull one in the family? I was neither exciting like my brothers nor perfect like my cousins. So I couldn't win, really. But I didn't mind. Over the years I had become immune to all this. Well, almost. At that particular moment in time, I wasn't feeling particularly hardened.

'Hello dear, it's your mother.'

I had long ago discovered that the trick to surviving phone calls from my mother was to dive straight in and ask as many questions about everyone else's life as possible in the hope that she might be deflected from asking too many about mine.

'How is David?' (*Moved to Paris.*)

'Where are Paul and Geraldine?' (*In Uzbekistan.*)

'How is Sheila?' (*Six months pregnant.*)

'How is Claire?' (*Engaged.*)

'How are the twins?' (*Both pregnant and engaged,*

18

one to a writer, the other to an organic farmer in West Cork.)

'How is John?' (*Separated, but at least that meant having been married.*)

'How are you?' (*Mad.*)

She took about twenty minutes to fill me in on how fabulous everyone else was, so I had time to gather my thoughts. I could have invented an interesting life for myself just to keep her happy, but really I couldn't be arsed. The only way of rebelling against my mother was to not rebel. My boring life irritated her, so I was happy to make my life even duller than it already was.

'Any news?' she asked.

'No.'

So that was that particular conversation over and done with. Now she could get back to telling me about how marvellous everyone else was. And she did. I eventually got rid of her by telling her that I had a huge pile of washing and ironing to do, and with that she let me go.

Chapter Two

Shortly after my revelation I started flat-hunting, convinced in my newfound enthusiasm for life, etc. that I would have a fantastic new place in no time at all. How wrong I was. I had been offered places but there was always something that made me tell them that I had found somewhere else: house pets, a psychotic housemate or the lack of a vegetable rack in the kitchen. Of course this was the sweet charm of stasis weaving its spell over me, but I was determined not to succumb to the easy option of staying put and equally determined to take the very next place that was offered, regardless of who or what I had to share with.

After eight weeks of fruitless searching, my enthusiasm had taken a serious battering. At the beginning of the ninth week I circled the only new ad in the *Herald*, made an appointment and turned up the obligatory two hours too early. When I arrived I thought there must have been some mistake. The advertisement had been for a single room in Phibsboro at €300 a month. I was expecting to view a box room in a tip the size of a Mini Metro. What I was not expecting was a rather nice three-story house with a basement. I rang the bell, full of suspicion. The door was opened by a stunningly beautiful woman. She was like a heroine from a pre-Raphaelite painting – tall, willowy and with a head of the most magnificent hair I had ever seen. It was long, abundant, curly and the colour, well, I can only describe it as the colour of autumn leaves. I guessed her to be roughly my own age – in other words, ancient.

'Hi,' she beamed at me, 'you're really early, that's great.'

She ushered me in with a flourishing wave of her arm and introduced herself as Angela. I used to take instant likes and dislikes to people. I prided myself on my infallible instincts about people and I knew from the second she waved me in the door that I was going to like her.

'I hope you're going to like it here,' she said as though she had already made up her mind about me. 'This is the sitting room,' she began immediately, whizzing me through all the rooms in the house at breakneck speed, 'here's the kitchen, washing machine, cooker, blah, blah, blah. I own a bookshop, by the way, small; I sell books on new age stuff, alternative health, that kind of thing. The house has been professionally feng-shuied, you know. Can you tell?'

I thought 'no' and said 'yes'.

'Rubbish, you cannot. It's all a load of bollocks really.'

And with that we went upstairs. She showed me two rooms. One was a lovely, large, sunny one. The other was a dreaded box room.

'I'm afraid you'll have to make do with this for a while, I can't afford furniture for the other room just yet.'

I didn't care, the rest of the house was nice and she seemed to have a bit more life in her than my seventy-five-year-old housemate. I think I deliberately forgot to question her about the signs of life in the room. The bed was made up and there was a rucksack of clothes on the floor. When she asked me if I wanted to take it I said yes a little too eagerly. Of course I asked her if she didn't want to see other people first, but no, she thought I seemed relatively sane and she really couldn't be bothered with any more flatmate-hunting stress. Angela suggested we celebrate by opening a bottle of wine.

Her wine collection was a revelation. For me the idea of a wine collection had always seemed like a contradiction in terms. I got a bottle, I drank it.

You could have flooded the entire north side of Dublin with all the wine in Angela's kitchen.

'So now tell me all about yourself, what do you do?' she asked as she uncorked an expensive-looking bottle of red.

'Isn't that usually the first question people ask when they're renting out rooms in their home? I could be a lap dancer or a drug dealer or anything.'

'Well, you don't look like either of those and I actually have a knack of being able to guess people's professions. Now let's see,' she said, taking a good look at me. 'Mmm, all black clothes so you're not an accountant or anything like that. They usually wear non-creasing polyester suits from M and S. Only architects or editors wear that much linen.'

'Bingo, I'm a junior editor,' I laughed.

'Really? God, I *am* good. Interesting job I'd say?'

'Nope. Well, I'm sure it is if you get some interesting stuff to edit. As a junior I get the dross that the senior editor doesn't want. At the moment I'm working on a novel about a priest and a nun who are having an affair. The nun's a bit oversexed, as is the priest, who decides at the last minute that he is in fact gay and in love with the nun's equally nymphomaniac brother.'

'Sounds very . . . have some more wine!'

The wine was delicious and one thing led to another bottle and then another and before I knew what I was about I had missed my last bus home.

Angela wouldn't hear of me ordering a taxi and insisted that I stay the night in my 'new home'. I reminded myself of my resolution to live a little and I reckoned that sleeping in my underwear in a strange house was a fairly good way to start. So I fell into bed in my soon-to-be new room and quickly drifted off into the sleep of the dead.

At about four o'clock in the morning I was woken by the front door opening and closing, followed by some scuffling about in the hall. I was slightly puzzled, but several glasses of wine can sometimes encourage you to ignore potential danger and so I convinced myself that it was probably nothing and tried to get back to sleep. However, when I heard footsteps coming up the stairs the old brain was jolted into gear and I froze. I leapt to the obvious conclusion: that someone had broken in. I was so paralysed with fear that I didn't even have the gumption to call out for Angela or at least arm myself with my trainers. Also the fact that I was in my underwear was a hindrance. No burglar was going to see me in my washed-out Dunnes Stores underwear. Pulling the duvet over my head seemed like the only sensible thing to do.

The steps got closer and closer and *OH* my *GOD* they were coming into my room, coming over to the bed, trying to get into the bed!

'Get out of my bed!' I screamed as loudly as my panic-stricken tonsils would let me.

'Jesus Christ, what the . . . hang on . . . *your* bed?' a confused male voice asked me. 'This is *my* bed, who the hell are you?'

'I'm Anna, who are you?'

'This is no time for introductions and this, by the way, is *my* bed so if you would just hop out now we'll say no more about it.'

I gathered from his slightly slurred speech along with the fact that it didn't dawn on him to turn on the light that he was as sozzled as I was. Obviously I was not going to make this helpful suggestion given the underwear problem.

'Come along now, off with you.'

I was about to yell for Angela when he suddenly exclaimed, 'Shite, Angela told me about tonight. You're not by any chance the new flatmate, are you?'

'Got it in one, pal. Now that we've cleared up the confusion could I ask you, whoever the hell you are, to get out of *my* room or I'll scream for Angela.'

'Oh you won't wake her, she would sleep through a nuclear explosion going off under her bed,' he said affably. And with that he stumbled out of my room and noisily made his way downstairs.

I awoke the next morning at the ungodly hour of eight o'clock, dressed, groped my way to the bathroom, looked in the mirror and saw that I was looking particularly unlovely. I couldn't even articulate a grunt of disgust as my tongue was glued to the roof of my mouth. I had discovered through trial and error that the only cure for this

25

was orange juice, so I trundled downstairs in search of some but because of my fuddled state I wasn't too sure where I was and so I walked into the sitting room by mistake.

In my stupor I had forgotten about the previous night's little adventure, but the reminder lay on the sofa, resplendent in underpants and socks. He was lying in what should have been an ungainly mess of legs, arms and duvet but he managed to make lying drunkenly on a sofa look graceful. This is what I had yelled at to leave my bed? He didn't seem to be particularly tall but he was very definitely perfectly formed with an olive-skinned, dark-haired Mediterranean complexion, and I confess to a tiny stomach lurch.

I have no idea how long I stood there drinking in all that loveliness, but it was obviously long enough for him to sense that someone was in the room as he woke up, farted, yawned, leered at me groggily and exclaimed in a gravelly voice, 'Another redhead, lucky old me.'

And so the Adonis illusion was shattered. I gave him the most withering look I was capable of at that hour and in that state and went off in search of orange juice. I was very thankful indeed that he hadn't seen me in my underwear.

I stumbled into the kitchen to inspect Angela's fridge. There was all sorts of weird and wonderful stuff in there – seaweed, odd-looking bean-type things and various foreign vegetables, but no shagging orange juice. If the wind changed my mouth was going to stay that way forever.

'Whatever it is you're looking for, you won't find it,' said a voice behind me. I jumped a little as I hadn't heard him come in. I turned around to say good morning and . . . God almighty, could he not have put a few more clothes on? His semi-nakedness was making me feel a little nervous and I felt myself getting a bit flushed.

'Nope, Angela is something of a freak when it comes to food. She goes through phases and right now it's a healthy one so unless you're looking for soya milk or seaweed you won't find it. She does, however, own one of these.' Now I had to turn around. The 'one of these' referred to a juicer.

'I'm fine, thanks, don't really want anything, I'd best get home.'

'Hang on, last night you were adamant that *this* was home. I'm confused. Don't you want me to squeeze you some juice?' He was smirking at me in what I think was supposed to be a suggestive manner.

'No, I'm fine, thanks.'

'I'm sure you are but you look like a thirsty girl to me. Allow me.' He stretched one very dark arm across me and into the fridge and whipped out a bowl of fruit and was whizzing it up while I stood and dumbly watched.

'Oh for God's sake, Marcus, how often have I asked you to put your bloody clothes on in the morning!'

It was Angela, looking slightly less pre-Raphaelite than the night before. She slumped into a chair and her head went down onto the kitchen table with a painful-sounding clunk, her hair looking like a small dog lying on the table. Marcus! What kind of stupid name was that? No doubt he had brothers called Giles and Sebastian.

'Okay, watch this,' said Marcus. He handed her a glass of his concoction. She downed it in one and I tell you it was like a miracle. The transformation was unbelievable. The smiling, beaming Angela returned. 'Ta da!' he exclaimed.

'So how are we all this morning? Anna, allow me to introduce you to Marcus.'

'Yeah, we've met.'

Angela got up and busied herself in her fridge of horrors.

'I think she likes me,' he said with a smirk.

'Of course she does, who wouldn't?' She gave him a huge hug. I decided it was time to make a tactful escape.

'Well, time for me to exit stage left. Thanks for the juice, nice meeting you, Marcus.'

'Likewise.' He smiled, unsuggestively this time.

'Sorry,' she whispered, 'I forgot to warn you about Marcus.'

'Warn me? Why, is he a serial slimer?' She looked a little puzzled.

'Marcus, slimey? That's hilarious. No, no, he's a real sweetie, I've known him for years, I met him

28

during my brief stint in art college. I dropped out because I'm a lazy fecker but he went on to do graphics. I suppose you could say that he's my best mate. Anyway, I'll talk to you again soon. I'd better get ready for work, Aoife is opening for me. Oh, keys. . . .' She rummaged around in a bowl on the table by the door, handed them to me with a 'move in whenever' and a breezy wave of her arm.

As the room was available straight away I decided to forgo my deposit on the old place and move in straight away. However, I thought it was necessary to clear up one or two details before I signed, sealed and delivered, so to speak. In other words, I needed to know if Adonis was going to be a permanent fixture.

'He won't be staying long . . . I hope. I mean I love him dearly, but I couldn't share with a guy, no farting, drying knickers in the bathroom or wandering around in a towel.' I suspected that Marcus wouldn't object to the latter at least.

'He's just split from his fiancée,' she explained in a confidential hushed tone, glancing back anxiously towards the kitchen. 'I offered him a place to stay until he found somewhere more permanent. The split was messy, though if you ask me it was no bad thing, as Isobel was a bit of a slapper and a total bitch.' I laughed and couldn't help telling her that this was neither the language nor the sentiment you'd expect from a purveyor of new age books.

29

'Bollocks, a tart's a tart whatever way you look at it. Though of course, he two-timed her,' she added hastily in an odd tone of voice. '*That's* the real reason they split.'

Once I had established that I would be sharing a bathroom with Marcus for a limited period only I was happy. I went back to my old house and broke the bad news. I packed my stuff on Sunday, drank a farewell cup of tea with the mammy and left for my new place and – I hoped – my new life.

There was no Marcus that Sunday evening so I could relax. I don't know what exactly I was expecting from my new place, but that evening I felt as though I was in a more normal home than I had lived in for a long while. There may have been no riotous party that night, but something told me that the dullness was lifting and that things might finally start to change.

Chapter Three

Monday morning arrived with a sledgehammer and shattered my newfound contentment. Changes may have occurred on the home front, but unless the premises of O'Sullivan & Hackett Publishing had been burned to the ground over the weekend, I still had to go to work.

I had a pile of shit in my in tray that you would not believe. As soon as I was finished with the nun and the priest and the Pope, I had to face the novelised memoirs of a soon-to-be released jailbird with dodgy paramilitary connections who had almost finished a five-year sentence for manslaughter. I had already communicated with him by letter and things were getting intense between us. He thought I was his pen pal rather than his editor and I think he was developing an epistolary crush on me. He frequently suggested that we meet for dinner when he got out, which did make me nervous, but on the other hand, I was curious to know were an ex-con would take a girl for a top night out.

'Well Anna, my dear, and how are you this morning?' Linda came sweeping in that morning in a breezy, magnanimous mood, so sweet she practically gave off the scent of roses. 'And what did *you* do with yourself over the weekend?'

'Moved house.' I usually tried to keep my responses to Linda's questions as brief as possible, as lengthy answers could lead to conversation.

'Oh lovely, at least you did *something* for a change. Well,' she said, 'look what the post has brought you.' She handed me a letter with a stamp on it declaring that it had passed the censor at Mountjoy. Tony. Again.

'You seem to have a bit of a fan there, Anna. Maybe you could get together with him when he gets out.' She tittered hysterically at her joke. James obliged, as he always did, by doing the same. I ignored them and placed the letter in my in tray, saying that I would save the treat for my morning tea, which I thought was a rather cunning thing to do as it would not only get me out of having to share my break with Linda and James, but would also impress them both by working through my break.

And so I brought my tea and three consolatory chocolate digestives back to my desk two hours later and prepared myself for Tony time.

Dear Anna,

Today I was feeling depressed and I wrote this poem and I thought I could include it somewhere in the book. What do you think? I'd be very grateful if you could let me know if you think it's any good.

Life is pain
That is what I have learned
I look at the outside world from the dark shores of
DESPAIR
And
HATE
That comes in the night on
Dark, silent wings.
Full of
DREAD
I wish I was
DEAD.

All the best,
Tony xx

Well, there was no confusion about how he felt.

I got home quite late that night as I momentarily forgot that I had moved house and got on the wrong bus. I only realised my mistake when I reached the terminus, which was, I think you'll agree, a brilliant way to end a fabulous day.

When I eventually got home I was greeted by the sound of a male voice singing rather loudly. I headed for the kitchen and there was Marcus cooking up a storm. He had the radio on and was singing over some opera in perfect Italian and with what I had to grudgingly admit was a half-decent voice. He heard me, turned around and continued singing *at* me. Feeling slightly uncomfortable at being serenaded I buried my head in the fridge looking for something to eat. Gone were all the strange things of Saturday morning and in their place were normal foodstuffs such as chicken, beef, cream, cheese, butter, herbs and recognisable vegetables.

'What happened here?' I asked.

'Angela won't take money off me while I'm here so I persuaded her to let me cook as a sort of payment. I took the liberty of stocking the fridge.'

'But all this meat and high-cholesterol stuff, isn't Angela vegetarian and healthy?'

'Not at all. She pretends to be, feels she has to make an attempt to live the lifestyle she sells, but wave a steak under her nose and she'll salivate just like any other carnivore.'

'And where am I supposed to fit my stuff?' I asked.

'Oh,' his face dropped a little. 'I'm afraid I was including you in the deal. I'm gate-crashing your house as well so I thought I would cook for us all.'

'There's no need to bother about me . . . I'm sorry, that sounded very ungracious. I really meant that there was no need as I wasn't expecting it and you don't have to, I've only just moved in, it's not really my home and—'

'I know what you meant,' he interrupted with a smile. It was another normal smile; that made two in three days. 'But you don't know what you'll be missing if you don't eat my offerings, they're usually delicious.'

'You're very modest, aren't you?'

'And you're very sarcastic. I don't believe in false modesty. I'm a good cook. So what do you think of my singing then?'

'Very nice.'

'Oh come on, you can do better than that. How about "magnificent" or "beautiful". You don't much care for me and my singing at the moment, but you will one day. I'm sure of it, you'll be *begging* me to sing to you.'

'Tell me, is it very tiring?'

'Is what tiring?'

'Carrying that huge ego around with you all day.'

He just laughed at me. He was as unprovokable as he was provoking.

'So is that bottle for drinking or just for decoration?' he asked, eyeing the bottle I was clutching. I opened it, poured two glasses and took mine in to watch *Eastenders* because some habits die hard. He continued to sing loudly, which I found irritating as I couldn't hear Pauline properly.

Angela came home shortly after that and politeness made me follow her into the kitchen.

'How's Anna, and how's the master chef?' she asked as she put her arm around his waist and leaned her head on his shoulder for a few seconds. They were almost the same height but she was a smidgen taller. He smiled back affectionately.

'Fine, thanks.'

'Any word from you know who?'

'Not today.'

She stroked his back, then pulled away as though she had just remembered that there was someone else in the kitchen who might feel slightly uncomfortable at all this affection.

'Can I have some?' she asked, gesturing at the bottle.

'Help yourself, though I can't answer for the consequences of your drinking cheap plonk.'

'I'll drink anything that's going. This,' she said, gesturing at the bulging wine rack, 'is thanks to my parents. They give me decent bottles for birthdays, Christmas, et cetera. They're in the trade. So what are we eating tonight then?'

'Green curry.'

'Made from scratch or did you cheat and use a jar?' she asked, looking in the the bin for evidence.

'From scratch, *of course*.'

'Isn't he great?' enthused Angela. Really, the fawning over Marcus's brilliance was getting a bit much but I kept my mouth shut.

It *was* delicious and I showed my appreciation by having a second helping. He looked at me with a mixture of confusion and admiration.

'What?' I asked nervously. Had I committed some sort of faux pas?

'I've never met a woman with as large an appetite as yours.'

'I'm a genetic mutant, did Angela not tell you? I don't even know how many calories there are in a rice cake. Tragic, really.'

All he said in reply was that liking his food was my first step on the road to liking him.

As Marcus had cooked, Angela volunteered her services and mine to do the washing up. He drifted off into the sitting room with a cup of tea made with love and devotion by Angela.

'Ah, he's really great, isn't he?' Angela asked all of a sudden as she attacked a particularly murky pot with a scrubber.

'He seems okay.'

'Okay? He's great,' she beamed at me.

'Well, I know the ability to cook is an unusual trait in a man all right. . . . '

'Ha ha. Don't worry, he'll soon charm you into adoration.'

'I'm not that readily charmed,' I laughed. 'Nor am I given to adoration.'

'Famous last words. Besides, no one has so far managed to resist his fatal charm.'

'So I gather he has a bit of a reputation with the ladies?'

'That,' she smiled ruefully, 'is putting it mildly. One twinkle from those eyes of his and most women fall into a swoon on the spot.'

'Surprised I'm still upright and conscious then.'

'Oh, be warned, our Marcus loves nothing better than a challenge, so you'd want to polish up that charm-immuno shield. The more you resist, the greater the charm offensive.'

'Never mind, I'm ready . . . and armed,' I added, flicking the damp dishcloth at her with a flourish.

'Armed for what?' asked Marcus. He had crept up behind us without our noticing.

'Jesus, Marcus, you should have been a nun!' Angela shrieked.

'There was a slight, or should I say, ahem, major impediment to that particular career path, apart from my general godlessness, that is.'

'Don't be crude,' Angela snapped at him. 'What I mean is that you have an unnerving ability to sneak up on people unexpectedly and at inappropriate moments. Did you go to a convent by any chance Anna?'

I nodded and visibly shuddered at the memory.

'Do you remember,' she continued, 'when you'd be talking about sex or body parts or whatever, and they would just manifest themselves at your shoulder and ask you what you were talking about, knowing full well what you were talking about as they had just appeared precisely *because* they had heard what you were talking about.'

'Yep, and they had heard it despite having been on the other side of the convent just as you said it. I used to wonder if they actually bugged the rooms – it was an unaccountable phenomenon.'

'I'm sure there was a logical explanation, Agent Mulder,' Marcus chipped in.

'Well, you'd think, wouldn't you, but I'm convinced that all nuns had an invisible hover board which was activated by swear words and the like – which, incidentally, it could detect from at least six miles away. Even a *"fu – "* was enough to activate these boards and so the nuns could appear just as you were adding the *" – ck".'*

'Ah, the joys of convent school,' Angela sighed.

'By the way, what *were* you fending off, Anna?'

'You,' chirped Angela before I had a chance to answer. 'I was telling her how women can run but they can't hide from your deadly charm, my dear.'

'No woman has ever run from my charm.'

'There's a first for everything.' At last I had found a cue for a smart-assed comment, thus saving my dignity.

'Anna claims to be totally immune to charm.'

'That's ridiculous … just you wait.' He turned and shook his fist threateningly at me and then ambled off happily back into the sitting room with more tea.

'I hope I haven't embarrassed you,' Angela said with a sheepish smirk. 'But I wouldn't worry if I were you. This kind of thing is water off a duck's back to him.'

To him perhaps, but not to me.

Chapter Four

The only thing about my exciting life that I have not yet shared is Tom. I don't really know what to call Tom. If I referred to him as a boyfriend I would have to surround that term with a particularly sturdy pair of inverted commas.

I met him at a party Trish threw for Julie's thirtieth. He was quite tall and good looking in a clever, James Spader-ish sort of way. He was neither very dark nor very fair. He looked like a college professor that all the girls get crushes on simply because he's under forty and still has most of his hair. He had a certain air about him that I found very attractive – though I admit that I had had quite a bit to drink that night. He seemed shy and reserved, yet at the same time he gave off the impression of being quietly confident. I imagined him to be the type you had to get to know you before he opened up – a sort of brooding, tortured soul, with a loving heart buried deep beneath multitudinous layers of disappointment and anguish – or something to that effect. And the more I made up his character for him, the more attractive I found him. But he told me quite a bit about himself that night and shattered my illusions in the process.

As it turned out, Tom was not a brooding soul but rather a maths lecturer in UCD who was currently writing a 100,000-word first person narrative with only two characters. I ought to have known better than to imagine that a would-be novelist would be interested in anything other than my editing 'skills'. I had long ago learned to avoid these types at social occasions, but Tom's good looks and the sorry state of my social life persuaded me to ignore the voice of sense that was shouting inside my head.

Before he left he asked me for my number and I willingly gave it to him, expecting never to hear from him again. Being asked for my number, though, was an event so rare, I lived off the excitement of it for at least a fortnight afterwards. By the third week, however, my pessimism seemed to have proved itself right. By the Wednesday of the fourth I had forgotten all about him, so you can imagine my surprise when, five and a half weeks after the party, he called. Now most normal people would consider a five-and-a-half week wait to be somewhat unflattering and even a little rude. However, being stupid and bored, I said 'okay' to his suggestion that we meet for a drink.

When we did meet up, Tom talked about how his book was progressing and I listened. Then we met up again, Tom talked about his book and I listened. Then we met up again, Tom talked about his book and I listened . . . . By the fourth evening I decided that it was make or break time with Tom.

We arranged to meet, as usual, in the Long Hall on George's Street at eight o'clock. Just like on the previous three occasions, I arrived before him – despite being twenty minutes late. I ordered two gin and tonics and sat down, putting the second gin opposite me. The reason for the second drink was my old-fashioned hatred of sitting in pubs by myself. If forced to do it, I always buy a second drink. It acts as a clear sign to people that I'm waiting for someone and as a warning not to ask if the other chair is taken. Though of course there was always at least one jester with a ready quip about taking my invisible friend out for a drink.

In order to pass the time I pulled an old favourite, *Persuasion*, from my bag and began to read while waiting for the unpunctual Tom. I turned to Wentworth's letter.

You pierce my soul. I am half agony, half hope. Tell me not that I am too late, that such precious feelings are gone for ever. I offer myself to you again with a heart even more your own than when you almost broke it, eight years and a half ago. Dare not say that man forgets sooner than woman, that his love has an earlier death. I have loved none but you.

Anne and I didn't have enough time to recover from this before Tom arrived.

'Hello,' he smiled, 'how are you?' No apology for the fact that he was forty minutes late.

'I'm fine, thanks,' I said, sounding a little breathless as I quickly shoved the book back into my bag. Now for most normal people this action would have offered a perfect conversational gambit. He might, for example, have asked 'What are you reading?' or 'Oh, is it good?' or even 'Are you a great reader then?' Unfortunately, Tom did not appear to be a normal person. As he sat down he noticed the gin and tonic sitting in front of him.

'Oh, I don't drink gin . . . um . . . .'

'No? Never mind, I do,' I said as I reached across for it. Tom was a firm believer in going Dutch and he had unsubtly woven into the conversation on our first date a diatribe against rounds and various other kinds of drink buying.

'So how are you then?'

'Fine, thanks. And you?'

'Grand, grand . . . .'

Silence was settling down for another cosy night in between us and I knew that once again it would be up to me to kill it, so with great reluctance and an enormous internal sigh I asked him to tell me how he was getting along with the tome. The transformation brought about in Tom by the phrase 'your book' was staggering. His little face lit up, reminding me that he had an extremely attractive smile – it was boyish and a little shy but very sweet.

'Oh, I'm really glad you asked as it seems to be going quite well at the moment – touch wood – and I was hoping that you would let me run a few ideas past you. You're the expert after all,' he chortled.

'Oh Tom, you are *such* a flatterer.'

He suddenly looked completely discombobulated. Clearly he didn't understand that an attempt at humour in conversation often prompts one's interlocutor to a similar attempt.

'Tell me all about it then,' I said with another inward sigh, but I think that a little bit of this one might have escaped.

'Well, the thing is . . . .' And off he went. My brain vaguely registered 'problems with first person narration', 'character deliniation', something about 'refraction and reflection' and I could have sworn he said 'sandwiches', but that could just have been me as I was feeling a bit hungry at the time.

I stared at him as he talked (on and on and on) and hoped that he wouldn't notice my slightly vacant and distracted look. Mind you, when he was talking about his beloved book, I don't think Tom would have noticed if my head dropped off and rolled across the floor.

'So what do you think?' he suddenly asked me.

Well, I *thought* that being on a 'date' with Tom made me feel very special indeed. And I'm not actually being sarcastic when I say this. I felt special because he made me realise that I had a supreme talent for apparently listening intently to someone when, in fact, I was inwardly thinking about something completely different. I had managed to pick up enough of what Tom had said to allow me to give him sensible 'feedback' but had successfully managed to filter out every other word. Amazing!

Tom drained his pint just as I had offered a final word of advice and it was very much a 'closing time' kind of draining – he slapped his hands down on the arms of his chair in a 'well, I'd best be off' type of way. But then he caught sight of my second, untouched gin and thankfully must have realised that it would have been unspeakably rude to just up and leave having got what he came for. So just in time he changed the gesture from 'I'm off' to 'I'm off to the bar'. I'm sure he felt trapped, but at least he had the consolation of not having to ask if he could get me anything while he was there.

As he was waiting at the bar I took the opportunity to have a good look at our fellow drinkers. In the corner I spotted a couple sitting side by side in silence, but they were holding hands. They looked so contented, I wanted to punch them.

'So how have you been then?' Tom asked politely when he returned.

'Oh, fine, you know, samo, samo.'

'Good, good.'

Silence.

'I've moved house.'

'Oh, really? Where to?'

'Phibsboro.'

'Ah, I used to love it there when I first came to Dublin. Is your new place nice?'

'No, it's a flea-infested rat pit.'

'Really?'

'No.'

'Didn't you mean a rat-infested flea pit?'

Silence.

'How's work?'

'Oh, same as ever. Still working on the book about the priest and the nun.'

'Sounds bad.' He paused, looking as though he was carefully considering something. 'There's a lot of rubbish being printed nowadays, isn't there?' he continued.

'I suppose there is.'

Silence.

'It's very smokey in here, isn't it?'

'Yes, it is.'

Silence.

Thankfully, my second gin was disappearing

more quickly than my first. I drained the last of it just as he did the same with his pint.

'Well, Tom, I think I should head.'

'Okay. I actually have a few papers that need marking so I should probably go home and get a start on them.'

'Good plan.'

Silence.

We parted outside the door.

'Well, good luck with the marking.'

'Thanks, see you soon.'

And off he went.

I stood at the number 19 stop with trepidation. I know it sounds silly, but I always believed the bus stops on George's Street to be jinxed as it was always there that I ended up waiting the longest. I used to share a flat with two other girls and we had a sort of a competition to decide who had waited the longest for a bus. Each day we would come home and proudly announce our waiting time. I was the record holder, having once waited for two hours and fifty-six minutes.

However, that particular evening the bus gods took pity on me and after a mere ten minutes they sent the 19A to rescue me and whisk me home from my non-date date. I reread Captain Wentworth's letter but then chastised myself for feeding unrealistic expectations. There was nothing really wrong with Tom, I began to reason with myself, but then I found myself unable to progress any further with this defence because there was nothing really right with him either.

The house was empty when I got home but there was a note on the kitchen table.

Angela and I have gone for quick pint in McGowans if you want to come along. Made plenty at dinner – thought you might be hungry – help yourself – in fridge. M.

And I *was* hungry, starving, in fact, so I tucked into the dhal with relish. Once my stomach was sated I felt a whole lot better. Who needs men, I decided happily, when you have delicious food.

Chapter Five

'Bastard customers, if I have to tell one more person that I cannot order and supply *Heal the Shattered Karma* in less than thirty-five seconds I am going to – what the hell is going on here?' Angela demanded one evening after a particularly unpleasant day at work as she cast her eyes over the bomb site that had been her kitchen and her two flustered flatmates.

I had quickly got used to Angela's work-related outbursts. She regularly came home and threw a mini-tantrum in order to exorcise the bad karma that had built up inside her throughout the day and I knew not to take them personally. She had explained to me once that the sort of bookshop she ran was particularly prone to the kind of customers most normal bookshops would have their security guards throw out. She had tried to minimise the problem by reducing her 'adult health' section, but when that proved a failure she simply resigned herself to daily doses of weirdness and perversion.

This particular evening Marcus and I had had a bit of a tussle in the kitchen. I had very kindly offered to make dinner for a change and he had gratefully accepted my offer. However, he wouldn't leave me alone to get on with it. He insisted on popping his head around the door 'just to check that everything is under control'.

'Of course it's under control, Marcus.'

'Do you really want to be doing that with the onions?'

'I do.'

'I think your oil is overheating there.'

'No it isn't.'

And so on and so forth. His pestering eventually turned into physical interference and when he tried to grasp a spoon out of my hand he made me bump into the handle of a pan of almost boiling water, which I naturally knocked off the stove and all over his hand. But as I explained to him, it was his own fault. Angela was therefore confronted by the two of us in a heated discussion of whose fault his injury was.

'She threw boiling water all over me.'

'You started it and it was *not* boiling, it was just off boiling. You'll live, you big girl's blouse.'

'Jesus Christ, what *are* you both talking about? Why does my kitchen look like . . . shit?' she demanded, having failed to find a more suitable word. 'For that matter, why do you two look like shit?'

'Anna decided that she wanted to cook for a change,' Marcus chirped with a smirk.

'Hang on, don't blame me for all this mess, you're the one who started interfering. If you hadn't kept lurking behind me, checking up on me, you would never have got in the way of that pan—'

'When I'm not here you two can tear each other from limb to limb for all I care, but this is *my* home and refuge. At the end of a day spent being a human punch ball for uptight customers I do *not* want to have to act as referee between two idiots fighting like children over how to cook a bloody onion. I am *not* going to be your mother.'

Oh dear.

'But it's all over and done with, right Anna?'

'Absolutely,' I said, grinning and nodding manically. 'Drink, Angela?'

'Oh God yes.' And with two mighty slugs of the magic potion the old Angela reappeared, thank God – Angela in a mood was a force I preferred not to reckon with.

'Well?' I asked smugly as Marcus took the first bite.

''Salright.'

'Oh for God's sake, Marcus, tell her it's delicious.' Irritability was creeping back into Angela's voice.

'It's delicious,' he muttered.

'Obviously, Marcus,' said Angela, 'given the look on her face, your approval is the ultimate accolade.'

'So where are we going tonight?' Angela asked as she leaned back in the kitchen chair and undid her belt a few notches. Out, on a Saturday night? I had forgotten all about this ritual that normal people performed on a regular basis.

'I feel like dressing up,' Angela said, sounding like a ten year old. Marcus didn't care where we went so long as they served beer.

'Does "dress up" mean that trainers are out?' I asked.

'Absolutely,' said Angela in what I hoped was *mock* disgust.

I'm not usually a 'dress up' kind of girl. I had spent so many years not having to that I didn't posses any clothes that could conceivably be classed as 'dress up'. Bollocks! Why didn't she just want to go to the local? When Angela started to run through the various designer numbers that she could wear and the glamorous places that we could go to I panicked ever so slightly. I debated about feigning sudden illness, but a small voice in my head reminded me how much I used to complain about not having a life. But now, when confronted with normality I found myself thinking fondly of the old dull Saturday routine. I liked Saturday nights in and they were better than hanging around some posey bar in town.

'Angela, if you don't mind I think I might give tonight a miss, I—'

'Don't be stupid, of course you're coming.' And that, as they say, was that.

At about eight o'clock Angela went up to get ready. We were going out in only two hours, which apparently didn't leave her much time. I went up to my room and looked into my monochrome wardrobe in the faint hope that there might be some forgotten article of fabulousness lurking in there. After about ten minutes of staring I realised that this was not the case so I gave up. I pulled out my favourite black trousers and a non-descript black top. I convinced myself that I was going for the classic, simple look. In other words, it was boring and safe, but at least this way I stood a chance of blending into the background.

A pathetic, bleating voice then started to call my name.

'Anna, help me!'

I pulled on my shoes (black to complete the look) and went to find out what was wrong with her. I knocked on the door.

'Come in,' she roared over Madonna. I went in and I don't think I had ever in my life seen so many clothes before. They were everywhere – on the floor, on the bed, on the chair, thrown over the wardrobe door, spilling out of a laundry basket.

'I have nothing to wear,' she wailed.

'Clearly you have a clothes shortage.'

'Have you not changed yet?' she asked, looking at me expectantly.

For my next trick I will pull a gorgeous outfit from my hat.

'Oh, what *am* I going to wear? Everything I own is horrible.'

'You must spend a lot of money on horrible clothes,' I laughed.

'Help me, please,' she asked like someone drowning, drowning in her own designer wardrobe. Bless her, she must have been desperate if she was willing to take sartorial advice from someone who dressed like she had a funeral to go to every day of her life.

'You know you could borrow any of this if you wanted, but everything would be far too big for you.' I know she meant this kindly, but she was making me feel plonkier by the moment.

After about forty-five minutes of her trying on designer clobber, we finally reached a decision on Angela's outfit. And of course she looked fabulous. She really was very beautiful and I had to tell her that she would look lovely in a black bin liner. Oddly, she was embarrassed by this. I assumed someone that good looking would be used to taking compliments. I went downstairs to wait for her to do her make-up. I knew it was going to take a while. Marcus was enjoying a beer and *ER*.

'Have one,' he said, throwing a can at me, 'we could be waiting quite some time.'

'If I looked like Angela I would relish not really needing to put any effort into getting ready to go out.' He gave me a funny one-eyebrow-raised look. However, I was relieved to see that he hadn't even changed his clothes, so at least he wouldn't show me up as well.

'You know,' he said as I sat down, 'I reckon I deserve an honorary degree in medicine from watching medical soaps. You can learn so much from them. I can diagnose Munchausens-by-Proxy from forty miles off.'

'So doctor, what's wrong with him?' I asked, gesturing towards the TV. A man writhed in agony and his guts seemed to be bursting all over the place.

'Clearly, he is suffering from a bad case of "guts spilling out of one like soup".'

'You're good,' I said, laughing in spite of myself. I asked him how his hand was.

'I'll live,' he said trying to sound sullen.

After what seemed like an eternity, Angela finally came downstairs.

'Ready in record time,' she beamed, 'only took me an hour and three quarters.' She seemed genuinely pleased with herself.

Our destination that evening was a bar of Angela's choice. It was one of those über-trendy places where a smile might be construed as an unfashionably excessive display of emotion. This was my personal drinking hell. I like pubs, not bars, and when in pubs I like to talk while I'm drinking, not stand around looking nonchalant. And in what I was wearing I felt like a nun. The elegant and simple philosophy was revealed for the sham it really was the minute I walked in the door. For a start I had too many clothes on. If I ran into the bathroom and maybe got some scissors and cut the back out I might have just passed muster. I looked at Angela and Marcus and realised with a sinking heart that I was out with a pair of beautiful people who seemed to fit right in. Even Marcus, who hadn't made any effort, looked dishabille rather than scruffy. I felt and looked like someone's dorky sister who was being taken out as an errand of mercy. My grump levels were rising by the second. At least I did what I had set out to do – blend into the background. In fact, I blended too well as I was walked over, bumped into and almost sat on. I decided the only sensible thing to do was get absolutely shit faced and sulk.

We were joined by a friend of Marcus's who seemed quite nice but not really worth coming out of my sulk for, as I couldn't help but notice that he threw many wasted glances at Angela. Angela was a bloody disgrace. She fired the odd comment our way in order to reassure us that she hadn't forgotten that she was, ostensibly, out with us. Really, though, we were like the cigarettes that some people smoke just so they have an excuse to ask for a light. Eventually I gave in and spoke, but it was only because his friend was very amusing. Poor sod, he was directing all his charm and wit at Angela, but she was more interested in checking out the talent. And she wasn't subtle about it. Her talent antennae started flapping all over the place the minute a group of lovelies squizzed themselves into the tiny space beside our table.

I could tell before they even opened their mouths that they were French. They were smoking very sexily and looking vaguely bored, even though they were probably having quite *un bon temps*. I used to think that all this was just a national stereotype until I turned up at a party once peopled largely by French people and guess what? They sat around on chairs in a little French enclave, smoking sexily, not saying much and looking disdainfully at the Irish drinking *le vin Australien* and dancing badly to Debbie Harry. Anyway, this particular lot were so lovely they made even the lovely Marcus look a bit scruffy. I wondered if in my all black and leather jacket I maybe looked a bit *deux maggots*, but I lacked the necessary fag dangling provocatively from bee-stung lips so I had no chance.

I noticed one of the men; he was particularly handsome, tall and dark with perfect, chiselled features. He even managed to carry off that horrendous Tintin hairdo so beloved of Frenchmen. He was standing right beside Angela and of course she hadn't failed to notice him. She went a bit shifty and giggly and was trying to mouth 'has he noticed me?' out of the side of her mouth, which made her look like she was having some sort of seizure. I leaned over and advised her not to do this.

Had he noticed her? Of course he had bloody noticed her. A blind man on a runaway horse would have noticed Angela. He kept glancing over, waiting for an opportunity, and indeed he got one without too much delay. I had to admire her direct approach. Once I had managed to indicate to her through a series of strange eyeball movements and subtle hand gestures that he had seen her, she simply swivelled around in her chair and threw him a beaming smile and a big, cheery 'hi'. And they were off, yak, yak, yak, flirt, flirt, flirt.

Then I noticed John's face. He looked like Bambi after his mammy died. This guy had it bad. He disappeared to the jacks, probably to restore his equilibrium, and I took that opportunity to do a little digging. Marcus seemed to misunderstand my curiosity and warned me off him. I tetchily told him I wasn't interested as it was obvious that he was hung up on Angela. My insightfulness seemed to amaze him and I explained to him a little loftily that we women could sense things. In other words, men are completely dumb and blind sometimes and that it didn't take a degree in rocket science to realise that John's mooney behaviour had nothing whatsoever to do with the fact that his beer had just run out.

'Angela goes for bastards,' Marcus explained with a shrug of his shoulders.

'What, like your man over there?' I said, gesturing to Tintin.

'You can't make snap judgments about people just like that,' he said, sounding more than a little priggish.

'Oh I can!' I responded with breezy confidence. 'You see, I have a lot of intuition and I'm never, ever wrong. I have instinctive reactions to people and I just know straight away whether I'm going to like someone or not.'

'Oh for God's sake, I've never heard such arrogant shite.'

'Excuse me, it's not arrogant shite, it's a gift. You're very rude.'

'Well it's a shite gift then. And I'm not rude, I just tell as I find.'

'That's just a complicated way of saying "rude".'

'Well if *honesty* counts as rudeness, then yes, I confess to being pig-ignorant.'

At which point John came back and told us that from the bar we looked like we were bickering like an old married couple. Neither of us found this particularly amusing.

A few hours later, as I was resignedly undergoing the short person's lot of being ignored at the bar, a very drunk Angela came up and threw her arms around me.

'I'm in love, I'm in love, I'm in love,' she trilled. 'Xavier's perfect so have to go home right now. Come with me.' I wasn't sure whether this was a request or an order.

'He's perfect . . . so you have to leave? Would you mind explaining that please?'

'Have to play hard to get cos I *reeeally* like him and have to open buggerin' shop in morning. Oh pleeeease come.'

My conscience was prodded into life by the sight of her; she was in no state to go home by herself. Forgetting one's prepositions is always a sure sign of gross inebriation.

'Okay,' I sighed, and with that she squealed her gratitude and gave me a slobbering wet kiss on the cheek that I could have lived without. When I went to get my coat and tell the lads that we were leaving I saw that Marcus had been accosted by one of the French ladies. She was sticky thin and looked a bit snotty. I took one of my intuitive dislikes to her. Obviously she was none too keen on me either as she shot me a filthy look and stomped off the minute I reached the table. I asked what all that was about, and apparently Marcus had told her that I was his girlfriend and was fiendishly jealous. I was slightly surprised that he had given her the brush-off, because despite being undernourished and poker faced she wasn't bad looking. He insisted on coming home with us, but I persuaded him (eventually) that there was no point in everyone's night being ruined by Angela's determination to go all aloof and mysterious with Monsieur Perfect. Not that anyone in that state could be mysterious – apart, perhaps, from how much they'd had to drink.

61

We left just as soon as Angela had given her number to Xavier. By some minor miracle we managed to flag down a taxi on its way back to a rank. Just as I was supporting Angela over to it, who should appear at the door of the bar but the lovely Xavier. Nothing would do but that Angela had to totter over because she couldn't remember if she had said goodbye nicely enough. I was left trying to restrain an impatient Dublin taxi driver, a breed that I have always thought should be kept in a zoo.

'I haven't all bleedin' night, love, either get yer friend in or I go on.'

'Angela – NOW. I cannot stop a moving vehicle by hanging onto the door handle!'

And off went the taxi. I spun around in annoyance to yell at Angela. She had disappeared. Fantastic. My humour was blackening by the second.

After a lengthy tangle with the bouncers I went back inside in search of her. No sign. I noticed that the French string bean had taken advantage of my absence to launch a second attack on Marcus. John was looking like a spare tool. Poor sod, destined for a raw deal at every turn. Some people are just like that, I suppose. French girl looked a little pissed off and a little frightened at my re-entrance. There was a good deal of hostile eyeballing from her and I wondered what on earth Marcus had said about me. I was more worried about Angela, though, and was going to make a second attempt at getting a cab but the gallant Marcus wouldn't hear of me going home alone.

'It's two o'clock in the morning. You can't go hunting cabs by yourself,' he said as though he were stating the obvious.

I laughed at him but was also slightly irritated by his unnecessary show of gallantry. 'Of course I can. I'm old enough to look after myself.'

'I'm sure you are, but I'm coming with you anyway.'

'God, you're *so* commanding.'

'It's a bit late in the evening to start flirting with me, don't you think?' Of course this irritated me hugely. I hadn't been trying to flirt with him and I really wished that the man wouldn't be so relentlessly assuming and arrogant. As we gathered our coats and when Frenchie thought I wasn't looking, she handed Marcus a piece of paper. Her phone number, perhaps? The brazen wench! Right under the nose of his girlfriend! There was much annoying manly guffawing between the two lads over this, which I decided to ignore.

I wasn't quite so lucky with the taxi the second time around. We seemed to be waiting for hours and I'm sure I must have driven Marcus mad by jiggling about from foot to foot in an attempt to relieve bladder pressure. The two a.m. cold was seeping into my very bones and there was only my battered leather jacket between me and pneumonia.

'I'm cold,' I found myself whimpering, and before I knew it, Marcus had taken off his jacket and had draped it around my shoulders. I was unused to such chivalry and was unsure how I ought to react.

'Now *you'll* freeze,' I said, trying to give it back to him, but he refused it. 'Let me guess, you're too manly to feel the cold?'

'No, I just don't want to have to carry you home to your mother in a body bag and explain that you were the casualty of a Dublin taxi rank.'

We arrived home to be greeted by some drunken babbling on the answering machine.

'Helloooo, 'smee, ahm in Xavier's [lots of giggling]. Marcus [in a pleading voice], could you open shop tomorrow, Aoife's on holidays, please, be your best friend, can't go into work dressed like this be in around—' and there the message ended.

Needless to say, Marcus was livid.

'Christ, I don't know how many times she's done stuff like this, I AM GOING TO KILL HER . . . but not before I polish off one of her very best bottles. You can help.' Who was I to refuse?

'You're very . . . masterful, aren't you?'

He shrugged his shoulders in response. 'My sisters call it overbearing, actually.'

'So how many sisters do you have?' I asked and took a huge slurp of Angela's wine, which even after several gins I could tell was too good to be drunk after several gins.

'Four,' he answered with a bit of a sigh.

'That's a big family.'

'Indeed. Some might say too big.'

'You don't really mean that, do you?'

'Nah, well, not entirely at least. Maybe just a little bit . . . sometimes.'

'Whereabouts do you come in the line up?'

'I, unfortunately, am the eldest.'

'Oh my God! The eldest *and* an only son. So how come you aren't in therapy?'

He laughed dryly and rolled his eyes. 'Being big brother to four idiot sisters doesn't leave me much time to assess their effect on my mental state. What about you? Any brothers or sisters?'

'Two brothers, one older, one younger, no sisters.' I said a little tersely, as I don't mind talking about other people's families but prefer never to mention my own.

'Jesus, middle child and only girl. Your position is far worse than mine.'

I laughed a little uneasily and reached for the bottle of wine.

'So I gather that was big-brother mode that I was treated to earlier?'

'I guess . . . I mean, *no*, I was being gallant to a damsel in distress.'

'I don't think anyone has ever called me that before.'

'I can imagine . . . probably knew they wouldn't live to tell the tale if they did.'

I laughed in spite of myself.

'You know I always really wanted a sister,' I announced out of the blue.

'Feel free to take a couple of mine.'

'Seriously, though, I always felt hard done by and when Nicholas – that's my youngest brother – was born my nose was put seriously out of joint. I spent nine months convincing myself that I was going to have a sister, so I was flabbergasted when things didn't go my way. I remember that I was so annoyed that when I was told that I had a little brother I swore solemnly that I would never, ever love him.'

'And did you keep your vow?'

'Absolutely, he's a nightmare.'

He laughed because he thought I was joking, but how wrong he was.

'No really, he is . . . .'

'Yeah, yeah. I have four nightmares but I wouldn't be without them. They're great for my ego, apart from anything else, as they think the sun shines out of my arse.'

'That's nice for you,' I said. I had a traditional Irish fear of the self-confident and I wanted to put a quick stop to any more self-eulogising.

'But I never let it go to my head,' he smiled as though he had read my thoughts. I realised just at that moment that Marcus's smile was as annoyingly disarming as it was unapologetic. I would come to learn that Marcus's family did indeed (mistakenly) believe that he was some sort of demi-god and so his alarming self-confidence was hardly surprising. Just then, though, in our kitchen, sharing a bottle of expensive wine, I only registered the unapologetic smirk and it made me feel ill at ease.

'I think it's time for bed, my lovely,' he announced after a short spell of silence.

I glanced behind me. 'Who are you talking to?'

'As you get to know me better, you'll understand that modesty isn't something I tolerate, particularly of the false variety.'

And to my shame, I felt my old-enough-to-know-better cheeks flush not only with embarrassment but also with something I vaguely recollected as pleasure.

Chapter Six

I went to bed at four thirty, fell into a coma and emerged from it the next day at ten thirty. I wasn't fit to move from the bed, and even though I badly needed water, the journey to the kitchen seemed too arduous to make so I lay there and suffered. By eleven o'clock my mind was going boggly with thoughts of water, so I made myself get up and made my way downstairs. I remembered that Marcus had to go in and open the shop for Angela so I succumbed to a momentary spasm of pity and brought him a cup of tea.

I knocked on the door and heard a faint groan from inside. I told him to make himself decent; I didn't want a repeat of my first morning there. A head emerged from under the duvet. He saw the mug and looked at me like I was Florence Nightingale.

'What time did I go to bed at?' he asked.

'Four thirty.'

'What was I doing till then?'

'Talking to me, or rather, at me, I think. But don't ask me what about. I should remind you that you have to open the shop for Angela,' I said with a bit of a smirk. I can't repeat here what was said in response to this.

'Don't suppose you know how to run a shop, do you?'

'Nope,' I answered with a big grin, so off he went an hour later, clutching his head in one hand and half a bottle of Paracetamol in the other. I found myself feeling almost sorry for him. Meanwhile, I went out, got a newspaper, then came home and cooked myself a delicious fry-up. After about my fifth cup of tea I was starting to feel human again. The sun was coming out after a morning of rain and I began to think about taking a wander around town in order to rid my head of the last of the hangover cobwebs. Off I went and I decided on my way that I would take a look into the shop to see that everything was alright, because lurking somewhere behind the enjoyment of a Sunday morning sloth was a sneaking sympathy for Marcus.

Angela's shop was a tiny little place just off Dame Street. However, every book ever printed on the mind, body and spirit was stuffed in there. It was a Mecca for the serious new age aficionados, but as I have already explained, she also got the freaks who just came in to tear the pictures out of Dorling Kindersley's *Illustrated Karma Sutra*. She also acted as a kind of information bureau. Her window was plastered with leaflets advertising various healing groups, fortune tellers, yoga classes, practitioners of alternative medicine and meditation groups. Basically if you wanted to find out about anything vaguely left field, Angela knew where to direct you. Marcus was sitting at the desk by the window, saw me approaching and gave me a wave and a big smile. Obviously he had perked up somewhat since that morning.

The place smelled alarmingly of incense and patchouli and there were quite a few people in there that looked as though they hadn't washed in about a month. Marcus, looking scarily com-petent, was helping a customer with her choice of books on reiki. I was impressed, well, sort of. I did question the suitability of The Beastie Boys as musak in that kind of establishment, but as he quite rightly pointed out, if he was going to endure a Sunday hangover in a shop full of hippies he at least had the right to choose music which might lessen their browsing time. I did notice that one or two potential customers stuck their heads in the door, looked mightily confused, then left.

'Anyway, I thought that you weren't too sure how to run a shop. Looks like you're a dab hand.'

'Well, I knew the only way to get you in here was to prod your conscience. You can forget about seeing Angela in here today. She has done this *once or twice* before,' he said with a rueful smile. I was forced to admit that for someone with a hangover who had just been dumped in it by a friend, he was remarkably good humoured.

'Where's Angela's kettle?' I asked, pulling out a bag of doughnuts that I had bought on my way in. I'm not all bad and even Marcus deserved a hangover cure. He looked grateful and a little bit surprised. As we were polishing off the last of the six doughnuts a couple came in. He had trouble written all over him. She had downtrodden stamped all over her. She would have been really pretty if she hadn't been drowned in floral print and hadn't looked so miserable. I couldn't blame her, though. He was all mouthy and cocky, not in an irritating Marcus kind of way, but in a horrible, aggressive way. The shop was so small there was no avoiding their argument.

'I won't be long, I promise. Why don't you wait outside or go get a coffee or something?'

'If I wanted a fuckin' coffee I'd have got one, wouldn't I?'

'I'm sorry, I just need to look for a book on—'

'Another book about shite-all. This stuff is all bollocks,' he said, picking up a random book from the table. 'I mean, what is this?' he wondered at *The Beauty of Me*. '*The Beauty of Me*,' he repeated disdainfully, 'the beauty of me arse.'

'Is non-existent,' I muttered under my breath.

He spun around. 'Excuse me, do you have something to say?' As I had a mouthful of doughnut I merely shook my head dumbly at him.

'Good! Keep it that way.' He turned to his girlfriend, who had by now gone from flushed to green about the gills. 'I'll be outside. *Five minutes*. If you're not finished, I'm off.'

He went out muttering away to himself, 'Fucking hippie crap . . . fruitcake . . . pain in the ass . . . stupid.' It was all very embarrassing. We studied the doughnut crumbs while the other two customers decided that they had to be somewhere else.

She came up to the counter and asked, blushing with embarrassment over her lovely partner, if we had any information on palmistry. My doughnut got suspended somewhere halfway to my mouth as I heard Marcus declare, 'I read palms myself, you know.'

You do? I thought

'You do?' she asked eagerly. She took a quick glance around the shop and saw that there was no one there. She looked outside and saw her boyfriend having a smoke and roaring at someone down a mobile phone. She thrust her hands at Marcus.

'Any chance of a quickie? I'll pay, of course.'

Marcus pretended to demure, telling her that he was really only a novice so he couldn't charge her. She didn't seem to mind, so he leaned over the counter and took her hands in his, turned the palms upwards and scrutinised them with a look of intense concentration on his face.

'Mmm, I'm really sorry, but your Mount of Venus troubles me.'

She seemed a little edgy at this.

'He,' Marcus said, gesturing at the bastard outside, 'is not the one for you.' This was audacious and I was made a little uncomfortable by his attempt to meddle with fate. There was a horrible silence as she slowly raised her head and stared intensely at Marcus. Then she let out a huge sigh of relief.

'Oh thank God for that. I should leave him, shouldn't I? I worried that maybe he was all I deserved, you know, maybe I had done something awful in another life that I was being punished for. You have no idea what it's like living with that day in, day out. He thinks I'm completely stupid. Oh thank you, *thank* you.'

I was gobsmacked. In five minutes he had sorted her life out for her and she was delighted. Then she left and walked off with yer man. She wore the satisfied look of someone hugging a secret to themselves, ready to drop a bombshell. He had no idea that he was about to be dumped.

73

Even though he was very clearly a bollocks, I was nevertheless uncomfortable with what Marcus had just done. There was still a chance, albeit a slim one, that he was simply not in a good mood and that he was normally really nice and that Marcus had gone and wrecked two people's lives without even a second thought. Of course I aired this reservation to Madame Marcus.

'Nonsense,' he said dismissively. 'Don't be so paranoid. No one really believes in all this rubbish,' he announced loftily. 'If she really does think that he's Mr Perfect, my telling her that he isn't won't make the slightest difference. She'll simply write me and my predictions off as a load of old crap. If he isn't Mr Right, which he clearly isn't, I'll simply have given her the helping hand she needed to give him the push.'

'Yes, but you seem to have ignored the fact that he seemed a tad aggressive and knows where to find the man who suggested to his girlfriend that he should be dumped.'

'Ahhh, hadn't thought of that.'

'Oh don't worry, I'm sure he'll come to realise that you did him a favour, really.'

'You don't mean that, do you?'

'No. Here, have the last doughnut and relax . . . and take one of these,' I said, handing him a flyer on martial arts classes.

I felt sorry for his growing unease so I tried to perk him up a bit by asking him to read my fortune.

Big mistake.

'Ah, yes, now *your* Mount of Venus is very interesting. I see a man has just entered your life.'

'No, don't tell me, tall, dark and handsome.'

'Well, dark and handsome anyway,' he said with his horrible, cheesy grin. The man's ego knew no bounds.

'Oh quelle surprise, and would his initial be M by any chance?' I asked, trying to sound sangfroid and bored.

'Well no, actually,' he said, dropping my hand. 'I was thinking of J.'

'J?' I was a little embarrassed and red faced.

'John . . . from last night. I know he's hung up on Angela, but I think he liked you and, you know, maybe if he started seeing someone else he might start to realise that there are other women in the world. He has no chance with Angela and—'

'Well, I'm sure your "dating therapy" is a *fabulous* idea but I'm afraid I'm not really free at the moment to act as the guinea pig. Nor am I willing to be someone's second best, and I'm fairly sure that your friend wouldn't appreciate your attempt to organise his life for him behind his back . . . and *I* already have someone, thank you very much,' I added hastily, having almost forgotten about Tom. And with that I decided to remember that I had something very important to do and made my exit.

I headed straight home, and as if she had telepathically picked up on the fact that I was not in a

75

terribly good mood, my mother rang. The phone was ringing as I opened the door and I dashed to it in the foolish hope that it might be someone I wanted to talk to.

'Hello, love, it's your mother, remember me?'

'Sorry, sorry, I meant to call you during the week but I was snowed under with work and everything . . . .'

'Oh, that's all right,' she said with an air of martyred resignation, 'I'm well used to it at this stage, Jason is as bad.'

'I gather you haven't heard from him in a while then.'

'No, but I'm not worried, you know Jason, he's well fit to look after himself.'

That was the funniest thing I had heard all week. Jason was the person least capable of looking after himself in the whole wide world. What he did have, though, was a knack of attracting people who believed it was their mission in life to look after him.

'How are you settling into the new house?'

'Fine, I like it here.' Then, suddenly and for no reason, the conversation swerved out of control.

'Have you been getting out much recently Anna?'

'I'm still single, Mother.'

'That's not what I asked. I hope this isn't going to be one of those difficult conversations?'

'Well you changed the topic.'

'Oh for God's sake, Anna, I only asked if you were getting out and about. Is a mother not allowed to show a bit of concern for her only daughter?'

'It's not *what* you ask, it's the *way* you ask, Mother.'

'What on earth are you talking about? What's so *strange* about the *way* I ask if all is well? Why are you always so difficult?'

'You always ask that question, "are you getting out much", and I know that there's another question lurking behind it. I'm not stupid.'

'Well then stop talking like you are! And of course I'm always going to ask "that question", as you put it. You don't get out enough for someone your age. You need to live a little, life will catch up with you before you know it.'

Of course, I knew she was right but these conversations always left me feeling depressed and inadequate. Of course I needed to get out more – but when your mother tells you that you're not getting out enough then you know you have a problem. Mind you, my mother wasn't really like other mothers.

'Anna, are you still there?'

'Yes, Mother, I'm still here.'

'Are you sulking?'

'No.'

'I'm not picking on you. I would just like to see you happy.'

'I am ha— what do you mean?'

At this interesting juncture the key went in the door and Angela came in looking a little less lovely than usual.

'Look, I have to go, Ma, I'll call you next week, I promise.'

'Of course you will,' she sighed. 'Just . . . take care.' And with that she hung up.

Angela tripped passed me and up the stairs, humming one of the weird tuneless ditties she was prone to. I guessed that she was floating on the wings of love.

Ten minutes later she came back down and looked slightly cleaner. Unfortunately the ecstasy had not washed off in the shower and so I was forced to listen to her enumerate the many wonderful things about Xavier. I could have written a thesis about how fantastic he was. He was wealthy, had a *fabulous* apartment and *fabulous* things and a *fabulous* body (I had to suffer detail overload on this point), a *fabulous* life and a *fabulous* sense of humour. Quite simply, he was altogether *fabulous*. She seemed quite oblivious to the fact that while she was enjoying all this fabulousness, her best friend had been doing her job for her. I listened politely for as long as possible then made my exit. I just wanted to sulk in a bath for a while, away from the fabulous Xavier and the smitten Angela.

I had bought some sort of relaxing lavender bath stuff on the way home that afternoon. Two drops were apparently enough to restore even the most wobbly of equilibriums so I put six drops in my bath, got in, sat back and waited for relaxation to flood over me. As I lay there, urging myself to unwind, Marcus came home. Surprisingly he came straight up the stairs and I heard him knocking on my bedroom door.

'Anna?'

I was curious to know what he had to say for himself but didn't want to talk to him, so I made splashing noises to alert him to the fact that I wasn't in my room. He then started talking to the bathroom door.

'I'm really sorry, I didn't mean what I said to sound the way it did, I wasn't really thinking—'

'Of course you weren't, you're a man; thinking is not generally regarded as the strong point of your species.'

'I just meant that if maybe John could find someone nice, not that Angela isn't nice, that maybe it would be good for him.'

'You're still making going out with me sound like a therapy session. Apology accepted, but really, stop right there before you dig yourself right back into your grave. Now go away, I'm trying very hard to relax. Go and listen to Angela for a few hours.'

And I really had accepted his apology. I tend to explode quickly, but like most short-tempered people I do have the advantage of not bearing grudges for too long. And then I got back to the difficult business of trying to relax.

To be honest, my mother's phone call bothered me much more than his crass attempts at setting his mate up. I wondered at my luck in getting the world's only mother who was upset because her daughter wasn't getting enough sex or drugs and who apparently didn't care much for rock 'n' roll.

My father had died when we were little and my mother was proud of the fact that she had raised three children all by herself. And she was right to be, but she was consequently intolerant of normality (though she did make an exception in the case of marriage and/or babies) and anyone who strove for it. Her phone calls always left me feeling a little depressed. I found it hard enough failing to live up to my own expectations without the added misery of knowing that I had disappointed someone else's as well. I reached out and checked the side of the bottle of relaxing stuff, as it seemed to have distinctly depressing side effects. I decided it was time to get out of this bath of misery before I drowned in it. As I went into my room I could hear the word '*fabulous*' drifting up from downstairs. I decided to leave Marcus to it; listening to Angela could be his punishment.

However, I was not to be left in peace. Ten minutes later there was a knock at my door. It was opened gently and Marcus tentatively asked if he could come in. What did he want this time?

'For God's sake come down here and help me. I can't take any more Xavier.' He looked pretty despairing and desperate so I relented and went downstairs, where I had to listen to Angela going on and on and on and on . . . .

Chapter Seven

One Thursday evening a few weeks later, after a particularly bad day at work, I came home to find the hallway littered with boxes and bags, CDs and books, clothes and shoes. Marcus came bounding down the stairs looking even cheerier than usual.

'Guess what?' he said. He appeared to be particularly pleased about something. 'I'm moving in properly. Isn't it great?'

'It's *fantastic*.'

As I was tripping over the numerous possessions that were littered all over the kitchen floor my interest was caught by a number of framed photos leaning against the wall. They were particularly good holiday snaps and I noticed the same girl appearing in them all. There she was in an olive grove, on a bridge looking into the water with a pensive expression on her very pretty face. She was blonde and ever so slightly feline looking; she reminded me a little of Vivien Leigh. As if in confirmation of a thought that hadn't yet formed itself, a slightly wistful voice behind me said, 'That's Isobel.'

I jumped away from them guiltily and apologised. 'I shouldn't have been looking at them, they're private.'

'Not that private,' he assured me, 'or I wouldn't have left them there.' Nevertheless, he gathered them up in his arms and went upstairs with them without another word. I noticed as he walked off that a loose photo had fallen out from between the frames. I bent down, picked it up and was about to put it carefully into one of his boxes. It wasn't of her, though, it was of him. I was a little taken aback. It was him, yet not him. I had seen him good humoured and smiling, but never like that. Someone who didn't know him might have found the face in that photo more than a little attractive.

He was smiling, not at the camera, but at whoever was behind it. I recognised the background as the same as in one of the shots of Isobel. I was puzzled. His look was one of love, contentment, affection, there was even a look of come hither in his eyes. If he felt all that for the girl behind the lens, then why or how could he have two-timed her? I looked at the photo again, and though I am ashamed to admit it, I couldn't help but wonder how it might feel to be looked at so adoringly.

'What's the sigh for?' It was Angela.

'What sigh?' I asked, as I hastily shoved the picture into a box. She saw what I did and calmly plucked it back out of the box. She said nothing, though I could feel my cheeks blazing in embarrassment. She simply raised her eyebrows ever so slightly, put it back in the box, put the kettle on and asked me if I wanted a cup of tea. To be honest, I found her silence more disconcerting than a good slagging would have been. Silence makes me feel as though I ought to feel guilty about something, but I soon snapped out of that mooney mood when I remembered that I was pissed off at being doomed to a single bed for the foreseeable future. Single beds are inherently depressing, but this one had the added misery of being shoved up against a wall and so every time I turned in the night the wall head butted me.

Angela went back upstairs to help Marcus unpack all his stuff and they seemed to be having a rare old time. I ate my beans on toast in front of the television and silently prayed that they would not be this jolly all the time.

The next day at work, while trying to explain to Linda why the rewrites of Olivia's book had not yet arrived without using the word 'bitch', an Interflora man arrived. He carried a magnificent bouquet of yellow roses. Of course we all knew they were for Linda, including Linda. She was still going out with the same guy so they were probably sent in celebration of that minor miracle. Her face lit up and she looked very smug indeed as she took them from the delivery man. But when she saw the name on the card, her face fell.

'It appears that they are for *you*,' she said, handing the card to me, huffiness and surprise fighting for supremacy on her face. I had to cough slightly to remind her to give me the flowers as well. Her eager curiosity was palpable. Even James seemed almost interested. But Linda couldn't have been more surprised than I was. Though I'm ashamed now to admit it, the irrational thought that they might be from Tom did flash across my mind. The card simply said, *Sorry for stealing your room.*

'Mind you,' James chimed in, 'I don't quite understand the theory behind sending flowers. I'm sure its historic roots must lie somewhere in the courtly traditions of the Middle Ages. But really, when you look at it logically, they die. Something so ephemeral could be construed as a representation of the transient nature of the feelings of the giver. Sending a book token would be better. Then they could buy something sensible and more lasting.'

'Obviously, James, the dictionary you swallowed as a child was missing the page with "romantic" on it.' I was certainly not going to explain to either him or Linda that these were an overblown gesture

85

of apology rather than of romance. Annoyance and irritation had managed to screw Linda's attractive face up into a little wizened prune-like thing and for that I could *almost* have hugged Marcus.

I left the office that evening on a slightly more upbeat note than usual so I suppose I had something to thank him for. When I got home that evening there was no sign of either of the other two. There was an envelope on the table for me with a note.

I'm sorry I couldn't give you the flowers in person but I had to make one of my visits home to Letterkenny this weekend. Really sorry about the room, I didn't realise that you wanted it. Hope the flowers might encourage you to forgive me!
Marcus

I undid the flowers from their ornate packaging and carefully arranged them in a vase. There were so many of them, the vase weighed a ton. Just as I was hefting them into the sitting room the front door opened and Angela let out a squeal of delight.

'Anna, your head appears to have turned into an enormous bunch of flowers. Who are they from?' she asked excitedly.

'Marcus.'

'Oh.'

'"Oh"?'

'I bet they're from Mad Flowers,' she guessed, whipping the card out from the mass. 'Just as I thought!' she laughed. 'That guy must have a standing order at that place.'

'I take it this is a grand gesture he makes a habit of?' I asked as I plonked them down amidst the mess of newspapers, books and dirty glasses on the coffee table.

'God yes. Our Marcus loves the floral gesture. Any old excuse and off he charges to the florist. I remember I accidentally burst into pre-menstrual floods over breakfast one morning and that day a gorgeous bunch arrived in the shop. I never really buy my own now, I just feign misery or illness or something.'

'It's a slightly weird trait for a man though, isn't it? Buying flowers, I mean. I've always assumed that men must suffer from some sort of genetic hay fever that makes even the shortest visit to the flower shop a horrendous ordeal.'

'Have you ever noticed how edgy men get when they spot another man carrying a bunch? You'd think they were triffids or something.'

'There speaks a woman from bitter experience.'

'Ohhh yes, indeed.' She glared significantly at the vase for a few seconds. 'But thank God for Marcus, eh?'

'Indeed, Angela, thank God for Marcus,' I echoed quietly.

Chapter Eight

Angela continued to mope over Xavier and was reluctant to admit that he might not be the man of her dreams. The possible reasons why he hadn't yet rung her had to be raked over on a nightly basis and both Marcus and I were obliged to contribute to the debate. The list of possible excuses consisted partly of the following:

He had lost her number.

Our phone was broken.

She hadn't sounded sincere when she asked him to call her.

He hadn't actually meant it when he said he'd call her. (This was Marcus's helpful offering and she didn't like it very much.)

He was nervous. (This, needless to say, was her suggestion and she got very tetchy with Marcus and I for laughing at it.)

He really, really liked her but wasn't ready to get involved with anyone just yet.

He had left the country.

He was working really, really late every night of the week.

He was ill.

He'd had an accident.

And so on and so forth.

'Well I think you should stick to the accident theory, Angela,' Marcus suggested one evening. 'His being dead is much better than indifference, don't you think?' Angela merely scowled in response.

She was driving us both mad until I accidentally hit upon the sure-fire way to shut her up: 'Remind me again, Angela, what star sign is Xavier?'

Angela had sworn off astrology ever since she'd discovered that Xavier was a Cancerian. Apparently, given that she was an Aquarian, the whole thing was astrologically doomed to failure anyway.

I hadn't heard from Tom in a couple of weeks so I just assumed that things had died a natural death. I wasn't moved to either disappointment or relief about this. I really didn't care one way or the other. However, I suppose that there was something a bit depressing about the fact that even someone as dull as Tom wasn't interested in me.

I was therefore very surprised that he rang me one otherwise dull Wednesday evening – much to Angela's annoyance, as she didn't like anyone taking up the phone when Xavier could be trying to get through. If the phone call came as something of a surprise, then his dinner invitation came as an even bigger one. I should have said no, but I couldn't think of an excuse quickly enough. Besides, I was curious to see if Tom was actually capable of wining and dining a girl. The spontaneity of the gesture was ruined, though, by the fact that he was giving me nearly two weeks' notice. He couldn't see me before that, he explained, because he had a ton of papers to mark. He didn't ask how I was fixed during that time so I guess he assumed that I would be hanging around waiting for him to call. He probably thought he was being polite, bless him.

I agreed to meet him on the Friday at eight o'clock. Angela's reaction to my news was most flattering.

'Jesus Christ! Marcus! Marcus! Where are you? Anna has a date!' She ran into the sitting room and practically jumped on top of him in her excitement.

'For God's sake, calm down, woman. I'm trying to concentrate here, there's a very serious myocardial infarction going on in Holby.'

'Well, *I* think Anna's news is more exciting than a bloody heart attack . . . this is *so* amazing.'

'Angela, my dear,' he began slowly, 'firstly, let me point out this is *televisual drama*, it is *not* real. As for Anna's big news . . . now that I think of it I do believe that it says somewhere in the Bible that one of the tell-tale signs that Armageddon fast approacheth is if someone other than Angela Meredith is having a date on a Friday night. It's somewhere next to the bit about the lamb lying down with the whatsit . . . Anna, get her a drink . . . or else take her off to your bedroom and do some girly squealing with her or something, anything, just take her away.'

Angela was indeed losing the plot. She wanted to take me in hand and do some sort of makeover. From anyone else I would have taken this badly because the obvious inference was that there was something inherently wrong with me. Which was quite possibly true in my case, but you don't want someone rubbing your nose in it. She was getting quite carried away, planning shopping trips, outfits, shoes. All I could do was laugh at her. Marcus emerged momentarily from his concentration to mumble, with just a hint of irritation, that I didn't need one. I was forced to admit that that was quite nice of him.

'Angela, this is Tom we're talking about here. I shouldn't imagine that we'll go anywhere more glamorous than Burger King.'

'Oh all right then. But you're coming shopping with me anyway as I need cheering up and I'm going to use you as an excuse.'

'Anything to keep you happy, my dear.'

'Late-night shopping tomorrow then. Want to join us, doctor?'

'Yeah, right.'

I met Angela the following evening after work and I saw with a sinking heart that she had changed into her trainers, which meant that she had serious shopping in mind. So off we went into Brown Thomas, me trailing after her like a bored child. The make-up counters were our first port of call.

Behind one of the counters stood a very sparkly young man who made the Elizabeth Arden ladies look as though they hadn't made much of an effort. Now I'm not an unliberal kind of girl, but some things just go against nature and male cosmetic assistants are definitely one of them. He clearly loved Angela as she could potentially earn him a week's commission in less than one painful hour. I was studiously ignored, as it didn't take a degree in make-up studies to see that I didn't know my Touche Eclat from my pore minimiser. Angela loved all things glittery and it was really quite charming to see her face light up as he waved a pot of gold glittery eye make-up at her. However, it was obvious that Angela spent far too much time and money in there, as he knew not only her skin type, but her name!

'Does it last?' she asked and we could both tell from the naked desire in her voice that she was going to buy half the counter even if he turned around and told her that everything was shite.

'Well,' he said with a flourishing wave of his hands across his face, 'I put some on this morning and you can tell that I still have it on.' He tilted his head up towards the light so we could admire it properly. His sparkly face twinkled subtly under the harsh neon lighting.

'Ooh, I'll take it,' Angela said a little breathlessly, as though he had just offered to sell her bottled orgasm. She was practically bobbing up and down in excitement. I think he sensed my puritan disapproval, as he whirled around suddenly and asked tersely if he could help me to anything.

'Er, no,' I sniggered.

'Are you sure? You know, Clinique do a fantastic basic skincare range.'

The bitch! Before any claws had a chance to come out, Anglea whisked me off upstairs.

I knew what she was up to. She kept pulling things out that were black (which she rarely wore) and in the wrong size (in other words, mine). After many dismissive shakes of my head or squeals of amusement at the hilarious price tags, she turned on me. She was getting angrier and scarier by the second.

'So, Anna, what *are* you going to wear on this bloody date? Do you like this guy or what?' She sounded as though this shopping trip for 'my bloody date' was a gigantic bore, even though it was her idea.

'It's *not* a date and I don't know. Besides, I thought this shopping trip was supposed to be about *you*.'

'What do you mean it's not a date?' she demanded, ignoring my question. 'He asked you out to dinner, didn't he?'

'No, he said "instead of going for a drink next time why don't we get something to eat." I'm not expecting to be whisked off my feet or anything like that.'

'Well if you turn up in those jeans he certainly won't even try. Anna, how do you expect someone to woo you and whisk you off anything when you turn up dressed like you couldn't give a toss one way or the other?'

I glanced in the mirror and suddenly felt depressed. I'm sure Angela hadn't intended to make me feel like shit, but she had just managed it nonetheless. I had never been overly concerned by my appearance. From the moment I was old enough to start buying my own clothes I had always aimed at blending with the crowd, because prior to that my mother had insisted that I stand out. She had unfortunately fancied herself as a bit of a dressmaker and amused herself when I was growing up by designing increasingly *unusual* and colourful outfits for me. She called them 'free-form garments'. In reality she couldn't sew to save her life and so I ended up going about in ill-fitting, badly sewn lumps of material that looked as though they had been put together by a blind lunatic. My brothers got off comparatively lightly, only having to endure the statutory Christmas offering of a knitted jumper in a mixture of whatever colours she could find in the bargain bin in the local wool shop. Mother claimed that trousers were too difficult to make. Oddly enough, the jumpers were usually torn by February.

Angela had her way in the end. She convinced me to part with a ridiculous sum of money for a relatively small amount of material. She had tried to bully me into taking it in pink, but childhood memories are not that easily overcome. I insisted that if I was going to be forced into parting with that much money I at least had the right to choose my favourite colour. So I took it in black. Well, what were you expecting? That I would suddenly discover my soft, fluffy side and realise that I looked charming and feminine in the pink version? And if you have any more ideas along those lines you may as well stop reading now. Life doesn't go the way it does in novels. Not even when it comes to minor details like clothes.

'Look on it as an investment,' Angela chirped as she pushed me towards the cash desk.

'I can't do it, Angela, the assistants are scary, they won't serve me, they'll know I don't have a skincare routine.'

I wanted to kill her for making me do something so against my nature, but it was lovely, so yes, I bought it.

Angela was clearly using Tom and I for some vicarious dating, as Xavier still hadn't made any effort to contact her. The excuses were getting more ludicrous as time went by. Her latest one was that the piece of paper on which he had written her number might have made it into the washing machine along with his trousers. What she wouldn't accept was that even if any of her outlandish excuses were true, being the owner of a particularly specialist bookshop made her very traceable.

But guess who called two days later? Xavier, Hallelujah! The transformation brought about in Angela by his phone call was staggering. Mind you, I thought it a bit much to ring someone on a Saturday after such a long absence and expect them to drop everything at your command. But she did. The three of us had planned a riotous Saturday evening – a Chinese and a movie. And she gave that up to go out with a wealthy and handsome Frenchman? Well, there's nought as queer as folk I suppose.

'Ermmm . . . .' She had nothing better to say in her defence. 'Come and help me decide what to wear.'

'You know, Angela, it's really quite easy to dress yourself. You just put your left arm in the left hole and the—'

'Yes, very amusing Mrs Smartass.'

'And don't even *think* about leaving any messages for us this evening. You are minding your own shop tomorrow, my dear.'

'Oh all right. At least, I suppose, that *will* help

me play a little bit harder to get than the last time. Anyway, why should you worry? It's Marcus who has to bail me out, not you. So are you two going out without a chaperone?'

'Guess so, neither of us have anything better to do. How sad is that? You know, I was convinced that moving into your place was going to magically transform my life,' I said.

'You mean it hasn't?' she asked in mock offence. 'You have two fabulous flatmates, one of them is witty, kind, urbane, clever and Marcus is quite pretty. There is no pleasing some people. The black or the red?' she asked, waving bras in my face. I was growing fonder of Angela by the day but this kind of thing I could do without. I have a very active imagination and sometimes the slightest thing can trigger it off.

'I suggest you wear that faded thing over there in the corner. That should ensure your safe return tonight.'

Angela tripped off happily two hours later to meet the perfect Xavier. He was taking her to Guilbaud's, which Angela mistook for an attempt to gain some lost ground. Now maybe I was being overly suspicious, but I didn't think you could get a reservation there just like that. Either he had this planned for some time, in which case his silence was deeply puzzling, or he had planned to take someone else there, something went wrong and Angela was a stand-in.

And yes, Marcus and I were both so much at a loose end we decided to go for the Chinese and the movie all on our own. I dithered about making myself look slightly more respectable by changing from my worn-out but comfortable trainers into my newer but less comfortable ones, but as it was only Marcus I decided not to bother.

'Ah, Anna, even drowned in black you look most radiant,' he offered as I came down the stairs.

'Oh God, not again,' was all I could manage.

'You know, don't you, that you're going to end up having a better time with me than you do with Tom.'

'Right then,' I sighed as I opened the front door. 'Come on and show a girl a good time.'

'I would if only you would let me,' he smirked.

'Arghhhh. Stop it.'

'Okay, okay, I'm sorry, I'll be normal, just for you.' And he was indeed relatively normal, for the rest of the evening at least. Of course there was minor bickering over which Chinese to go to and which film we would go see but all in all the evening passed off without major incident. We were both quite happy just to eat, watch the world walk by on the street and pass the odd comment on the other diners. I thought that sitting in silence with someone you know has its advantages over having to sparkle in front of someone you're trying to impress.

'Neither of us is this quiet when Angela's around,' he said out of the blue. 'Wonder how she's getting on with the amazing Xavier? So what about Tom?' he added after a slight pause.

'What about him?'

'That doesn't sound too enthusiastic.'

I found the idea of Tom inspiring enthusiasm very amusing and started to laugh.

'What's so funny?'

'The idea of anyone being enthusiastic about Tom.'

'Ouch.'

'Now I feel bad. It's not that he's unpleasant or a bastard or anything, he just seems a bit . . . one dimensional. He seems to be interested in very little apart from his book and mathematical equations. And I don't quite know if *we're* an equation, to be honest.'

'There's your answer then.' I looked at him blankly. 'I mean,' he continued, 'if you were an equation you wouldn't be sitting here with me wondering whether or not you were one.'

'I know what you mean, but I prefer to give people the benefit of the doubt.' As I said this, he almost snorted beer out through his nose.

'Do you indeed?' I knew what he meant but chose to ignore him. 'So is there anything you actively like about this guy? Do you have anything in common apart from a shared love of his magnus opus?

'We don't even share that. To be honest, it's a load of pretentious old bollocks.'

'Insightful criticism. But you should have at least two things in common with someone in order to get on.'

'Is them the rules? But I can't agree with you there, I don't think you have to have absolutely *everything* in common with someone in order for them to be right for you. In fact, it would be very boring. For example, "I like X", "Oh, so do I." What would you have to talk about?'

'So are you telling me that it's healthier to have nothing in common?'

'No, I'm saying that it's healthier to have differing interests.'

'Does football count as a "differing interest"?'

'No.'

'Why not?'

'That's more a morbid fascination than an interest.'

'Anyway, I'm not the best person to be giving relationship advice right now.' He suddenly looked miserable, perhaps even a little wistful, and I found it difficult to reconcile this dejection with my preconceived notions about two-timers. I had always imagined them to be a uniformly cruel, heartless bunch and never dreamed that their actions could break their own hearts as well as those of their loved ones.

'Well, I guess we all make mistakes.' It was such a trite thing to say, but I couldn't think of anything better. I didn't know him well enough to point out that his sadness was his own fault, but on the other hand, my principles wouldn't allow me to offer him any more sympathy than this. I was surprised, however, to see a quick flash of annoyance and anger flash across his face.

'Sure, we all make mistakes, we're all human, et cetera, et cetera. But a year-long affair? I think that counts as something more than a "mistake", don't you?'

'Well, yes,' I said tentatively, though I was irritated by his outburst. Did he want me to be angrier with him, more indignant?

'There's no supposing about it. I think that sneaking about behind someone's back for that long takes considerable organisational skills, so I'm afraid the "I didn't mean it, it just sort of happened" excuse doesn't really wash with me.'

I was feeling increasingly uncomfortable and confused, so I remained silent.

'Jesus, I'm sorry, Anna, I don't know what's come over me. I'm sure you don't want to sit here on a Saturday evening listening to some whinging bore moaning on about his sorry love life.' He paused for a little and stared at his plate and then, as though he realised that this wasn't quite explanation enough, he continued, 'It's just that even though it happened quite a while ago, she can still make me angry.'

'Isobel?' I asked incredulously.

'Yes, of course Isobel. How many fiancées do you think I had?'

Now I was really confused. 'But why should you be angry?'

'Why? Have you heard a word I've said?' he demanded accusingly.

'Of course I have, Marcus. I just don't understand why you would feel entitled to be angry.'

Now it was his turn to look confused. 'Is this some weird sort of female solidarity thing where you have to stick up for the woman, no matter what? How would you feel if your fiancée had a year-long affair with one of your colleagues?'

'Angry.'

'Exactly!' he exclaimed, throwing his hands in the air.

'But . . . oh!' It had suddenly dawned on me. '*Isobel* had the affair.'

He looked at me as though I were slightly wanting. 'No, my dog ran off with another owner. Of course Isobel had the affair. I thought you knew about this. Angela told me that she had mentioned something to you ages ago.'

'She did, but she told me that you cheated on her.'

'What is she like!' he laughed.

'So if Isobel had the affair, why on earth did Angela tell me otherwise?'

'Angela is one of my oldest and dearest friends, but sometimes she can be unbelievably stupid. You see, for her, if someone cheats on you it must be because of something you did wrong, or something you didn't do and so the shame of it is enormous. It would never cross her slightly unhinged mind that the person doing the cheating may just not be a very nice person. She probably thought that she was somehow defending my honour.'

'I owe you an apology.'

'What for?'

'For assuming that you were a low-down, dirty, cheatin' love rat.'

''Salright,' he mumbled through a mouthful of rice. 'How on earth did we get onto this subject anyway, because, if you don't mind, I'd quite like to change it. As you can see, it brings out the worst in me.'

'It's actually quite a relief to see that you're capable of being flustered.'

'Oh I'm that all right, when it comes to her. Now are you going to eat that spring roll, because I've just fallen in love with it.'

Before I had a chance to answer him he reached over and grabbed it off my plate. I didn't have the heart to give out, as I could tell from the look on his face that he considered eating it to be one of the happiest moments of his life.

'Well, what did you think?' he asked as we emerged from the cinema a few hours later.

'I've no idea. I fell asleep halfway through.'

'You fell asleep!' With a very rapid gesture he raised his hand and tucked some stray hair behind my ear.

103

'I've had a tough week, leave me alone.'

'You look like a cat.'

'Thank you.'

'No, I mean cats always look hazy and contented after a good nap. You know how they're so pleased with themselves that they sometimes start rubbing themselves against your legs.'

'Forget it, you'd have more chance with a cat.'

'Oh well,' he shrugged, 'it was worth a try.'

On the way home Marcus stopped off at a late-night pharmacy and bought two sets of ear plugs. He handed one of the packets to me. I asked him what they were for.

'You might need them later,' he said, slightly grim faced.

'Why?'

'Just take them,' was all he said.

At about four o'clock in the morning Angela came crashing in. Two sets of feet 'tip-toed' very noisily up the stairs. Not long after her door was slammed shut I reached out in gratitude for the earplugs.

The next morning Angela headed off to work and Marcus and I were left to entertain the lovely Xavier, who was fairly god-like, I have to admit. They say no one has the perfect body. Wrong! Xavier did. However, he could have done with a few inhibitions to go with it. After months of sharing with Marcus I had (almost) got used to him swanning around in his shorts. Xavier, however, went one step further. As I came out of my room that Sunday morning I was confronted with the sight of a completely naked Xavier casually wandering across the landing into Angela's room. I felt like an eight-year-old reading a sex education book for the first time.

'Allo,' he said nonchalantly as he closed the door. This was too much. Bad enough that I had just endured full, glorious surround-sound sex without the fun of participation. It was bad enough that I knew the rhythms of his performance, now I had to view the equipment. Call me old-fashioned, but I usually expect a formal introduction before I progress to full-frontal nudity.

I heard him make his way downstairs and into the kitchen, where, from the banging of pots and pans, I gathered that he was making himself an interesting breakfast. After half an hour or so the television was turned on in the sitting room and I could hear the sound of football. Angela had clearly told him to make himself at home and now I wouldn't be able to enjoy my Sunday morning routine of breakfast and the *Hollyoaks* omnibus. However, I was too hungry to lie in my bed and sulk so I went down to have my breakfast in the kitchen, which he had left in chaos after concocting his nice breakfast.

The worktop was covered in broken eggshells, splodges of jam, a few splashes of milk, coffee grinds and enough plates and pans to prepare for a small dinner party. As the only person in the house willing to spend money on decent coffee, he had, naturally, helped himself to mine. The eggs were mine, as was the expensive jam and the half-loaf of brioche. He had polished off the last of it. What I didn't spend on clothes, I spent on luxury food-stuffs. That was my thing, and I was livid that half of them were all over the kitchen floor and the other half were inside his majesty. I knew that if I complained to Angela she would merely shrug her shoulders and think that I was being anal over a bit of jam and buy me a replacement jar of Chivers. But this was the equivalent of helping myself to some of her designer gear and then throwing it in a bundle on the kitchen floor. But she wouldn't get this. Marcus was the only one who vaguely under-stood my food thing. But then, he would never have done anything like this.

Chapter Nine

Monday morning arrived bathed in crisp winter sunshine. If there's one thing I hate more than a Monday, it's a sunny Monday. They're such a slap in the face. I sat down at my desk with my usual coffee and jam doughnut ready to go through my usual morning routine of looking at the paper on the Internet and slowly coming to life by drinking my coffee and doing an idiot's crossword. James, of course, did Crossaire in *The Irish Times* and was continually trying to convert me. Generally speaking we had quite an amicable arrangement whereby neither of us spoke and each allowed the other some mental alone-time. That particular morning, however, my routine was broken by the unusually early arrival of Linda. Every now and again she liked to surprise us by unexpectedly turning up before eleven o'clock in order to make sure we were actually doing what we were paid to be doing. Thankfully, due to the loud clickety-clack of her heels on the carpetless stairs we always managed to stash the papers away just in time . These were the only occasions on which I experienced any sense of solidarity with James.

So in breezed Linda that morning sporting another new outfit, a sleek new up-do, a new set of Tanya Turner talons and a huge 'I've had lots of sex' smile. I think James was able to smell the sex in the air because he always got more slavish and puppyish around her on such occasions.

'So how was your weekend in the country, Linda?'

'Oh, Dromoland was wonderful, James, thank you for asking!' she squealed while throwing me a hostile look as a reprimand for not having made a similar enquiry.

'So what did you two get up to then?' she asked, glancing from James to me and back again. As if she needed to ask. The answers were invariable.

James: 'I went to see some ridiculously obscure Mongolian movie that is only showing for one night in the IFC because I am the only person in Dublin who actually wants to see it.'

Anna: 'Nothing much.'

'Really? What about this "Marcus" who sent you the flowers . . . ah dear, oops, I've let the cat out of the bag, haven't I? I'm such a silly!' she said, simpering at James, who confirmed her sense of her own adorable girlishness by smiling fondly at her.

'I'm so sorry, Anna, I really am a curious one. I confess that I was so intrigued by your beautiful flowers that I snuck a look at the card when they were sitting in the staff room sink. I *am* terrible, aren't I?' she giggled. '*Mea culpa*, so who is this mysterious Marcus? You really are keeping him under wraps Anna, aren't you? Whatever for? Is he married?'

'I live with Marcus,' I said, trying to sound both repressive and deliberately ambiguous in my phrasing, 'and there is nothing particularly mysterious about him.'

'So why was he sorry? I seem to remember something about a room.'

I was just about to tell her that she was a complete bitch with no shame, but just before my courage ran for cover, the phone rang and, being the unofficial secretary, I answered it.

'Olivia!' I squeaked in transparent despair. 'How are you? . . . Oh dear . . . But I thought we had sorted that one out . . . Well, I know, I do understand, but . . . Yes I know that you're the creative one . . . Well, unfortunately I think it *is* too late to add an extra three chapters at the end . . . Well, I think James probably *would* agree . . . I'll just put you on hold while I check if Linda is free.'

Puff! All Linda's charming girlishness disappeared in a cloud of annoyance. I handed the phone out to her, trying not to look either scared or defeated. 'Erm, Olivia would like a word with you, Linda.'

'So I gather. Put her through to my office,' she barked as she stomped off.

Twenty minutes later my phone rang.

'Anna, could you come through to my office please?'

She told me to shut the door behind me, which was one of the first warning signs that she wanted one of our all-too-regular 'little chats'. My very worst fears were confirmed when I noticed that she had provided tea and a plate of biscuits. Linda liked to play bad cop in these little scenarios and in the absence of a good one she provided a plate of biscuits. I noted with a slight feeling of consolation that she had at least nestled two Mikados in with the pile of Maries.

'Take a seat. Have a biscuit,' she said, pushing the plate across the wide table towards me. I took the two Mikados with a defiant insouciance. Ha ha! I knew that in spite of all her sophistication she liked nothing better than a Mikado with her tea. My act of daring was rewarded by a look of disgruntlement that flitted across her face.

'Anna, we seem to have been having a lot of problems with Olivia's book, haven't we? She has confided in me that she feels she cannot place her confidence in you as an editor and that, I'm sure you'll agree, is not a good thing.' She paused, obviously waiting for some kind of response from me. I took a slug of tea and bit into the second Mikado.

'Wouldn't you agree?' she repeated tetchily.

I took my time to finish my mouthful of biscuit. 'Olivia is reluctant to accept the need for any further editing. In fact, she is reluctant to accept the need for any editing at all.'

'I think we might have something of an attitude problem and that concerns me. Let me ask you something, and I hope you'll give me an honest answer. Do you like this job?'

I wasn't feeling up to indulging in honesty with Linda, so I lied and told her that I did indeed like my job.

'Well, that doesn't always come across, you know. In fact, I would go so far as to say that it *never* comes across. I feel I spend far too much of my very limited time reminding you how lucky you are to actually have a job in publishing. You should be doing your utmost to develop your skills, but instead you seem to be hell-bent on doing nothing better than antagonising writers.' Then all of a sudden she performed one of her amazing personality changes and turned from wicked stepmother into stern-but-kindly headmistress.

'Do you think perhaps that your own failure as a writer is making your editorial judgment a little . . . .' she searched for a polite word meaning 'crap', '. . . jaundiced?'

'How on earth did you know I wrote?'

'It's on your CV.'

Of course! Damn that stupid CV! It also claimed that Anna Malone made twice weekly trips to the gym, was a regular theatre goer and an active member of the Green Party since 1997.

'Well, I don't write any more.' I was annoyed to hear myself sounding petulant rather than defiant.

'Well, bingo, there's your problem! You're clearly full of resentment against those who can,' she cried out, obviously delighted with her instant diagnosis. But however right or wrong she might have been I wasn't going to be totally defeated by her. I had to make some effort to stand up for myself.

'Linda, I'm not full of resentment against anyone, I simply happen to think that Olivia has written a bad book that doesn't need editing so much as binning.'

Linda wasn't used to contradiction from anyone, least of all from me.

'Are you questioning my judgment then in taking on Olivia's book?'

'No, of course not, it's just that . . . .'

'Well, I'm glad to hear that. I don't take on writers if I don't believe that they'll go very far indeed.'

Olivia was going to go very far into oblivion but nowhere else, but I managed to suppress my reaction of hysterical mirth to Linda's faith in her.

'Anna, I really don't have time to continue this *chat* any longer, though I see that some further discussion will be necessary at some point, but that particular chat will have to wait for another time. We both have a lot of work to get on with now, *don't we?*' In other words, Linda was now bored and so she dismissed me with a queenly wave of her taloned hand.

'So how was your little chat then?' asked James with barely disguised schadenfreude.

'It was lovely, James. We talked about make-up and boys and I had two Mikados.' Ha, that wiped the smirk off his silly face.

'But they were the last two,' he whimpered.

'I know!' Now *I* was smirking.

The following day Linda did one of her infamous pulling-a-deadline-out-of-the-hat tricks. She'd let you doddle along with a book, assuring you that there was no immediate rush, when in fact she would forget all about it and then out of nowhere she would ask you if it was ready for the printer and get really pissed with you if it wasn't. Then she would set a deadline for the end of the week, no excuses acceptable. And this was to be one of those weeks. Linda decided that Olivia's opus was to go to the printers sooner than ASAP. I tried to reason with her, reminding her that it was too late for Christmas publication anyway so the printers wouldn't even look at it till the New Year, but in response to this she merely offered one of her steeliest glances and after the debacle of the day before I quietly and wisely resigned myself to a few late nights.

As I predicted, the printer laughed heartily but slightly menacingly when I rang him that afternoon.

'Forget it, Anna, not even for you,' he managed to say once he had stopped spluttering with a mixture of hilarity and rage. And with that he hung up the phone. However, I reckoned that it would be foolish to go back to Linda. She could deal with the printer at the end of the week.

At precisely five fifty-three that afternoon James leapt up from his seat, declaring that he had been concentrating so hard he had lost track of the time. As he grumbled over the loss of those valuable minutes I suggested that he might like to put in for overtime.

'Do you think I should?'

'No, of course not.'

'Then why did you suggest it? You know, you can be very odd sometimes, Anna.'

'I know, James, I'm sorry, but it helps to keep me sane in this place. Make sure you close the front door properly,' I yelled after him as he raced down the stairs.

In spite of my resentment, I enjoyed working after office hours much more than I did during them because the phone didn't ring, James wasn't there, Linda wasn't there and, more importantly, I could sneak the odd game of solitaire when Olivia's book became too much to bear, which was quite often. In other words, I could pretend that I had a normal job.

At about eight o'clock that evening I was actually working quite hard, believe it or not. I had the radio on, not loud, but loud enough to drown out the distracting noise from the street below. I was concentrating on untangling both a particularly long and difficult sentence from itself and Owen and Mary from each other when I glanced up to see a man hovering in the doorway, staring at me. I jumped and his face broke into a smile.

'You must be Anna!' he beamed at me.

'And you are?'

'Tony! I'm Tony.' He was smiling far too eagerly for my liking while slowly edging his way into the office.

'It's after eight o'clock. How on earth did you get in?'

'Well, I just happened to be passing, saw the light on, tried the door and it was open so I just came on up. Was that not okay?' He suddenly looked anxious, but the calm way in which he sat down in the seat across from my chair and took off his jacket belied his apparent concern.

'The office is closed. I'm working overtime so I can't really see anyone right now.'

'You seem nervous or something, Anna. Are you? Are you nervous of me?' he asked with apparently genuine incredulity.

'No, it's just that I have this book to get out by the end of this week and I really should get on.'

115

'You're a hard-working girl. I hope they pay you enough.' He slowly began to put his jacket back on. 'Would you like to meet up for a drink after you've finished?'

I wasn't expecting *that*.

'I . . . can't.'

'"Washing your hair" by any chance?' he chuckled.

'No, I promised my flatmate I would, ah . . . .'

'No worries. I can take a hint. It's very nice, by the way.'

'What is?'

'Your hair. You have really nice hair.'

'Thanks,' I mumbled, trying to make it plain that I didn't really want his compliment, while at the same time being careful not to offend a man who had done time for manslaughter.

'Well, some other time, perhaps.' But he was still lingering at the door. I was getting impatient.

'I'll see you next week, Tony,' I said while staring with rude and pointed concentration at the screen. I felt the atmosphere in the room freeze for a split second, then he turned and left.

Needless to say I didn't stay long after that. As I came down the stairs I noticed that he had left the front door open. I pulled it after me and quickly made my way down the street towards my stop. It could well have been my imagination, but I thought I saw his burly figure quickly turn the corner ahead. But, as I say, I may have imagined it. It had, after all, been a tiring day.

Naturally, the bus gods decided that they would entertain themselves that evening by watching me grow old at the bus stop. By the time I stepped on a bus my mood had sunk so low that asking for the ticket was nearly enough to send me off into spasms of hysterical weeping. But I just about managed to hold myself together till I got home. Just as I opened the front door Angela yelled out to ask if it was me. I just managed a wobbly 'yeah'.

'Oh good!' she beamed as she emerged from the sitting room, a glass in one hand and a bottle of red in the other. 'You can help me with this – drinking in company makes me feel less like a lush. You look like shit, by the way. Did you have a bad day?' She had progressed to the kitchen and was filling the largest glass she could find, right up to the brim. 'Here you go, a nice glass of mood-enhancer. Oh, Marcus told me to tell you that he made extra and put it in the fridge for you. It was really good, don't ask me what it was but it tasted nice . . . oh my God, speaking of Marcus, how could I forget, guess who rang him this evening?'

'Who?' I asked, trying not to sound too weary.

'Go on, guess,' she prompted.

'I can't.'

'Ah, you can. Go on.'

'*Really*, I can't.' I felt guilty about the hint of tetchiness in my voice, but it was out of my control.

'*Isobel*,' she spat as though the name were profane.

'Oh,' was all I could manage.

'Yes indeed, "oh". This is terrible.'

'By the way, I think you should know that I know about Marcus and Isobel.'

'Of course you do, I told you,' she said, looking at me like I was a cretin.

'No, I mean I *really* know. I have to say, though, Angela, that I admire your loyal and valiant attempt to hide his shame.'

'Well, I did my best,' she demurred, ignoring my irony.

'So where is he now then? Has he gone to meet her?'

'Good Lord, *no*. I have absolutely forbidden him to do that. He's gone running or swimming or footballing or something like that. I think the exercise will do him good,' she added, generously refilling our glasses. 'So, what's your excuse for a long face?'

'In a nutshell – a psychopathic boss and two psychopathic authors.'

'Oh dear . . . drink up and come and watch TV with me. And have some food. You'll feel much better.'

I did what I was told and did indeed feel much better. However, when I lay in bed that night, misery returned with reinforcements. I had never been the most ambitious of people and so, till O'Sullivan & Hackett, had been quite good at switching off the minute I stepped out of an office door. Now, though, I not only took work home with me, I ate with it, slept with it, had the odd bath with it and even took it on holidays with me. Linda may have been right about the importance of editorial experience, but I was beginning to wonder if it was really worth it. She had stung me that afternoon more than I cared to admit when she threw my failure to write in my face.

Recalling her jibe, I began to think about the contents of a cardboard box I had stashed away under the bed. I mentally flicked through the pages and notebooks, receipts, bus tickets and other scraps on which I had jotted down the odd sentence or idea. Not content with doing just that, I switched my light on, leaned over the side of the bed and hauled the box out. It was covered in dust and a sock had somehow landed on the top. I gave it a quick wipe and lugged it up onto the bed with me and began to rummage in it for something good. But I couldn't find anything. Every piece of paper I looked at had something pretentious or foolish or just plain awful written on it and I resolved to dump it all the very next day. I shoved the box back under the bed in a fit of pique and huffed downstairs for some water, as the red wine had left me very thirsty.

As I was forcing a second glass into me I heard a key in the door and instinctively looked up at the clock; it was half past twelve. Marcus glanced down the hall and saw me.

'Sorry, I just wanted to check that you weren't Angela.' From the smell of him I could tell that his run hadn't taken him beyond the nearest pub. 'That sounds really disloyal, but she was doing my head in earlier and I had to pretend to go for a run to get away from her. I'm slightly hammered by the way, I give you fair warning.'

'I know it's the most annoying question in the world, but are you okay?'

'Do I look okay?' he barked at me. 'Oh God, I'm really sorry, Anna. I'm being a grumpy bastard, aren't I?' he asked, slumping into one of the chairs.

'Oh, that's all right, it makes a pleasant change from being an infernally cheerful one,' I replied, closing over the kitchen door. 'Tea?'

'Go on then. But shouldn't you be in bed getting your beauty sleep?'

'Marcus! I'm shocked, clearly you're not okay – not only are you grumpy, you have just told me that I need beauty sleep. Dear oh dear.'

'Ah, crap!' he laughed. 'What's happening to me, Anna?' he wailed dramatically while cradling his head in his hand.

'Oh, never mind. The lack of smarm is really quite refreshing, you know,' I told him as I put his tea in front of him. 'You should try it more often.' I paused and then began a little more tentatively, 'Angela mentioned that she had forbidden Isobel any visitation rights, is that why you ran away?'

'Yep. I have absolutely no intention of seeing Isobel just at this moment in time, but I could do without Angela going on and on and on. I know she means well, but I just wish she would stop reminding me every two seconds about what a bitch Isobel was. I loved her, maybe I still do a little bit, but I can't think straight sometimes – and the anti-Isobel diatribes don't really help much.'

'How long were you two together?' I asked.

'Five years. But if I was honest I would have to admit that really only two of those were what you might call happy.'

'Really?'

'Yeah.' He trailed off for a few seconds. 'I had fancied her for ages before we got together. I thought she was the most gorgeous, sophisticated and intelligent woman I had ever met. When we actually did get together all our friends thought I was the lucky one. *I* thought I was the lucky one and that she was undergoing some sort of temporary lapse of sanity. A couple of years later she began to think the same thing – during one of our increasingly frequent rows she told me that she found me slightly dull and I think she may even have used the word "uninspiring" to describe our relationship.'

'My God, that was harsh,' I couldn't help but exclaim. 'Sorry, I interrupted you.'

''Salright, the unintentional vote of confidence is very much appreciated,' he smiled. 'Christ, I feel terrible about moaning like this.'

'Stop worrying. Sometimes it's better to talk to someone you don't know so well. I don't know Isobel so I'm not going to have an opinion one way or the other.'

He seemed to study this piece of wisdom for a few minutes. 'You know, you're really all right,' he said as though it had only just dawned on him. Perhaps it had.

'Well, I do grow on one, I suppose.'

'You can grow on me . . . .'

'Stop!' I yelled, putting my hand up. 'I don't want to hear. You're clearly feeling much more like yourself so off upstairs with you now.' He opened his mouth to speak again but I clapped my hand over it. 'No more.' The Marcus I was used to had reappeared from behind the cloud of glumness, but I worried that my interruption might have disturbed the flow, so to speak.

When I got back into bed I still couldn't sleep, but then the copious amounts of tea I had just drunk didn't help. I found myself fascinated by this woman I didn't know who could so deflate one of the most ebullient and self-confident people I had ever met. The tiniest part of me was compelled to respect such a powerful personality. It was this same part of me that secretly admired Linda's extraordinary talent for seducing any man she had a mind to. However, the image of Marcus's crumpled face at the kitchen table quickly did away with any such admiration.

The next morning Marcus greeted me with an extra-large smile and I instinctively understood that I was to forget that the night before I had caught a glimpse of an entirely different man.

Chapter Ten

The evening of my dinner with Tom rolled around and I wasn't surprised to find myself indifferent to the whole thing. If he had rung and said that he couldn't make it, I don't think I would have been too upset. Angela, however, more than made up for my lack of enthusiasm and it took quite a while to convince her that I was well fit to dress myself and to go away and leave me alone. I'm surprised she didn't want to supervise my shower just to check that I had washed behind my ears.

I felt so lethargic after my shower that I could quite happily have crawled under my duvet for a little sleep. I sat on the bed and stared guiltily at my new dress, hanging on the back of the wardrobe door.

The price tag hung down its front, looking at me accusingly. I got up and took it off its hanger, snipped the tag off quickly and pulled the damn thing over my head. The minute I had it on I felt stupid. I glanced in the mirror, and for all its exquisite tailoring and soft material I felt that I had never looked worse in my life. Sophistication and glamour didn't come naturally so I felt stiff, uncomfortable and unnatural in it. I took it off and began to pull on some safe black trousers, but I couldn't get the cost of it out of my head and so I decided that I would have to wear it, even though it meant sacrificing my own comfort.

When I came down the stairs, Angela bounded out of the sitting room.

'My God, you *do* scrub up nicely.'

I flushed and shrugged off the compliment with bad grace. I reached for my jacket from the peg beside the door.

'No, wait a second. Marcus!' she yelled. 'Come and have a look at Cinders here.'

'Angela, I'm not an exhibit in a bloody zoo,' I hissed at her as I began to put the jacket on. She made a grab for it and I grabbed it back.

'Give it here . . . no . . . let go . . . ow . . . just take it . . . .'

'Girl on girl action in my own hallway. There is a God.' I jumped at the sound of his voice and Angela took the opportunity to whip my jacket out of my hands, leaving my own with nothing to do but dangle clumsily at my sides.

'So what do you think of my transformation of Anna here?'

'Well, Ms Svengali, Anna looks lovely, but then again she always does.' And with that he ambled back into the sitting room.

'Have a good time,' he called out, 'if you can have a good time without me.'

'It's possible, you know,' Angela shouted after him. 'He always says the right thing. Thank god for Marcus, eh?' And once again I found myself thanking God for Marcus.

I had arranged to meet Tom outside The Mermaid Café at eight o'clock. I had chosen the restaurant because I guessed that if it were left up to Tom he would have booked us a table at Pizza Hut. As usual I arrived before he did but I was buggered if I was going to hang around outside on the street waiting for him, so I went on in and ordered myself a drink. When I sat down the skirt of my dress rose to what, to me, seemed like an obscene number of centimetres above my usually covered knees. I'm sure that for most women the dress would have seemed quite a respectable length, but the world hadn't seen my legs since about 1986 so I felt awkward with them on display. Angela had let out unintentionally surprised exclamations of admiration when she first saw them in the shop, but I had remained sceptical, and as I tried to cover my knobbly knees with the napkin I realised that I should have just stuck to my guns.

Ten minutes later, Tom arrived late and unapologetic.

'Ah, you arrived before me,' was his only comment.

'I usually do,' I replied, revealing slightly more irritation than I realised I had felt. Tom seemed oblivious to the arctic chill in my voice.

'Have you eaten here before?' he asked, scanning the menu. 'It's a bit pricey, isn't it. Ah well, I suppose I don't do this kind of thing very often so I'll think of it as a nice treat. Hmm, I think I'll have the risotto.' The risotto was, of course, the cheapest dish on the menu.

And in that epiphanic moment I realised just how awful Tom really was and I was growing tetchier by the minute. I'm sure the dress wasn't helping my mood as I was forced to continuously shift about uneasily in my chair, trying to yank it down subtly. At one point my gyrations caused the chair to topple over to the left and I had to slam my right hand down very quickly on the table in order to stop myself from falling right over. Tom looked at me strangely. He had just finished saying something so I said 'I agree' in an emphatic tone in order to make my odd movement seem like a deliberate gesture of agreement.

'You agree that Fermat's last theorem may be proven?'

'Yes, indeed I do. If you say so.'

He shook his head in bemusement and turned his concentration on his risotto. I had to wonder at Tom. Here he was in a restaurant with a virtually naked woman who was wobbling around on her chair and randomly agreeing with statements of mathematical theory and all he could do was shake his head quietly. What was wrong with him? Was he being polite by pretending not to notice my odd table manners or could he simply not be arsed saying anything that might lead to conversation about me rather than him? And then, as though in confirmation of this theory, he immediately launched into one of his favourite topics of conversation – his three o'clock tutorial group.

'They really are a very bright group and today's class was the most interesting I've had in a long time.'

'You said that two weeks ago.'

'We were discussing binomial chickens when an alligator came in and asked for directions to Istanbul.' Trust me, you don't want to know what he actually said about binomial theorem as it would bore you to tears.

'Marcus would really like this place,' I found myself thinking aloud. 'Must ask him if he's ever been.'

'Sorry? What? Marcus? Who's he then? Anyway, as I was saying about that fifth chapter, I thought that . . . Anna, are you in there? You seem to have drifted off.'

'I'm so sorry, Tom, I'm afraid I did. I was just thinking how delicious my meal is and how much my flatmate, Marcus, would enjoy it here. How's your risotto? Is it nice? It looks delicious. Would you like to try some of mine? No? You don't know what you're missing. And what do you think of this wine? You've hardly touched yours. Don't you like it? I think it's just so . . . .' I waved my hands in the air as though the word I was looking for was sitting just above my head. I grasped it. '*Perfect*,' I said with a shade too much emphasis.

And suddenly I felt very depressed.

'Yes, the wine is pretty good,' Tom agreed. 'In fact, it reminds me of a scene in chapter ten that I wanted to run past you. I'll bat a few ideas around if you don't mind.'

'I do mind, Tom.'

'The character has a glass of wine in front of him and he stares at it, thinking about its colour, which leads him to . . . sorry, what did you just say?'

'I said I do mind,' I repeated patiently.

'What? Why?' he looked flabbergasted.

'Tom, can I ask you something?'

'Sure.'

'Why did you call me?'

'Because I wanted to meet up with you,' he offered tentatively.

'It's not a trick question, I just wanted to know what you thought about our . . . .' again I struggled for the right word, '. . . meetings.' He wore that strained, hunted expression that passes across men's faces when you ask them that dreaded relationship question, 'where is this thing heading?'. And I suppose, in fairness, I shouldn't have grilled him like that; we weren't, after all, actually going out together.

'I enjoy our chats and I suppose,' he added hesitatingly, 'I thought we were kind of seeing each other.'

Now it was my turn to look flabbergasted.

'Seeing each other? What on earth gave you that idea? You haven't even tried to kiss me let alone anything else.'

'Well, I thought I might tonight.'

All I could do was laugh in response. Tom was clearly too gormless to be offensive.

'Well, I suppose that's reassuring. At least I know you don't find me repellent or anything.'

'Oh, I certainly don't think that,' he assured me with a wink and what I can only imagine was intended as a gallant little smirk.

'Oh good,' I sighed and excused myself to go to the bathroom, where I shut myself in a cubicle and leaned my head against the door, feeling torn between an urge to laugh hysterically and an equally strong one to cry. *What was I thinking of?* I asked myself.

'What's up?' came a voice from the next cubicle.

'What?'

'You just asked yourself what you were thinking of.'

130

'Oh great, now I've started talking to myself. This evening just gets better and better.'

'It's a guy isn't it?'

'How did you guess?'

'When women bang their heads against bathroom doors and spend far longer in them than is strictly necessary, it usually suggests man bothers.'

'So why are *you* in there then?' I asked.

'Hey, I asked you first. But if you must know, my boyfriend has just asked me to marry him.'

'But that's great . . . isn't it?'

'Dunno, that's why I've been in here for ten minutes. I'm sure he's wondering what's happened to me. So what has yours done then? Has he made a similar mistake?'

I laughed. 'He's just told me that he had thought about kissing me tonight.'

'Why are you in here debating? Wave him goodbye, my friend.'

'Yeah, I guess you're right.'

'Does he make you laugh?'

'No.'

'Is he kind?'

'I actually have no idea.'

'Is he generous?'

'He's probably splitting the bill as we speak.'

'Well there you are then. There's nothing worse than a dull and stingy man.' She got up and flushed the loo. 'I'm afraid I can't stay and chat any longer because there's a man out there waiting to have his heart broken.' I heard the door open and the click of stilettos across the bathroom floor and out the door. I emerged from the cubicle of indecision shortly after that, but when I sat down again at the table I couldn't see what had happened to my new friend. I would never know what became of her or her boyfriend.

In my absence Tom had indeed asked for the bill and was poring over it as I sat down.

'I didn't have desert,' he reminded me, 'so your share comes to twenty-five seventy-five and mine comes to twenty-one ninety-three.'

'It's so handy splitting the bill with a maths teacher,' I quipped.

'Lecturer,' he corrected me, either oblivious to or ignoring the thinly veiled sarcasm in my voice. 'So, what shall we do now then?' he asked cheerfully. 'Shall we go for a drink? Or maybe we could see a film?'

'Tom, if you don't mind, I'd just like to go home.'

'Okay,' he said affably, 'we can always see a movie next time.'

I looked at him in confusion. Surely I had made myself clear earlier on?

'Tom, I don't think that there will be another evening. I'm sorry, but I just don't think that you and I have a great deal in common . . . .'

'So you'd rather we didn't see each other again?'

'Em, well that about sums it up.'

He looked blankly at me for a few minutes and then, as though the thought had just dawned on him, he wailed, 'But what about my book?' Now he looked genuinely upset. Should I have been angry? Insulted? Amused?

'Tom, your book will be fine. You don't need me for that.'

'I suppose so,' he said dejectedly. Then a thought suddenly occurred to him. 'Could I send the finished manuscript into O'Sullivan and Hackett?'

'Yes,' I sighed, 'why not.'

I wasn't willing to let the bus gods toy with me that evening so I treated myself to a taxi home. The taxi driver was blessedly silent so I was able to sit back and clear my head. I wondered if I had done the right thing by giving Tom his marching orders; after all, I wasn't exactly inundated with offers. Impending lonliness was already making me look more kindly on him. I found myself wondering about the girl in the toilets and hoped that she had said 'no'. It was mean spirited, I know, but I would have felt cheated somehow if having acted on her advice she hadn't done likewise.

The taxi pulled up outside the house and I tipped the driver handsomely in gratitude for his silence. When I opened the front door I was greeted by Marcus's ridiculously loud laugh coming from the sitting room. I was feeling far too miserable to deal with Marcus, so I quietly made my way up the stairs.

'Angela, is that you? Where are you going with my chocolate?'

'It's not Angela, it's me,' I called out and hurried on up.

'Anna! What are you doing back so early?'

I was standing outside my room and I just wanted to crawl into bed with Captain Wentworth, but I didn't want to seem rude or make a big deal out of nothing – which was what Tom and I had been. I leaned over the banisters.

'Let's just say that things didn't quite go according to plan. Look, Marcus, I'm knackered and I just want to go to bed.'

'Come down and talk to me.'

'Where's Angela?'

'Gone to the shop for supplies.'

'She'll be back soon, I'm sure you'll survive on your own till then.'

'Ah, please, come down . . . I'll give you some of my chocolate.'

'My mother always told me—'

'Never accept sweets from strange men. I haven't heard that one before.'

'Well what do you expect if you insist on being a strange man? Seriously, though, I just want to head to bed.'

'You wouldn't by any chance be running away from Angela's cross-examination, would you?'

I nodded.

'Fair enough, I know all about *that* feeling,' he smiled. 'But just so long as you won't lie awake moping.'

I promised him I wouldn't, then I went into my room, closed the door and lay on the bed, moping.

Chapter Eleven

Christmas seemed to gallop up behind me that year and I didn't see it coming till it hit me in the face.

I hate Christmas.

Linda was busy organising her annual Christmas soirée. O'Sullivan and Hackett didn't have Christmas parties because they were too bloody stingy to fork out for a few mince pies. To be fair to the woman, Linda organised these dos at her own expense in order to make up for this lack. She invited the staff and various authors (including Olivia) around for some plonk, bitching and Marks & Spencer finger food. Not exactly a top night out, but there was no excuse good enough to get you out of it. If you rang and made your excuses from a casualty department she would expect you to ask the ambulance to drop you off when you were all tidied up. Matters were made even worse that year by her insisting that everyone bring a 'friend'. Now I knew what all that was about. Ever since my Interflora delivery, Linda had been all huffy curiosity as to who could possibly find me attractive enough to send me flowers. This was her way of finding out. Of course, my dilemma was who the hell did I bring to this thing? Tom? No way, I wasn't going to resurrect that old dinosaur. And to be honest, I wouldn't want anyone to think that we were going out together. He would be exactly what they expected my boyfriend to be – dull. I had hoped that James would, as usual, be going solo, which would have made my turning up alone almost acceptable. But the Christmas miracle had happened in O'Sullivan and Hackett – James had met a young lady and he was bringing her to the Christmas do!

'So how long has this been going on, you sly old dog you?'

'There's nothing going on just yet. I only met her last week.'

'But you've been out together, on a date?'

'No.'

'So this will be your first date?'

'Well, I don't think that "date" is an appropriate term. But yes, this will be the first time that we will be doing something together.'

'God, James, the O'Sullivan and Hackett Nightmare before Christmas. You do know how to sweep a girl off her feet.'

'Cliona is not that type of woman.'

'Well she wouldn't want to be, would she? Will she bring a good book so you won't have to worry about her not knowing anyone?'

'No, she's quite sociable,' he said with a straight face.

Although I was greatly amused by the fact that this Cliona had been foolish enough to agree to come to this thing, I was also nettled to think that I would be the only single person there. Linda was still going out with the same guy she had been going out with in October. I was looking forward to this so much I almost burst. I thought about bringing Angela, but decided against it for both altruistic and selfish reasons. It wouldn't be very fair on Angela, as this could very well be the most boring party of the year and Linda might decide that I was gay and start touching me all the time. I was moaning to Angela about my dilemma that evening when she came up with the not-very-helpful suggestion that I ask Marcus along as a pretend boyfriend. I really didn't think this was a good idea, as I pointed out that I would probably just look irritated by him all night.

'Nonsense, you'll look as though you've had a heated row, which will make you look passionate, and Linda will be made to think that you have an

138

exciting and tempestuous relationship and she'll be most jealous.'

Marcus chose that perfect moment to come in and throw himself on the sofa. He demanded to know who was going to be jealous and why and before I could stop her Angela asked him if he would mind accompanying me to my office soirée in the guise of my boyfriend.

'Absolutely,' he said without a second thought. He was obliging anyway, I had to hand him that, but I was nonetheless quite pissed off with Angela as he now knew that I knew of no other males that I could ask to perform this onerous task. I felt somewhat pathetic.

The night of the do arrived and Angela annoyed me greatly by attempting to perform another makeover miracle on me. She hovered in my doorway, offering unwanted and unnecessary advice.

'Angela! Unlike you, I am perfectly capable of dressing myself. Please go away, now!'

'If I leave you to your own devices, you'll end up looking as though you're going to do your shopping in Tesco.'

'Right, that's it, one insult too many, get out, get out, get out!' I took her by the arm and forcibly removed her from my room and closed the door in her petulant face.

'Well don't blame me if you look all wrong.'

'No, dear, I blame that on the sperm and egg that made me.'

Marcus had been working late that evening and so I arranged to meet him in a pub in town where we both helped ourselves liberally to some Dutch courage. We reached Linda's house and rang the bell. Slade was blaring from the front room. I prayed for God to at least spare me Shakin' Stevens.

'So are you ready to be so besotted of me you simply can't keep your hands off me?' As the door was opened he quickly flung his arm around my waist. I thought at that moment that I was standing at the gates of hell. The soundtrack was about right anyway.

'Anna,' screamed Linda in a worryingly jolly manner. 'And who is your lovely partner?' She was unreservedly eyeing Marcus. The nerve of the woman. He was mine . . . sort of.

'This, Linda, is *Marcus*.' I don't know why I said it like that. Together with the gesturing wave up and down made it seem like I was introducing the latest model in robo-boyfriends. *The M.A.R.C.U.S. comes fully equipped with flower-buying ability and is guaranteed for one year to say the right thing at all times.*

She was floored. I know she wanted to scream, 'Anna has a boyfriend? It's another Christmas miracle!'

'Aha, Marcus! Would you be the same Marcus who sent those wonderful flowers?'

'Well, unless there's something Anna isn't telling me, then yes, that would be me,' he said, pulling me towards him and running his hand affectionately up and down my arm.

'Come,' Linda purred, hooking her arm through his spare one, 'let's find you a drink. Anna, you can leave the coats in the first bedroom to the left upstairs,' she commanded, handing me the coat she had just taken off Marcus.

'Jesus Christ, she's a bit much, isn't she?' He had managed to escape her clutches for two minutes in order to 'bring Anna a drink'.

'She nearly didn't let me go, told me that she thought you were well capable of getting your own.'

'Well, at least she thinks I'm capable of doing something. Anyway, I would have thought you would have relished the admiration.'

'I'm not the total egomaniacal wanker you seem to think I am.' It was said with a slight smile, but I suspected that I had offended him.

About an hour later James arrived and I thought I had better go and be polite. Actually I was dying to meet the woman willing to go out with him. She turned out to be quite attractive, really, in an academic sort of way. She was blonde, just as James preferred, but she had one of those horrible short, sensible bobs so beloved of female academics. I suppose they show off the unusual and ethnic earrings that seem to be just as de rigueur among the brainy set. I reprimanded myself for stereotyping and pointed out to myself that she was probably looking at my ridiculously high boots (which

Angela had insisted on lending me) and assuming I was an airhead. James introduced us. Cliona turned out to be a lecturer in UCD, so maybe stereotypes do contain a grain of truth.

'Hi Anna, nice to meet you. I like your boots.'

Unfortunately, that was the extent of her conversational input. She was struck dumb after that and allowed James to do all the talking. And in fairness, so did I. He was boring the pants off me (and possibly her) going on and on about some dramatisation of *Finnegan's Wake* that he had gone to see in the Project. Apparently it was a very interesting but loose interpretation and was a multimedia spectacular.

'Yawn, yawn, yawn. James, it's bloody Christmas. Stop intellectualising, treat yourself to a day off,' I said. Cliona was shocked. James just laughed in a patronising way, which let me know that my ignorance didn't surprise him.

'James, I'm an old-fashioned girl. When I go to the theatre I like Shakespeare and Oscar Wilde and things like that. If I want to interpret something I go into work and study Linda and her various moods.' James then started waffling about colonialism and traditionalism and imperialism and every other 'ism' he could think off. Even Cliona seemed bored as she wandered off mid-stream to look for more drink.

Her place was taken by one of the directors. James went into crawling mode and I was left in a dilemma. My presence was surplus to requirements but I couldn't very well stomp off in a huff from a senior member of the board. I looked around the room to see who was doing what, where and with whom and spotted Marcus cornered by Linda. She was a bit too close for comfort, especially his. I could see what she was up to. They were perilously close to a door frame, all of which had been festooned in a mixture of real holly and plastic mistletoe. Then the thought struck me that Linda hadn't introduced us to any gentleman friend. Could they have broken up? Was she perhaps lining Marcus up as the next victim? Shit. I had to rescue him. His only means of putting any space between him and Linda was to move backwards, ever closer to the mistletoe and kissing-Linda-hell. He caught me looking at him and I could see the panic in his eyes. Not even Marcus deserved this.

I turned back to the conversation between James and Mr Hackett. I was just about to excuse myself when Mr Hackett decided that I existed.

'And what do *you* do?'

'Junior editor,' I said, trying not to sound like I couldn't get away quick enough.

'Lovely, how nice. And what are you working on at the moment?'

A lovely book about nuns and priests and artists who are at it like rabbits with sex addiction, you patronising old fart.

'I'm just in between projects, Mr Hackett,' I simpered.

143

'Lovely, lovely, lovely.' And off he tottered towards Trish. He probably wanted to know what the weather was like on the island of Lesbos as he was thinking of taking his holidays soon.

Great, I was released. Just as I was heading over to rescue Marcus, James grabbed my arm.

'Not dashing off on me, are you?' Where the hell was Cliona? 'You know, Anna,' he said, ignoring my emphatic 'yes', 'I think that underneath it all you're really very interesting. I mean, you're clearly not stupid.' Good Lord! Was James chatting me up? 'They really are nice boots, aren't they?' He paused slightly and then announced, 'I have two tickets to a concert next week . . . young German composer, does really interesting work, incorporating kitchen implements into the score, giving the quotidian reality of domesticity a wider symphonic scope, thereby accentuating its relevance in a world lost to issues of globalisation and technological expansionism, and I wonder if . . . .'

Oh James, whisk me off to bed now!

'Cliona!' I roared at her when she returned as though she was the best friend I hadn't seen in ten years. 'James was telling me about the wonderful concert he's going to take you to next week!' She looked puzzled and he looked embarrassed. I probably looked like I had just had a lucky escape.

I ran off as politely as I could and resolved to forget this little incident. I whizzed round, ready to help Marcus, only to discover that he had disappeared again. There was no sign of Linda either! Oh no, had he succumbed? I saw Trish with Mr Hackett. I was so worried for Marcus's safety that I had to gird my loins and interrupt. She had last seen him walking backwards into the kitchen pursued by a manic-looking Linda.

As I turned around to follow him I collided with Olivia.

'Olivia! Hi! How nice to see you!' I was almost hysterical now.

'So I hear that my book went off to the printer at long last.' She was obviously in high good humour as she was almost smiling. 'Mind you,' she continued, 'I was somewhat disappointed that it wasn't brought out in time for Christmas, but I suppose it's not really bestseller material, a bit too raw, perhaps . . . close to the societal bone, you know.'

God almighty, she thought she had written the next Booker winner. She spat the word 'bestseller' as though being one was a book's worst fate. She was too highbrow for all that nonsense. 'Mr O'Sullivan, how are you?' she beamed. Good, she was distracted, I could make my getaway.

At last, I made it to the kitchen. There he was, in a corner again. I think my heart melted a little at the sight of him. I was used to seeing him confident and sometimes even full of himself, but he looked scared and was trying very hard not to let it show. Linda obviously hadn't noticed, but I knew him well enough. He was frantically jingling the coins in his pocket – a sure sign of distress. I knew that this rescue would require a sacrifice of my dignity, but I selflessly marched up with a huge smile plastered over my face and put both arms around him. If that didn't mark my territory clearly enough for Linda, then nothing would. I saw her face drop a little and she threw me a most venomous smile. She hadn't a bloody leg to stand on. He was my boyfriend so he wasn't up for grabs. I had to literally hang on to him, as I think if I had let him go for even ten seconds she would have eaten him alive.

'Time to go, hon?' I asked.

As Linda went upstairs to fetch our coats she shot me a look along with her 'Happy Christmas' that spoke eloquently about what I could expect from her on Monday. As I was poking around my bag for my scarf and gloves I saw out of the side of my eye that Marcus was pilfering some of the plastic mistletoe. We were waved off at the door by Linda, Marcus keeping a firm grip on my hand till we were at least a good mile away.

'Thanks for the rescue, by the way. Hang on, you're losing your scarf,' he said, picking the trailing end off the ground and winding it around my neck.

'I never thought I would see you in a situation you couldn't charm yourself out of.' I was laughing at him, but not in a nasty way.

'She's your boss, I was worried that if I was too brutal, it might rebound on you. But now do you at least see that you're the only woman who can resist me?' I explained to him that her thinking that I had someone when she didn't would now make her hate me forever.

'Where are we going, by the way?' He suggested walking towards town and getting a taxi along the way. I began to grumble about being tired but revived miraculously when he offered to carry me part of the way.

'Just as well,' he laughed, 'I'd do myself an injury.'

'What are you saying? I'm not exactly mountainous.'

'You are positively sylph-like.'

'That's better. Listen, I feel I ought to apologise for this evening.'

'Not your fault,' he said with a shrug of his shoulders. He was totally relaxed again. Nothing seemed to ruffle his feathers for too long. 'Besides,' he continued, 'it seems to have brought its rewards.' When I asked him what he meant by that, he said he hoped that I now realised that he wasn't a total tosser.

'I suppose I have,' I said, smiling, 'I think now that you're only a half tosser. I'm only messin', thanks for coming.'

'Any time. You looked like you needed rescuing yourself at one point.'

'Oh God, you mean James, don't you? Marcus, I'm doomed, he thinks I'm interesting. That's the highest accolade he can bestow on anything. He was about to ask me to some experimental concert before Cliona came back with drinks. Hang on . . . Cliona, that means that in his head James could be two-timing her with me? Do you think it could have been the drink?'

'Perhaps.'

'But James? Yuk.'

'Obviously it's your eloquence that attracts him.'

'I'd rather go out with a dalek, you'd get more emotion out of one.'

We walked on towards town but the queue at the rank on Camden Street was too daunting, so we decided to try at Stephen's Green, which turned out to be even worse.

'What now?'

'College Green?'

'Let's go.'

As we walked down Grafton Street I glanced in the windows at the displays that had been there since late October. It was another three weeks till Christmas, but to my mind the decorations already looked jaded and tawdry. However, just as I was indulging this particularly profound thought, Marcus announced, 'Christmas is great.'

'What are you gibbering about? Christmas is bloody awful, everyone hates it.'

'You can be such a grumpy old man sometimes.'

'Thank you.'

'How can anyone not like Christmas?'

'What's to like?' I wondered as I studied a mannequin in the window of Brown Thomas that appeared to be wearing a piece of string and carrying a jewel-encrusted shopping bag.

'Well, I suppose when you put it like that, other than presents, food, drink, presents, meeting up with friends and family that you haven't seen in ages and presents, I suppose it is all a bit useless, really.'

'You see, the meeting up with family is what makes the rest of the year seem so magical to me . . . .'

'Christ, you *are* cynical.'

I was a little stung, but rather than try to defend myself against the charge I opted for compounding my errors.

'For God's sake, Marcus, no one has warm, snugly Christmases . . . like the ones I used to know.

No sooner had I said that than he started to sing 'White Christmas', loudly, right at me in the middle of the street. How did I react to being serenaded? Why, I did what any sensible person would do – I hitched my skirts and ran at breakneck speed down Westmoreland Street.

I only stopped running when he realised that I wouldn't stop till he had stopped. So he stopped.

'Marcus, your Christmases sound like something from the Waltons.'

'Well call me Jim-bob then. But why do you dislike it so much then, Scroogella?'

I paused before answering him. I wasn't quite ready to confess how lonely Christmas made me feel, how year after year I had nothing better to do than trail back to Armagh and Mother's disappointment. I couldn't tell him that Christmas was no better than an extended Valentine's Day.

'It's just all too commercial,' I muttered instead.

Happily, the conversation was cut short by Marcus suddenly sprinting off after a taxi that was dropping off its fare and he just about managed to get to it ahead of the stampede heading its way.

A short while later, outside our front door as I was searching in my bag for the keys, he whipped the stolen mistletoe out of his pocket and waved it over my head.

'Well?'

'Well what, Marcus? I don't think so.'

'Oh go on, it can be my "thank you" present.'

'Your what? You mean all your niceness this evening was the result of an ulterior motive? What, you want a snog as payment? If I had known this was coming I'd have gone by myself. "Thank you" present my arse!'

'Such charm and eloquence! But who said anything about a snog? Listen, I've pecked the cheek of every female I know. It's an important, and quite an enjoyable, Christmas tradition. And if you think that I'm so desperate that I would have to spend a whole evening at my flatmate's horrendous work party, fending off her insane boss just so I could get a snog out of the said flatmate, then you are very much mistaken. I'm not that desperate for female attention, my dear. So come on then, give Santa a kiss.'

'Marcus, you make Santa sound like a pervy old man, so if you don't mind, I'll decline this particular Christmas treat.'

'You don't know what you're missing.'

'I'll carry the burden of disappointment as best I can.'

'You're no fun, do you know that?'

'Yes, Marcus, I do. But thank you for reminding me.'

Just as I finally found my keys at the bottom of my bottomless bag, a taxi pulled up outside the house. The back door opened and Angela sort of fell out of it, and the lovely Xavier stepped out after her (slightly more elegantly, because the French never really get paralytic; bastards).

'Hellooo you two, did you have a lovely time? I did. Xavier is such a sweetie.' She thought she was whispering, bless her, but not only Xavier but the whole row could hear her.

'Come on you.' She lurched backwards and threw her arm out and with the luck of the drunk she successfully grabbed his hand. 'You two look like an old married couple having a row. Oh, mistletoe, what *have* you been up to? Give it here.

Think I might need it more than you two by the looks on your faces. Night, night,' and off she went upstairs, dragging the beautiful Xavier after her. 'By the way,' she called down to us from the top of the stairs, 'we're having a New Year's Eve party, so keep your diaries free!'

Chapter Twelve

Marcus drove Angela and I to distraction that weekend with his ghastly Christmas cheer. He demanded that we get a Christmas tree and decorations and I was just waiting for him to suggest we roast chestnuts round an open fire. He nagged at Angela till she agreed to allow the horror of Christmas into our home, but only on the understanding that neither she nor I would be expected to buy, help with or admire any of his efforts.

'Fine, you two be a pair of miserable old boots, I'm off to get myself a merry little tree.' And off he went tree hunting, whistling as he went out the door. I was delighted to find an ally in my hatred of Christmas. I asked her why she hated it too. 'Probably for much the same reasons that you do.'

'Family?'

'Well guessed. I'm the black sheep of our family, really, simply because I'm not a doctor, solicitor, engineer, et cetera, et cetera. Despite the fact that I basically run my own business I was branded a drop-out ever since I abandoned college and haven't yet been forgiven for it. Being single doesn't help, of course. My brothers and sisters are all either very successful and/or married. And my living on the north side simply isn't mentioned. Don't get me wrong, the annual present of fabulous wine is very much appreciated, but I have to question whether it's worth the attendant hassle. If I had a nice, sensible job I'd be fine. Actually, they would love you.'

I wasn't too sure whether this was a good thing or not. I suggested to her that perhaps we had been mixed up at birth, as my mother would think her lifestyle a vast improvement on mine.

'Maybe we could swap parents?' Angela suggested.

'Wouldn't inflict Mother on anyone.'

'Likewise.'

'Guess we'd better just get on with the ones we have.'

'I suppose so,' she sighed.

Marcus came back a few hours later dragging a real tree behind him.

'Oh look, Angela, the hunter-gatherer has returned bearing a magnificent tree.'

It was massive and Angela had a fit when she saw it.

'It's going to take over the whole sitting room, you idiot. How did you get it home?'

'Manly strength,' he beamed. 'We've got decorations and everything,' he enthused, 'John's just getting them out of the car, he'll be in any minute.'

Angela looked a bit pissed off at having to share her house with this monstrosity (the tree, that is, not John), but I just laughed. Marcus looked so pleased with himself, like an overgrown child, and sometimes his good humour was infectious.

'Look, Anna is smiling in spite of herself, she's being infected with the Christmas spirit.'

John came in then, laden down with bags of decorations. I took them from him and gently urged him into the sitting room. He had spotted Angela drifting into the sitting room and seemed to have frozen to the spot. God, this guy had it bad. I had to practically drag him into the room and push him into a chair. He wouldn't relinquish his hold of the decorations and he visibly wilted when Angela tossed a breezy 'hello John' his way. I couldn't understand her behaviour towards John. She wasn't exactly rude, but she acted almost as though he didn't exist. If she had taken the trouble to notice poor John she would have seen that beneath the painful reserve he was really nice and could be very funny, in a low-key, subtle kind of way. I think that was John all over – he was low key and Angela seemed unable to register anything other than loud and brash. And yes, I do include myself in this. And yes, he was good looking. He was a grower; you wouldn't notice him in the street, but once he got talking his face grew animated and he had a damned sexy smile, slow and wide, and an even sexier laugh, a deep, low chuckle.

I was prevented from getting too carried away by my musings by the phone, which, as usual, I answered. It was Xavier for Angela, so off she tripped into the kitchen, leaving the despondent John at least free to let go his grip of the shopping bags and talk to us.

'Now Anna, get your nose out of that book,' said Marcus in his best *Blue Peter* voice. 'Too much reading is bad for you,' he said as he snatched the book from my hands. 'Now, what job would you like to do?'

'Oh, I know,' I said, clapping my hands excitedly, 'how about . . . none!' I grabbed the book back off him.

'Oh come on you old grump, you're not going to sit and let John and I do all the work.' He snatched the book from my hands once again. 'What is it this time, anyway? *The Mill on the Floss*. No wonder you have a long face, it looks bloody miserable.' He flicked through it and I was relieved that he didn't seem to notice my own scribblings in the blank end pages. In my pretentious undergraduate days, I had been wont to write profound things in my books.

'There's a lot of death in here, isn't there . . . I'm going to make mulled wine. Anna, you have to help. You're not getting your book back till you do.'

I groaned into a cushion and told him that I hated mulled wine, which I do. It's pointless. Why take a drink that is perfectly fine on its own and make it disgusting by adding random and incompatible ingredients?

'And besides, why me? You're not going to ask Angela, are you?'

'She has no good nature to work on. And I think,' he said, nodding at an excited Angela whizzing past the door and up the stairs, 'that she may be otherwise engaged this evening.' John started to look glum again.

'Anna, come up here NOW,' Angela screamed from the top of the stairs.

'Oh what a pity, seems my services are required elsewhere.'

'Jesus, why are you women incapable of dressing yourselves?'

I went upstairs to find Angela in her usual going out frenzy of indecision. Xavier had asked her to go to his work party, which was taking place in a couple of hours. I did wonder why it hadn't yet struck Angela that Xavier's dates were always on dreadfully short notice. She had actually only discovered what he did for a living very recently, which was some sort of financial analyst for some organisation or other.

As usual she looked achingly beautiful, and looking at her I felt something like a mammyish

157

pride. When I saw how eager and happy and lovely she looked, I felt an urge to kill Xavier.

As I feared, the effect of her on John as she came in to say goodbye was overwhelming. I had heard him chatting away to Marcus as we came down the stairs, but the minute she walked in the door, he shut up. I really wanted to go up and shake the man. He didn't seem capable of even *trying,* and with Angela the old adage about faint heart and all that was very definitely true. Angela simply didn't notice shy, retiring types, and to be fair, the way John acted around her, who could blame her for ignoring an apparently dull, silent and gloomy man?

He got a breezy 'goodbye' and a vague smile; she was like a queen smiling benignly on one of her lesser subjects. And he had to watch the woman of his dreams walk off into the arms of a distinctly dubious character. Marcus and I glanced at each other and I knew he was thinking the same thing as I was. In order to rescue John from catatonic depression I decided to sacrifice my cynicism and my dignity and help them make the house look like a stupid fairy grotto. I let them struggle with the tree while I made some revolting mulled wine. Of course I kept a little wine aside for me to enjoy in its pure form. I found myself actually getting quite bossy with the lads over what went where and probably got on their nerves as I kept insisting that they take things down and put them up elsewhere and then deciding that they were actually best in their original positions.

When, finally, the tree was done, Marcus was insistent that I put the star on top, which was clearly a stupid idea as the tree was about ten feet tall.

'I'll lift you up,' he offered with a strange cross between his cheesy and his boyish smile.

'I'll help,' offered John, who was at this stage slightly squiffy on mulled wine and maudlin spirits.

I was just about to refuse when Marcus swept me up and John shoved the star into my hand. I stuck it on and was then lowered back down. As my feet touched the ground again I caught Marcus's eye. He smiled at me and I felt just a tiny frisson of something, discomfort maybe? I'd say I was probably just woozy from the wine.

We were quite exhausted after our exertions and we flopped into the chairs to admire our work. Even I had to admit that we had done a good job. It's funny how Marcus and I had got so used to our designated seats that even when Angela wasn't there we still sat in the same spot. He had developed an irritating habit, though, of stretching his arms out along the back of the sofa. John sat in Angela's chair and it was almost as if she had left something of herself behind in it, as the minute he sat in it he grew glum again. He asked questions about her latest conquest. I didn't think it would be much consolation to him if I pointed out that she was the conquered rather than the conqueror. It would only aggravate his sense of chivalry and that would make him just as depressed as his jealousy was doing.

John didn't stay much longer after the depression set back in. I decided to raise my suspicions about Xavier and it turned out that Marcus agreed with me.

'You agree with me? Unbelievable!' He just laughed. 'Angela is a bit queenly around John. I wish she would open her eyes and see what she might be missing.' I then eulogised a little on his smile and laugh, which for some reason didn't seem to please Marcus too much.

'Okay, okay, I get the message, he's any woman's dream,' he said, just a little snappishly.

I was about to snap something back when the phone rang. It was for Marcus.

'Bad news, I'm afraid. For all of us.' He drew in a deep breath. 'My sisters are descending on me the day before Christmas Eve.'

'Oh my God! All twenty-five of them?'

'Well, three at any rate.'

'What on earth for?'

'Shopping, apparently. And it gets worse.'

'Go on, break it to me.'

'One of them is bringing two children,' he grimaced.

'Let's have a drink.'

'Good idea. God help us all.'

Chapter Thirteen

The horde descended on us at eleven thirty the morning before Christmas Eve.

'Brace yourself, Anna,' Marcus warned as he made his way with mock trepidation towards the door. When he opened it three women, one teenager and two small children standing there launched themselves at him.

'Any room at the inn?' one of them asked as they all bundled in and offered him hugs and kisses.

'You look great, Marcus!'

'No, he looks like shit.'

'Orla, how many times do I have to ask you to stop swearing in front of the children?'

'Sarah! How is my favourite sister?' Marcus

asked, giving the teenage goth a large hug.

'I thought *I* was your favourite sister.'

'Hello, who are you?' one of them asked me.

'Oh, I know who she is, that's Anna, right?'

'Anna, nice to meet you. Say hello, girls,' said one of them to the two little girls, who duly chimed two polite hellos.

I noticed that one of the women was lurking quietly behind the rest of them. She was extremely pretty, but her blonde hair stood out amongst all the dark heads. She clearly was not one of-them. Mind you, the way Marcus was looking at her was sufficient proof that this was no relative.

'It's not Chloe, is it?' Marcus asked her when he had finished with his sisters.

'It is indeed!' she giggled. 'Nice to see you again, Marcus.'

'But the last time I saw you, you were this big,' he smiled, holding his hand at waist level.

'Not quite!' she laughed and gave an almost imperceptible toss of her hair.

'So how did you and Orla enjoy traipsing around Europe?' he asked, directing the question to Chloe only. He raised his voice to be heard over the din that was starting up again.

'Marcus, where are we all sleeping?'

'Do you have anything to eat?'

'Oh my God, guys, come in here and take a look at all this food!' an excited voice called from the kitchen.

'Excellent!' exclaimed the woman who had demanded food. She rubbed her hands together and trotted off towards the kitchen.

'Marcus, where do you keep your tea?'

'Ooh, tea, good idea, stick the kettle on!' cried another one, making her way to the kitchen.

'No, I want coffee.'

'Tough, I'm making tea.'

'I'll make my own then.'

'Ruth! Where are your manners? Remember that this is Anna's home as well. Anna, I apologise for my sisters, they're a very rude bunch.'

The one they called Ruth then turned to me and smiled. 'God, I *am* being rude! We haven't even been introduced. Well, there's no point in waiting for Marcus to do the honours, is there?'

'He appears to be otherwise engaged!'

'Marcus, leave Chloe alone!'

'Ha! That's a good one, more like Chloe leave Marcus alone.'

'Chloe and Marcus, leave each other alone.'

'Anyway, I'm Ruth and *I* am Marcus's favourite sister, and these are my two, Sophie and Rachel.'

'And I'm Orla, and *I* am Marcus's favourite sister. And this quiet wee one here is Sarah, everyone's favourite sister!' she said as she smiled fondly at Sarah, who I guessed to be about sixteen. She offered a shy smile and a blush in return for her sister's mark of affection.

'Nice to meet you, Sarah,' I said. 'I like your bag.'

'She made that herself. She's very talented,' Marcus said proudly.

'And finally, Anna,' said Orla, 'this is my old friend Chloe. We've known each other for donkeys.'

'I hope you don't mind me gate-crashing, Anna', Chloe smiled apologetically at me.

'So what's the plan then?'

'Let's go into town!'

'Oooh, can I go to BTs and try on silly dresses?'

'Oh yeah! And we can torment the make-up ladies while we're there!'

'Let's go!'

'Well, enjoy yourselves, ladies,' said Marcus.

'You're coming with us, young man! We've always gone shopping together at Christmas. It's tradition so there's nothing you can do about it.'

'If you think that I'm going to hang around waiting for you lot to try on dresses, you've got another thing coming.'

'Well, why don't you go off and do some boy stuff and then we can all meet up later for coffee or lunch or something?'

'Anna, would you like to join us?'

'Ah . . . .'

'What about Sarah, where is she?'

'Sarah!' they all screamed and Sarah duly appeared back in the kitchen from where no one noticed she had disappeared.

'There you are! What would you like to do in town?'

'I just want to do a couple of the bookshops if that's okay?'

'Oh, Anna will know where to take you,' said Marcus. 'Would you mind showing Sarah around? But maybe you have plans?'

I shrugged my shoulders. 'I don't, actually, I'd be glad to. Though maybe Sarah would prefer to go by herself?' I asked, giving Sarah a chance to assert her independence.

'I don't mind,' she mumbled.

'That translates into "I'd love you to join me",' Marcus laughed. 'Well, you two are well suited anyway, you can bore each other to tears about your favourite dreary Victorian novelists.'

'Great, now we're all sorted, let's go!'

And with that we all bundled out of the house and off towards the bus stop.

When we got off at the other end, we split up into two parties – Ruth, Orla and Chloe headed off to Brown Thomas, while Sarah and I decided to make a start in Waterstone's.

'Well, if you two don't mind, I'll tag along with you as I think that clothes shopping is above and beyond the call of normal brotherly duty.'

'The children!' Ruth suddenly exclaimed.

'What about them?'

'What will I do with them?'

'Well, if you feed and water them regularly they should grow.'

'No, smartass, I mean I can't take them clothes

shopping. They hate it.'

'Wonder why,' Marcus murmured, then he promptly offered to take them.

'Oh, you're the best! I haven't tried on a dress without these two for months!'

'They'll get bored,' Sarah grumbled.

'Nonsense, not when they have their favourite uncle to entertain them.'

'You're our only uncle, Marcus,' Sophie reminded him.

That day turned out to be one of the most tiring but enjoyable days I had had in a long time. Sarah was more than happy to be dumped in the classics section while Marcus took Sophie and Rachel off to the children's section. Sarah proved to be a typical bookish teenager with a penchant for gloomy nineteenth-century writers, so we got on like a house on fire. She stocked up on cheap editions of Hardy and the Brontës, but on my advice she tempered the gloom with a bit of Austen. I found it funny, but also quite flattering, that by the end of the day she looked on me as some sort of oracle. She accepted my recommendations without question and put back choices that she felt I was less than enthusiastic about.

By four thirty Sarah had run out of money and so with great reluctance she put back the copy of *Vanity Fair* that she had been about to buy and we went off to retrieve Marcus from the nightmare of the children's section. We found him looking slightly frazzled. Rachel was kneeling quietly on the floor poring over a copy of *Meg and Mog*, but Sophie had unfortunately discovered a children's encyclopedia and seemed intent on verifying every single fact in it by referring to what she believed to be the superior knowledge of her uncle.

'Marcus, why are there *seven* Wonders of the World? And what happened to the Vikings?'

'I don't know, petal, what does it say in the book about them?'

'Where is the *Mona Lisa*?'

'It's in Paris.'

'What is it?'

'It's a painting and you can read all about it in your book . . . oh thank God! Am I glad to see you two. Help me! You know, Sophie, Anna's much cleverer than I am. You should ask her some questions and I bet she would know the answers.'

'I've just remembered that I meant to look at something upstairs, won't be long!' I smirked and dashed off.

'Oh, cheers! Leave me to deal with Magnus Magnusson here.'

I ran back upstairs to buy the copy of *Vanity Fair* and quickly ran back downstairs.

'That's for you, Sarah,' I said, handing the bag to her. She looked taken aback and then she thanked me with excessive effusion when she saw what it was. She explained to Marcus that she really, really wanted to read it but had run out of money and had put it back. Then for some reason Marcus looked at me with the sort of fond look you might give your favourite pet. It made me feel slightly uneasy and I had no idea how to react. Thankfully, though, Marcus was immediately distracted by Sophie.

'Uncle Marcus, it says here that Lough Neagh is the biggest lake in Ireland. Is that true?'

'Yes, it is.'

'How do you know?'

'Because it says so in the book.'

'But how do you know the book is right?'

'I just do, chicken.'

'Okay . . . Marcus?'

'Yes,' he sighed.

'Can I have this book?'

'No.'

'Why not?'

'Just.'

'That doesn't make sense because it isn't a proper sentence.'

'Oh, all right then, anything to keep you quiet. But you must promise that if I buy it, you won't ask me any more questions.'

'Okay.'

'Promise?'

'I just did.'

'And what about you, petal? What have you got there?' he asked, leaning over Rachel, who was still absorbed.

'*Mog*,' she answered with barely a glance in his direction.

'Would you like me to buy it for you . . . so we can get the hell out of here,' he added under his breath.

'Yes. But don't swear,' she replied.

'Uncle Marcus?' Rachel began as soon as we emerged onto Dawson Street.

'Yes, my sweet?'

'Can we feed the ducks now?'

'It's practically sub-zero and you want to go and stand in a park and feed ducks?'

'Yes.'

'Marcus, what's "sub-zero"?' Sophie asked.

'It's very, very cold is what it is.'

'Can we feed them?' Rachel asked again.

'I don't want to go to the park,' Sarah grumbled. 'It's too cold.'

'See, Sarah agrees with me and Anna does too, right Anna?'

'Actually, I would quite like to feed the ducks.'

'You're a bit old for the ducks, aren't you?'

'Marcus, one is never too old for the ducks.'

'Oh for God's sake, let's go buy some flamin' bread then,' he sighed in exasperation.

'Language, Marcus!' I corrected him with a smirk.

'Marcus, the idea is to *feed* them, not dive bomb them,' I chided him ten minutes later as he fired enormous wads of Dunnes sliced white pan at the poor unsuspecting creatures.

169

'Marcus, stop it! You're scaring them away!' Sophie admonished him and I took the bread from him.

'Think I'll take charge of this till you learn to behave, young man.'

'Sorry, I'll go and sulk on the bench with Sarah.'

'You do that.'

Sarah had refused to join in, and in fairness, only children and adults over the age of twenty-five can admit without embarrassment to enjoying feeding ducks in the park.

Sophie, Rachel and I had a great time, however. They screamed delightedly when a whole battalion emerged from the water and swarmed around our feet. Marcus was getting no joy out of Sarah, as she had clapped her Walkman on her head and was buried in her new purchases.

'Can we go now?' he moaned as he ambled back towards us and the ducks.

'No!' we all said.

'Here, have another go at feeding them,' I suggested, handing him a reasonably sized piece of bread.

'I'm hungry!'

'Have some bread then, you big moaning baby.'

'The ducks are getting more bloody attention than I am.'

'You don't see Sarah complaining, do you?'

'That's different, she's a teenager and is perfectly contented with a bit of a sulk and brood over her Hardy or whatever it is she's reading.'

'Come on,' I coaxed, handing him another bit of bread, 'have another go, you never know, you just might enjoy it.'

'Anna Malone. Are you flirting with me?'

'Yeah.'

'Oh look at bully boy there, he's not letting the others get any! Greedy bast—, I mean, bad duck,' he said, and before long was enjoying himself as much as we three were.

Angela and Xavier had arranged to exchange their gifts over a meal in the Tearooms that night and she admitted that she was quite pleased to be missing the mêlée at home. Having said that, though, there was much happy squealing and greeting between them when she came home from work. Everyone except Marcus and Chloe congregated in Angela's room to chat while she got ready for her grand evening out. Orla and Ruth rifled Angela's wardrobe and tried on outfit after outfit until almost every stitch that Angela owned was strewn across the floor.

'Well, ladies, I must love you and leave you,' she announced eventually and off she went.

Meanwhile, downstairs in the kitchen, Marcus was busy cooking for us all and Chloe was 'helping' him, by which I mean that she was leaning on the counter, nursing a glass of wine and admiring how finely he could chop an onion.

I couldn't quite figure out how Marcus took Chloe's obvious admiration. He would never *not* flirt with anyone because that would be rude, but I got the impression that evening that his heart wasn't quite in it. The effort seemed to be mostly Chloe's. However, that's not to say that the whole thing was one sided. It looked, to me anyway, that he was just going through the flirting motions, if that makes sense.

Too many hours and too many glasses of wine later, we all tumbled into our beds, sleeping bags and sofas, but were unfortunately woken too few hours later by a ridiculously chirpy Marcus.

'Rise and shine, sleeping beauty.'

I pulled my duvet as far over my head as it would go.

'Anna, come on, we have an early start. I did warn you.' Marcus was tugging at the duvet, but to no avail.

'Noooo, go away and leave me alone. I'll get the bus.'

'No you won't. Come on now, get up!' With a violent tug of my duvet, he pulled both me and it off the bed and onto the floor.

'Oh dear. Are you okay?' he asked, picking me up and trying to check my head for damage.

'I'm fine, I'm fine,' I snapped at him, pulling my head away. 'What time is it?'

'Six thirty.'

'Urrrgghh!' I moaned, cradling my delicate head in my hands. 'I didn't know there was a six thirty in the morning. You're evil, you know that, don't you?' I started to get back into bed.

'Oh no you don't.' He started tugging at my covers again, and again dragged me onto the floor. 'Thank you, Marcus, the large bruise on the left-hand side of my face will now at least be nicely balanced by the one on my right.'

'I'm so sorry! I'm an idiot.'

'Yes, you are. Now make me some tea.'

Nobody else seemed to be up and I didn't see why he had to inflict his early morning chirpiness on me. At least at that ungodly hour I would be able to get a headstart on the bathroom, so I hopped in ahead of the crowd and washed away the blurriness.

Meanwhile Marcus had busied himself by making the largest breakfast I had ever seen. The boy did have his good points after all.

'Breakfast with my three favourite ladies. What could be better?' he wondered as Sophie and Rachel thundered into the kitchen.

'Marcus, would you stop, for the love of God. It's too early in the morning for smarm.'

'What's smarm?' asked Sophie.

'It's something that your Uncle Marcus does. And he is very good at it. He practises *all the time*.'

'But what does it *mean*?' she persisted.

'Being *smarmy* means saying nice things to people,' Marcus told her.

'Oh . . . Mammy, you're smarmy!' she exclaimed happily as her mother came in with a huge towel wrapped around her head and a grumpy expression on her attractive face.

'What?' she snapped. 'What's she talking about? Marcus, what have you been saying to her? Where's the coffee?' I looked in awe and trepidation at the very nice person of the evening before, transformed into a monster of morning grump even more terrifying than Angela. Marcus nudged me and whispered that she was even worse than I was in the mornings.

'What do you mean?' I expostulated in a whisper. 'I'm not *that* grumpy in the morning.'

Marcus let out a loud spluttering laugh.

'Anna, during the day you are truly lovely, but in the morning you make Godzilla look sweet tempered.'

'That's not a nice way to talk about your sister, Marcus,' quipped Orla, who had just come in.

'Would you all stop bloody shouting,' Ruth snarled. She was messing unsuccessfully with a coffee percolator.

'No, Orla, I'm talking about Anna. Ruth, I've already made coffee,' Marcus said.

'Marcus, you're so rude sometimes,' Orla said. 'You know I only drink percolated in the morning,' Ruth said.

'Jesus, Ruth, you're such a fussy moan,' said Orla.

'Don't swear in front of the children,' Ruth said. 'They don't understand. Give me that percolator, I'll do it,' Orla snapped.

'Don't snatch! They do understand. Sophie, what did Orla just say?'

'She said "Jesus".'

'And why should she not say that?'

'Because it's a bad word.'

'Well, it's not a *bad* word as such . . . .'

'Anyway, you swore only five seconds ago,' Orla interrupted.

'I did not!'

'Yes you did, you said "would you all stop bloody shouting". Which we weren't doing, by the way.'

'Oh.' Pause. 'Orla, are you trying to make coffee or dishwater? Put more coffee in the thingie.'

'Ruth, would you sit down, shut up and stop giving orders.'

'Orla, you're not being very smarmy,' Sophie chipped in.

Marcus looked remarkably unfazed by the chaos around him. I found myself simultaneously confused and fascinated by this family noise. I had never experienced anything like it; the shouting in my family wasn't underscored by this lot's unspoken, loving tolerance of each other. I couldn't hide my confusion and Marcus noticed my glances from face to face as I watched the exchanges between the sisters played out like a tennis match. I glanced over at him at one point to see that he had been looking at me with amusement.

'You get used to it,' he said with a smile.

I felt myself break into an answering smile, but then his glance flicked away towards the door.

'Sorry, I hope I'm not holding you all back. I'm so slow in the morning. It takes me ages to get ready.' Chloe beamed an apologetic smile around at all of us and then let it rest unapologetically on Marcus.

It was little wonder that it took her so long to get ready in the mornings. Chloe was the most groomed woman I had ever seen; Angela would have looked a mess standing beside her. Even at that ungodly hour she managed to look as though she was ready for a night out. Not one of her glossy chestnut strands was out of place, she had no pillow creases on her face, no sleep in her eyes. And to top it all, she seemed like a nice person so I couldn't really vindicate the slightly chilly feeling I felt towards her. Marcus's fawning could only be excused by the fact that Chloe was one of those women who could probably make even the most devoted of partners and husbands leap to attention and rediscover their inner gentleman.

'Orla, Ruth, budge up there and make room for Chloe. What would you like, Chloe?' he asked with much more solicitation than any of the rest of us had got and immediately started to fuss about the kitchen, trying to salvage some breakfast from the wreckage of our selfish bingeing.

'Oh, just some coffee . . . and some fruit if you have it.' She smiled and I noticed that all the women except Orla looked a little shifty and guilty, as though her healthy habits highlighted our own piggery.

I amused myself by watching Marcus being more than polite to Chloe. He stood by the worktop and chatted with her as she ate her meagre breakfast. I couldn't really hear what they were saying, because even though our kitchen wasn't enormous, I couldn't hear anything apart from the racket at the table. However, there was much hair flicking and smiling and laughing and, remembering Austen, I couldn't help thinking that the whole thing 'had such an appearance as no English word but flirtation could very well describe.'

Chloe eventually finished her three grapes and two sips of black coffee and Marcus ordered us all to be ready in ten minutes or he would go without us.

'Oh God, I'm so useless, I haven't even started to pack yet,' Chloe apologised and suddenly it seemed that we were not in fact in any great rush at all.

'I should probably go and get petrol before we start, so take your time, Chloe.'

'It's a shame you didn't mention the lack of urgency when you woke the rest of us at ten to six,' said Ruth, caustically airing my own thoughts.

I decided to use the extra time to go over the pile of books I had taken with me to make sure I had made a wise choice.

As I was dithering in my room, I overheard Chloe and Orla in the bathroom next door. I think they were brushing their teeth and having a conversation at the same time.

'So exactly how long has it been since the fiancée?' I heard Chloe ask.

'Not long enough, Chloe,' Orla responded with a warning tone.

'I'm only asking! I'm not going to leap on him or anything. I'm just curious.'

'I know you are, too curious. Remember, I've had to mop up the consequences of your curiosity before. Seamus didn't get over you for years. Probably still hasn't. Besides, Chlo, I'm not sure you'd have much of a chance.'

'Chlo' answered with a snort of derisive laughter.

'I'm serious, Chloe. I could be very wrong, but I don't think you have much chance of anything more than a bit of harmless flirting. Besides, I wouldn't want you getting your claws into him. He had a bad enough time with Lady Isobel, who I hear has only just taken a break from tormenting him on a daily basis. Going from her to you would possibly drive him into therapy for the rest of his life.'

'Why thank you, Orla! What a kind friend you are!'

'Chloe, my flower, I think that you are the lovliest person in the whole wide world, but knowing your track record with men as I do . . . need I say more?'

'You can be such a bitch sometimes, Orla, and I hate you.'

'No you don't. You love me. Now get a move on. If you brush your hair any more it will all fall out.'

A car horn blew outside and we all scrambled downstairs and milled around the two cars. Ruth was the other driver and we all waited to be divided up between them. I naturally gravitated towards Marcus's, as did Chloe – throwing a provocative smirk at Orla as she did so. Ruth's children proved themselves very weird by demanding that I go in their car.

'Ask Anna nicely, girls,' their mother chastised them. So they did, very nicely, and I couldn't refuse.

Chloe looked pleased, but Orla did not.

The journey turned out to be surprisingly pleasant. The coffee had returned Ruth to her normal self and I couldn't help but be flattered by my fan club in the back seat.

'My two seem to have taken a great shine to you, Anna,' she said as they dropped off to sleep just outside Carrickmacross.

'Yeah, it's odd all right. But don't worry, I'm sure they'll get over it.'

'How do you like sharing with Marcus then?'

'Well, let's just say he has his moments . . . .'

'A polite way of saying that he can be a right pain in the ass,' she laughed. 'But he means well. I'm surprised he doesn't bombard you with the charm. Did you see his performance with Chloe this morning? He was always like that, though, bless him. Even in infant's school he used to come home and all he could talk about was all the lovely girls in his class.'

'So I guess he must have had a good many girl-friends?' I prompted, curious in spite of myself.

'He hasn't had as many as you might imagine from the way he goes on. He's very flirty all right – as I'm sure you've noticed. He would flirt with a stick if nothing better presented itself. But he's only had three or four *serious* girlfriends, well, as far as I'm aware anyway. He doesn't attach himself too readily and when he does, he really does . . . that's why we all hate Isobel so much.'

'She doesn't seem to ring him as much these days, if that's any consolation.'

'But she still rings?'

'Sporadically.'

'She trampled all over him for five years, but he's such a soft-hearted idiot I wouldn't be surprised if she finally gets her way again.'

I knew it shouldn't have made any difference to me whether or not Marcus and Isobel reunited, but for some reason I felt the tiniest flicker of panic somewhere in my stomach when she said this. But it didn't last long and I had forgotten it almost as soon as I recognised it.

We arrived in Armagh almost three hours later and I thanked Ruth profusely for the detour she had made on my account.

'Good Lord!' she exclaimed as she pulled up the drive.

'Is your house a palace?' Rachel asked.

I suppose I should now explain that when my parents married they sank all their savings into a semi-derelict Georgian farmhouse. My father had been a full-time art teacher and part-time DIY expert and my mother was a full-time arty type, so the prospect of renovating a ruin filled them with great enthusiasm and pleasure. It did look wonderful now, but that was because of the years of hard work and denial (theirs *and* ours) that had gone into bringing it back from the dead. When my father died various well-wishers tried to persuade Mother to sell the house and move into something more manageable, but she refused. She told the well-wishers that there was still far too much to be done and to mind their own business. I think she might have felt that Da would have been disappointed if she had given up on their pet project, so I suppose, in a way, her finishing it was quite a romantic gesture. So she carried on and slowly, over the years, in between knitting us horrid jerseys, she turned the derelict heap into something approaching a house and home.

As a child, this house had been a source of slight embarrassment. Because of where I lived, the other little girls in my class assumed that I was a bit posh. On the few occasions that I invited friends around to play or to a party, they would stare about them with obvious and rude curiosity at the shabby furniture, at mother's knitting basket, at the framed nudes from my father's student days. Despite the huge fire and the streamers and banners, the dining room always remained determinedly cold and austere and the cake and the rice crispie buns always seemed to shrink as soon as they were set down on the huge dining room table. The little girls always fidgeted in their chairs around that table and I always assumed that their uneasiness had something to do with me. I never imagined that a table could cause such a reaction.

When I stepped out of Ruth's car I was surprised to see Marcus's coming up the road behind us. He pulled up and got out.

'I suddenly realised that I never got a chance to say happy Christmas,' he explained. 'So, happy Christmas Anna.' As he said it he pressed a small parcel into my hands.

'Oh, but I didn't get you anything. I'm so sorry, I didn't think—'

'Don't worry,' he interrupted me. 'It's only a tiny thing. And I can think of something you can give me in return.' He leaned in very suddenly and planted a smacking great big kiss on my cheek.

'Got you!' he smirked, then jumped back into the car and drove off.

I caught a glance in the back window and saw that Orla was smirking. Chloe, however, was not.

Chapter Fourteen

I let myself in the door and was greeted by the shocking sight of a huge canvas on the wall, daubed with large splodges of muddy paint. I had never seen it before and it was hideous. I guessed that it might be part of some new venture of Mother's. I called out for her but she wasn't in, so I stood and examined it a little longer. But it still made no sense to me. Just as I was trying to determine whether a blue and green blob was, in fact, a small screaming face, the door opened and the artist herself greeted me.

'Anna, love, it's great to see you,' she said, giving me a perfunctory hug. 'Come and help me unload the car. What do you think of my painting then? It's actually only just finished. I think I may have rushed it just a bit at the end, but I was so keen for you all to see it. I've been taking lessons. Did I not mention them to you? Oh, I was sure I had.'

'It's very interesting.'

'Oh good, I'm glad you like it. I've called it *In the Dead of the Night*.'

It sounded like the title of one of Tony's poems.

'So how have you been? Was the journey all right? Town is bananas. Do you think people might be stocking up for the New Year or something? Jason will be here later on today, by the way. He's bringing his latest with him, but I can't remember her name. Paul and Geraldine will be here on Stephen's Day . . . and not forgetting Ronan, of course,' she added, failing to hide a certain steeliness in her smile.

'Ah, bless, how could we forget little Ronan?'

'So where are your friends Annabel and Martin spending their Christmases?'

'Angela and Marcus are with their families.'

'God, are you not all getting a bit old to be trailing home for Christmas . . . not that you're not very welcome and all that, but when I was your age, your father and I were just setting up this place.'

Mother was one of those strange mothers who express their love by finding fault and their pleasure at seeing you, but attempts to drive you away. As it was Christmas Eve, however, I decided to extend peace and goodwill by holding my tongue, but I think my failure to react irritated her, as she continued to pick away at me throughout the day about the fact that at the age of twenty-nine I had nowhere better to be at Christmas. I was about to go upstairs with my bag when she stopped me and informed me that I would have to sleep on the sofa bed in the sitting room, as she had given my old room to Paul and Geraldine. Visitors always caused problems in our house because although we had a good many rooms, we didn't have enough beds or radiators.

'What do you mean you've given my old room to Paul and Geraldine? They're not even coming till tomorrow.'

'Well, I have no intention of changing sheets on Christmas Day.'

'They won't be gassed, Mother, after one night of me in the bed. Anyway, I still don't see why I have to give my room up. Why can't they take the spare room?'

'Because Jason and Delphine are getting that.'

Sometimes I really wished for a nice Catholic mammy who would be shocked at the very idea of a couple of only five minutes sleeping in the same bed.

'So who's getting Jason's old room?'

'Ronan.'

'Why should he get it? Why can't he have the sofa bed?'

'Use your head, Anna. I can hardly ask a four year old if he would mind waiting till everyone else had gone to bed before he did the same.'

'Oh, but it's perfectly okay to ask me?'

'I *was* going to say that you are not four, but I wonder sometimes.'

'Why can't Paul and Geraldine have the sofa bed then?'

'*Because they are a couple*,' she said with a barely concealed 'nudge nudge, wink wink'.

'Lord, why can't you just disapprove of sex the way you're supposed to?'

'Anna, would you please stop being so childish. And the sofa bed is perfectly comfortable apart from anything else.'

'Good, then Jason and Whatsherface will be very comfortable in it, won't they?' I said as I defiantly stomped up the stairs.

'Anna, get back here now. They are having your room and that is that. You don't need the privacy.'

'Of course I don't, what was I thinking? What would a sad all-alone like me do with privacy?'

'Oh please don't start, it's Christmas Eve.'

'So?'

'For God's sake, Anna!'

'What do you expect? I seem to be for ever giving way to your precious sons. Maybe I should be a bit more like Jason with his five-minute girlfriends. Maybe then I might get a bit of respect, hell, I might even get a real bed in a real bedroom.'

'*Maybe* you should stop feeling so sorry for yourself and stop ranting and moaning all the time.'

I broke off mid-flow, feeling as though she had just slapped me. I couldn't think of any better way to respond than to offer a sulky denial. I really wanted to storm upstairs and slam a bedroom door, but because I had nowhere to go, I began to feel foolish and slightly ashamed of my outburst.

'Come and have some coffee. I've made a chocolate cake.' With an unexpected and unusual gesture of tenderness she put her arm around my shoulder and gently guided me into the kitchen. The chocolate cake was sitting proudly on the table and I smiled, as her baking skills had always gone some way to compensating for her tendency to try to live the 'good life'.

She sat us down with two mugs of really strong coffee and two large slices of cake.

'Well, do I still make the best cake in the world?' she asked as I took the first bite. As my mouth was full I could only nod dumbly in reply.

'Tell me what the matter is, Anna.' I looked up from my plate, surprised as much by the concern in her voice as by the request itself.

'I don't know what would make you think there was anything the matter.' Which was, of course, a stupid thing to say, and I had to stop talking quite suddenly as I was uncertain now of any steadiness in my voice.

'C'mon,' she said, gently putting her hand on mine. 'I may be a demented old lady, but I'm still your mother and I'm afraid we all come with an in-built sixth sense,' she smiled.

I was torn between an urge to cry good and hard and an equally strong one to tell her to mind her own business. Emotional exchanges with Mother had been few and far between and those few we *had* shared had left me feeling drained for some time afterwards. I stared silently at the crumbs on my plate and remained silent.

'Every time I ring you seem determined to pick a fight – don't interrupt, you know it's true. And you seem to forget sometimes that I did give birth to you and raised you, I know you better than you think. Even as a little girl if you were sad you would shout at me and hide under your bed rather than look for a hug.'

'What a strange child I was.'

'Well, you had your moments, dear, I must say. But my point is that I know that you can't hate me as much as all your shouting should lead me to believe. I know you're unhappy and I just wish you would tell me why. You never know, I might even be able to do something about it.'

'Doubt it. Unless you can wave a magic wand over my head and give me a new life.'

'It's not that bad now, is it?'

'Oh come on, Ma, you're never done implying, not very subtly, mind, that it's dull as hell. Work is a nightmare, Linda hates me and thinks I'm as thick as two short ones, James is a malfunctioning humanoid and all the authors I have to deal with fit in somewhere along a scale from crazy to psychotic.'

'And what about your own writing? Do you still do that?'

'How did you know?'

She laughed. 'You are many things, but secretive is not one of them. You were always scribbling as a child and you left all your notebooks stacked up on your desktop—'

'You didn't—?'

'Of course I didn't read them. What do you take me for? You know, your English teachers always thought the sun shone out of your you-know-what. They loved your stories. When the other kids were writing about school sports day you were writing about Miss Penelope Smyth-Witherington's first cotillion ball and the like.'

'Miss Who? I have no recollection of her whatsoever. How do *you* remember her?'

'You showed me the story, believe it or not. I think you were quite proud of it – and rightly so. If I remember correctly, Miss Smyth-Witherington was being pursued by Mr Henry Fortinsque but she wasn't interested because she planned to travel around the world, and when Henry pointed out that a lady couldn't do that, Miss Smyth-Witherington promptly cut her hair and bought herself some breeches.'

'So was poor Henry left languishing?'

'I'm afraid he was.'

'Oh dear.'

'But then in the *next* story, Henry realised that he couldn't live without his beloved Penelope, even if she was a bit improper, and he went off after her.'

'Oh good, I like a happy ending.'

'So do you still write?'

'No, I kind of gave it up.'

'You "kind of gave it up"? Well, that was a silly thing to do. You should take it back up again.'

'It's not that easy.'

'Yes it is. But I bet you woke up one morning and got it into your head that you were no good and decided there and then just to stop.'

'That about sums it up, yes.'

'Well, that's very stupid. How will you know if you're any good at writing if you don't write? Maybe you are rubbish, but there's only one way to find out, isn't there?'

'But even if I do that, it's not going to magically transform my life. It'll only make it more frustrating.'

'God almighty, why must you be so defeatist all the time?'

'Because I don't see any reason not to be.'

'Sometimes, girl, I really, really want to strangle you. I know you think that I'm unimpressed with your "boring" life, but, as always, you get it wrong. What drives me insane is not the fact that you don't do anything with your life, but the fact that I know you want to but you seem to have dug yourself into some sort of rut and don't seem to want to do anything about it. If I thought that you were happy just sitting around, waiting for life to happen, that would be fine.'

'That's not fair. It's nothing like that. And I never said my life was boring. Not everyone wants to run off with the circus or go meditating in the Burren or go and set up an organic pig farm.'

'I never once said that they should. But I don't expect a daughter of mine to sit back and let her life wash over her as if there were nothing she could do about it.'

I was saved from the bother of a response by the sound of the front door opening, followed by my brother Jason's voice calling out a hello.

'We're in the kitchen, love,' Mother called out with palpable delight. 'Jason, how are you?' she asked while engulfing him in a massive embrace. 'And you must be Delphine!' she beamed at the tiny, waif-like creature lurking in the doorway. In response Delphine offered a pensive little smile and a fluttering wave of her tiny hand. She had a far-away expression in her huge, pale blue eyes and when she turned them on you she seemed to be looking through you rather than at you. She looked like the slightly bonkers but fragile heroine of a subtitled movie and had 'rescue me' stamped all over her. When Mother asked her if she would like some coffee, Delphine surprised us all by answering in a Cork accent that could have cut paper. She surprised us even more when she polished off two large slices of cake with her coffee. Clearly there was nothing gamine about her at all.

I slipped off and left Mother to get to know

Delphine a little better, but as soon as I got up from the table I realised that I had nowhere to go. While I sat and disconsolately surfed the television in the sitting room/my bedroom, I remembered that I hadn't yet opened Marcus's gift. I picked it up from on top of my rucksack and smiled at the appalling job he had done with the gift wrap. There seemed to be more Sellotape than paper, but when I finally broke through the tape I found a leather-covered notebook and a pen. The notebook was beautiful, but I couldn't understand why he had given it to me. He often teased me about always having my nose stuck in a book, but I didn't think he suspected me of attempting to write myself. There was a small card inside the notebook, which I opened. It had a picture of a Victorian family Christmas scene on it. One particularly winsome child with ginger hair was frolicking with a dog and he had written my name and an exclamation mark over her head. Inside he had written: *I saw these and thought of you. Hope I got it right? M.*

It seemed a shame to spoil the lovely creamy paper, but on the other had, it looked a bit naked without any words on it. Naturally the present made me think about the giver and I found myself remembering our very first encounter and I smiled. And because I couldn't think of anything better to write in my new book, I wrote about that.

Chapter Fifteen

I was woken on the morning of Stephens's Day by Jason, who had come into the sitting room with his breakfast in order to watch *Mary Poppins*.

'Jason, would you please bugger off. I'm trying to sleep.'

'This is the sitting room, Anna, common space, you can't throw me out.'

'"Common space"? What are you on about? This isn't like your squat in Zurich.'

'Exactly, so you can't hog a sitting room and claim it as your bedroom.'

'Oh, touché, Jason.'

I got up, wrapped the duvet about me and waddled into the large, cold kitchen where I curled up on the battered old sofa Mother kept in there and had, in the past, used as a bed for the occasional stray cat she took in to nurture. 'Anna, get up, it's ten o'clock,' Mother roared as she came in shortly after I had just managed to nod off again. 'I'm putting on a wash, do you have anything? Anna,' she began prodding at me, 'do you have any washing? Come on, get up. Paul, Geraldine and Ronan are arriving later, we haven't much time to get ready.'

'What do you mean? How long can a bomb shelter take to build?'

'That's not very Christian of you,' she laughed.

'Well, you're not a Christian, so it shouldn't bother you.'

I got off the sofa and went to hunt for my washing, but in my fuddled state I bundled up clean clothes along with the dirty and shoved them all in the machine. When I woke up and realised what I had done, it was too late to do anything about it and I realised too that I would be forced to wear the jumper that Mother had made me for Christmas. It was pink.

I had felt surprise and trepidation when she handed me a squashy parcel, while declaring proudly that she had made it herself. It had been a while since she had given me clothes for Christmas and I had thought that she had finally come to know better. The image of a 'free-form garment' flashed across my brain.

I opened it quickly in order to get the horror over and done with and so I was not a little surprised when I pulled out a delicate, beaded cross-over cardigan. If I had been into colour, I would have thought it a beautiful shade of dark rose pink. If I had liked girlish clothes I would have thought it lovely. I genuinely admired and praised the work that had gone into it, but I couldn't keep the surprise from my voice. The last time I had seen one of Mother's efforts at a jumper it was having a hole picked in it by Jason.

'It's beautiful, thank you.'

'But will you wear it?' she asked eagerly. 'That colour always suited you,' she said wistfully.

'Of course I'll wear it,' I smiled as I carefully folded it up and put it to one side.

That morning I had no choice but to wear it. Mother had both environmentalist and financial objections to over-use of central heating and so left it off for as long as possible. If I didn't wear it I would die. Mother practically had hysterics of pleasure when she saw me in it.

'Anna! You look lovely. Oh, I did do a good job, though I say so myself. And I got the colour just right. It suits your complexion so well. It makes you look pale and interesting rather than washed out!' she cooed as she fidgeted with the shoulders, trying to make it sit more elegantly on me.

Bless her, I think she thought she had won some sort of victory and I realised that it would be churlish to point out that I was only wearing it because I had stupidly put everything else in the washing machine.

Just after lunch I settled down in front of the television with a large mug of tea and a large wedge of cake, all ready to enjoy the last few hours of calm before Hurricane Ronan arrived, when the doorbell rang. Jason and Delphine were upstairs doing God knew what and Mother was outside, having found some urgent task to do from her never-ending list of urgent gardening tasks.

'I'll get it then, shall I?' I asked myself. I assumed that Paul and family had arrived early, so I was taken aback when I opened the door to see Marcus standing on the doorstep.

'Marcus!'

'Jesus Christ, Anna! You're wearing *pink*!'

'What on earth are you doing here?'

'And it's lovely to see you too. Here, take this,' he said, handing me bottle of wine. 'Well, are you going to ask me in or do you normally entertain your guests on the doorstep?'

'Sorry, come in. I just wasn't expecting you. But what *are* you doing here?'

'What are you doing wearing pink?'

'It was a present.'

'Oh good, that's a relief. Just so long as it's nothing to do with a new personality. So long as the old Anna lurks beneath the new fluffy exterior, it's fine by me.'

'Well, if you're quite done being charming, you still haven't answered my question.'

'Are you this rude to all your guests? It's Christmas, people visit each other.'

'Why?' I persisted. 'You only saw me two days ago.'

'Do you know something?' he laughed. 'I pity any poor fool who ever gets it into his head to try to whisk you off you off your feet. Random gestures are not meant to be questioned, just appreciated. Now you're supposed to offer me some tea, or even a drink if I would prefer it, to which I will reply that I am driving so a tea will do very nicely, thank you very much.'

'I take it you'd like some tea?'

'Well done! I would indeed.'

I didn't want him there. I should have been pleased to see a friendly face, but I wanted for nothing more than him to suddenly remember that he had to be somewhere else – and remember before my mother came in from the garden.

'This is an amazing house. How old is it?'

'Dunno, very old.'

'Who did the painting?' he asked, eyeing Mother's masterpiece with apparent admiration.

'You mean you like that?'

I think Mother's 'potential boyfriend' antennae had picked up on the presence of a man in the house, because she miraculously appeared in the kitchen the minute Marcus sat down at the table. And just to make things worse, she transformed before my very eyes into Mrs Bennett.

Her painting wasn't really *that* good . . . what did he do for a living? A graphic designer . . . great

197

job . . . very talented . . . would he like to stay to dinner . . . no, the roads wouldn't get bad for ages yet . . . quite safe till at least ten o'clock . . . very lucky with the roads around Armagh . . . Donegal not that far away . . . make it home safely by mid-night . . . any food allergies? . . . how long had he lived in Dublin . . . seven years, a long time, seven-year itch, ha ha ha . . . what was it like living with me . . . she could imagine, ha ha ha . . . was he sure he had no food allergies . . . very pleased to have him . . . he was welcome any time . . . would he like some more tea . . . and what about some cake?

I was waiting for her to ask how many thousands he earned a year and then declare that he would do very well for me.

'Marcus, would you like to see the garden?' I asked abruptly and loudly. Both Mother and he looked at me as though I had just said something very odd indeed. Mother probably wondered at this sudden interest in her garden and I'm sure Marcus wondered why I thought he might be interested.

'If you would like to show it to me, then I would like to see it,' he said politely, but with some confusion.

'Come on then,' I said, leaping up from the table and dragging him away from his tea.

'So why the anxiety to show me the garden? It's lovely, but I'm not what you would call an expert.'

'Sorry about Mother. She can be a bit much sometimes.'

'She seemed perfectly friendly to me.'

'A bit too friendly. You know you don't *have* to stay for dinner.'

'Anna, would you like me to leave?'

'I'm sorry, I didn't mean to offend you. I just don't want you to feel bullied into staying.'

'I don't, but if the thought of me staying upsets you as much as it seems to, then I wouldn't dream of imposing myself on you any longer than necessary.'

I hung my head in mute embarrassment.

'I came because I missed you,' he said.

'You did?'

He laughed at my obvious confusion. 'Yes, indeed. There was too much love and adoration at home and it was all getting a bit cloying, so I thought I'd drive down here for the afternoon for a bit of guff and the odd withering comment. It makes for a refreshing change and for some reason I seem to have grown oddly accustomed to having my ego punctured on a daily basis.'

'Would you mind if we just sit outside for a bit? It's not really *that* cold.'

'No, indeed. Compared to the North Pole it's positively balmy.'

'Oh!' I exclaimed suddenly.

'Oh?' he imitated me.

'Your present! I almost forgot. Thank you, it's beautiful.'

'You're very welcome.'

'What made you choose them?' I asked shyly.

'Like I said in the card, I saw them and thought of you.'

'Yes, but why?'

'Well, you always leave your books lying around the house and sometimes I pick them up to see what nonsense you're reading and I've noticed that some of them have scraps of writing on the blank pages at the back.'

'You've never . . . .'

'Read them? Of course not! I'm a gentleman.' But he was grinning at me rather suspiciously.

The sun emerged briefly and shone right into my face. It took away the worst of the cold and we were quite happy to sit outside for another little bit. I enjoyed the peace and calm, but not for long. I heard a car draw up to the door and Geraldine's thick Monaghan accent shouting a greeting to Mother and Jason. Then she was in the garden, invading my quiet space.

'Anna, hi! What are you doing out here, it would freeze the balls off a brass monkey. Ha! ha! And who is your wee friend? Come inside. You're look-ing so well Anna. I would barely have recognised you. What have you done to your hair? The colour looks . . . less red, but not *dull*, of course. Lovely. I sometimes thought your old colour was a bit much, bit too ginger, but it's lovely now, really subtle.' (I hadn't done anything to my hair.)

Then, as though struck by a highly amusing thought, she burst into loud shrieks of laughter.

'Oh, hear me!' she twittered. 'That probably sounded really bitchy, but you know I don't mean anything by it . . . and aren't you going to introduce me? I'm Geraldine, Anna's sister-in-law.'

I didn't give Marcus a chance to introduce himself before I launched into my counter-attack.

'You're looking very *healthy* yourself.' Then, as though it were a complete non sequiter, I offered, 'Christmas is such a killer, isn't it, with all that lovely food,' I said, staring intently and obviously at her waistline. 'Sorry, I'm very rude, this is Marcus, my flatmate.'

Geraldine didn't really like anyone apart from herself. She just about tolerated her husband and child, so it was no surprise when she didn't fall instantly beneath the Marcus charm. Just as she was grumbling about the cold and turning to go indoors, a small, screaming, swearing ginger rocket came out of nowhere and launched itself at my legs.

Darling Ronan.

'Fuck off! Fuck off! Fuck off!' he roared and was apparently delighted with himself as he laughed insanely and butted his little head against my knees.

'And a happy Christmas to you, Ronan,' I responded, gently but firmly taking his shoulders and holding him a little away from my knees. 'So what did Santa bring you this year?' *You little fecker* I added internally.

'Fuckin' Santy!'

Geraldine offered a half-hearted reprimand and sauntered back into the house. The presence of Ronan meant that she was no longer the centre of attention. Little Ronan was my godchild, but he hadn't done much to kindle any latent maternal instincts. To be fair to the child, when I got him away from his parents and was able to exert a little authority, there was a transformation of sorts. He would calm down and allow his nicer characteristics to show through. But that afternoon he had clearly overdosed on Smarties and Coke and was acting like a demented devil-child. Marcus seemed to find it all vastly amusing, but I was mortified.

'Did you bring your football, Ronan?'

Instead of answering he spun his head around and around.

'Yes? Great. Let's ask Marcus to play.' In response Ronan turned to Marcus, bared his teeth and growled at him.

'I bag goals,' I announced.

'Not fair!' Marcus sulked.

'It's usually best to let Ronan win, by the way.'

'No chance, I'm going to put this guy through his paces,' he said to Ronan. 'Let's go find your ball.' He took him by the hand back into the house. Ronan tried to kick his shins only once, which was quite unusual for him and clearly a sign of affection. I heard Marcus tell him that if he did that again he wouldn't play with him.

After a good deal of manic running around the garden by them and some standing around by me, Ronan seemed to have expelled most of the demon spirits and collapsed into an exhausted but happy heap on the grass. Marcus had shown him how to stick his jersey over his head when he scored a goal (he scored twenty, but I put that down to poor defence from Marcus) and he didn't want to take it off, so I had to guide him very carefully back into the house. Just as got to the kitchen door he let go of my grasp and went in ahead of me, roaring his little head off. 'Goalllllll!' he screamed.

Geraldine was holding court at the kitchen table when we came in. I could hear her from outside.

'Really, Maura, I do advise you to make a will. I mean, Paul and I both have one . . . you never *know*, do you?'

Geraldine assumed that because Mother lived in a big house she must have a 'big house' mentality, which, to be fair, she didn't. But Geraldine did – in spades. She hoped – and none too secretly – that Mother would leave the 'estate' to Paul, the eldest son. Whatever else her faults, Mother had no time for this kind of nonsense and took great delight in dropping hints to Geraldine about her plans to leave the house to a charitable institution when she went.

'No, Geraldine, I'm quite all right as I am and I have no intention of going to the knacker's yard just yet. Do have some cake with that tea,' she spat through understandably gritted teeth.

Geraldine shot me a very dirty look as we came in, then she grabbed Ronan in a bit of a temper and yanked the jersey down off his head, at which he set up a wail.

'Please, darling, don't cry.' His response was to tell her to you know what off and to crawl under the table to stick his jersey back over his head and have a good sulk.

'It's the ADHD,' said Geraldine in a tone that distinctly resembled pride. 'He needs to set his own agenda and decide for himself when to come out from under the table.' Yeah, whatever, Geraldine.

'Oh Maura, that's not beef you're preparing, is it?'

'Yes, Geraldine, it is. Why?'

'Paul, I told you to tell Maura!' she chastised her husband.

'Tell me what?' asked Mother, looking from one to the other.

'Well, Maura,' she began with an apologetic little smile, 'I've just turned vegetarian . . . no, really, it's fine, just give me whatever vegetables you had planned to do and I'll be fine. I don't mind plain potatoes at all and sometimes peas can be just the thing, especially fresh ones . . . but of course, frozen are equally good.'

'I think Marcus and I will go look for a pub,' I announced over the din.

'You can't, dear, dinner is almost ready, and besides, there's someone I want you to meet, he'll be here soon.' I noticed that Mother was just a little flushed when she said this. *Great*, I thought, *another lunatic for the asylum.*

Geraldine was busy getting squiffy and talking about death and nursing homes. Mother was doing her usual trick of sublimating righteous rage into cooking. I don't think I had ever seen potatoes mashed with such vigour. Paul being Paul ignored everyone and everything outside his own head. Ronan was setting his agenda very loudly and Jason and Delphine were upstairs doing who knew what with and to each other. For once Marcus was looking bemused and didn't seem to know quite what to do with himself. Mother was actually strangely flustered and contributed to the mêlée less than was her wont. Something was up. Call me astute, but I guessed it had less to do with Geraldine's inconvenient conversion to vegetarianism and more to do with the imminent arrival of our mystery guest.

At six o'clock on the dot the doorbell rang and my mother practically beat Paul out of the way in order to get to the door before he did. She came back with a shy but proud little smile on her face and a man by the hand. Good Lord! Twenty years after the death of my father, she had gone and got herself a new man! Geraldine's jaw dropped; she probably wondered how this might affect the inheritance.

'Everyone, this is Patrick,' Mother beamed.

Patrick was a tall, ageing hippie type complete with bald patch and grizzled grey ponytail. His leather biker jacket, his Grateful Dead t-shirt and his face had all seen better days, though at least in the latter I could see the remnants of good looks. Jason and Delphine chose this moment to re-enter the earth's orbit and drifted into the kitchen in search of food and looking a little dishevelled.

'Jason, Delphine, this is Patrick.'

'What d'you do?' asked Jason, getting straight to the main point.

'I'm a rider,' he replied with a good-humoured smile. My mother's face was beaming up at him with pride and adoration. This was embarrassing. She was acting like she had hoped I would act when I eventually brought home Mr Wonderful.

'A rider?' queried Jason, looking thoughtful and confused. 'What, like bikes or something?'

'No, books, I ride books.'

'Oh, a *writer*,' squealed Geraldine in delight, stressing the *t*. 'What's your second name?'

'McMahon.'

'Patrick McMahon, mmm,' she mused 'have you written something I should know, Patrick? I'm really very ignorant. I haven't come across your name, not that that means anything, of course.' She twittered all this in a voice of incredible sweetness. Mother was fuming.

'Patrick is a *poet*, Geraldine,' she explained a little repressively.

'Oh, well, of course I wouldn't know anything about poetry. But Anna might,' she said as she spun around and threw me one of her sweetest smiles. 'Anna's an editor, Patrick, so I'm sure you two will find plenty to talk about.' Everyone, including Patrick, looked at me expectantly, waiting for me to clarify just exactly who Patrick was.

I could have garrotted Geraldine, not only for how she was irritating my mother, but also because I tend to lie to people about my job when I suspect that they might have a book in them. They're compelled to pick your brains on behalf of their opus in the way that people at parties ask doctors about the mystery illness that's been plaguing them for the last twenty years but which has not yet managed to carry them off.

'I . . . em . . . .'

'Aghhhh!' Marcus suddenly screamed in agony. When no one was looking, Ronan had sorted out his agenda, found a fork from somewhere and had just tried to shove it into Marcus's leg. Ronan found Marcus's pain highly amusing and so did Geraldine. Her merry laughter set her bloody son off and he thought he had done something wonderful. Paul emerged from his dream world momentarily and picked the miscreant up and whisked him out of the room.

'Shitefucker' yelled the little love.

Mother searched frantically in the freezer for peas while I plied Marcus with more whiskey and mumbled 'sorry' over and over. For what, though, I wasn't sure. Perhaps it was for Ronan, my family, everything. Poor Patrick looked embarrassed and guilty, as though the house had been a sea of calm before he walked in. Eventually relative calm was restored and Geraldine promised to send Ronan off for adoption in the morning. She laughed, but my mother looked slightly shocked. She never did have much faith in the strength of Geraldine's maternal urge.

We sat down to dinner when Marcus assured us that he would live and asked me for God's sake to stop apologising.

After a difficult evening of Geraldine, Jason and poetry I began to look forward to sharing a rickety old sofa bed with someone who probably thought that it was going to be a big treat for me. As none of my things were dry and I had no intention of going semi-naked, I was forced to borrow one of Mother's delightful flannelette nightgowns. Marcus, unfortunately, didn't seem to share my sense of modesty and was, as usual, clad in nothing more than shorts and a smile. He looked very relaxed as he lay there with his hands behind his head and I had another of those fleeting lurches in my stomach that I couldn't call pleasant. Yet I couldn't quite call them unpleasant, either.

I knew that I didn't look exactly glamorous, but there was really no excuse for Marcus's rudeness – he took one look at me and burst into hysterical laughter.

'It's not *that* bad,' I said with an air of sniffy righteousness.

'I'm sorry, how rude. I've never seen you look so lovely. Pink frilly flannel really suits you.' And off he started again. Sometimes, like just then, his laugh was too infectious to resist, and in spite of myself I began to laugh.

I got into the bed, trying not to make it too obvious that I was clinging on to the very edge in order not to get too close, as I knew he would get the wrong idea. However, the fact that I was lying at a strange slant and that every muscle in my body was stiff with the effort made it quite noticeable.

'You needn't worry. I have no *intention* of molesting you this evening. That thing you're wearing is protection enough, I'd have to send a search party ahead to find you beneath all the frills. But here's a little extra,' he said, whipping a pillow out from behind him and lying it between us, 'just in case I take leave of my senses during the night.' But clearly the idea of that happening was highly amusing, as he still couldn't stop laughing. In fact, he was getting hysterical and I warned him that I was going to have to hit him. I was becoming irritated and was about to take the moral high ground and ask if he considered me so inherently unattractive that he couldn't see past the night attire. But then I realised how (Marcus being Marcus) he might misconstrue that question, so instead I reached into my bag and pulled out my book, *North and South*. I always reach for my old favourites in times of crisis, and let's face it, having to share a bed with Marcus was something of a crisis.

'I can't believe you,' Marcus exclaimed, dragging me out of my reverie. 'This is our first time sleeping together and all you want to do is read?'

'You forgot to finish your sentence.'

'Excuse me?'

'You left "and last" out of your sentence. This our first *and last* time to sleep together.'

'You think?'

'I don't think, I *know*.'

'Anyway, what *are* you reading?'

'It's called *North and South*,' I said with a heavy sigh.

'What? As in that awful eighties mini-series with Patrick Swayze?'

'No,' I answered with another sigh, 'as in the nineteenth-century novel.' I adopted a look of deep concentration, hoping that he would leave me alone. But oh no, he was full of chat.

'So, what's it about then? Educate me. What could possibly be more interesting than sharing a bed with me?'

'How long have you got, and you don't really want to know, do you?'

'I just want to keep you talking. I don't like being ignored in favour of someone who's been dead for a thousand years. But I'm curious.'

'Well, all right then,' I said, setting the book down. 'It's about a mill owner and a young woman—'

'Oh don't tell me, they meet, they fall in love, encounter a difficulty, part, reunite and then finally get married. You see, anyone can write one of those old novels because that's all that ever happens in them.'

'You're talking rubbish.'

'Well that's an eloquent argument you have and you've almost won me over . . . oh no, don't start reading again, you still haven't told me the plot,' he laughed as he tried to snatch the book out of my hands.

'Why should I? You've just dismissed one of my favourite books as a load of old rubbish. I don't see why you'd be interested.'

'Because it interests *you*, that makes me curious. So what about this mill owner?' he asked, reading the blurb on the back, trying to coax me out of my huff. And I relented. 'He and Margaret, the heroine, meet under what you might call inauspicious cirmcumstances. Her father is a clergyman who has lost his faith and leaves their cosy home to head up to the grim North to act as tutor to this grim mill owner who wants to improve himself. The grim mill owner and the haughty heroine are distinctly hostile, but you know that they're really attracted to each other and the grim mill owner realises it when she flings herself in front of him in order to prevent him being mobbed by an angry crowd of grim mill workers. He takes this as a sign of love, but it isn't.'

'Men, eh?'

'She still can't stand him, or so she thinks. He's supposed to be very ugly, but you're constantly reminded about his height, his perfect teeth and his broad shoulders, so I think we can safely assume that like all ugly heroes he is not, in fact, very ugly at all. You see, I always think that the ugly heroes are the handsomest.'

'Because they're attractive in spite of their not being attractive?'

'Exactly!'

'So does she end up with him in the end?'

'Oh yes.'

'Well, that's a weight off my mind. So do you think that there's a John Thornton out there for you?'

I didn't, but for fear of sounding cynical I simply said I didn't know. Was there a Margaret out there for him?

'Hope not, I hate the name Margaret. It's one of those names that always make you think of your mother.'

'But your mother's name isn't Margaret.'

'I know, but isn't it an inherently motherish name?' I had never thought of it before, but I found myself smiling in agreement.

'But to answer your question, no, I don't think that there's a perfect someone for everyone.' I was slightly shocked by such cynicism from him. 'But I don't mean it in a cynical way. What I mean is that I don't think anyone has the right to demand perfection because no one is perfect and if you expect perfection then Mr or Mrs Perfect is equally entitled to expect perfection from you. Don't you think?' Before I had time to answer he was off again. 'And I don't like this idea that you can make up a shopping list of qualities that the perfect someone must have if they are to be, well, perfect. It takes the surprise out of life. I mean, you never know, do you, when, where or who? If you concentrate too hard on trying to find someone with the X quality you think you want, you risk not seeing the person with the Y quality which would really suit you much better than the X you're determined to have . . . if you see what I mean.' Then he paused for breath.

Really, the man was full of surprises. I thought it strange indeed that it was with him that I was now having one of those rare moments in life when someone perfectly articulates a muddled thought that had been trying to form itself in your own head. I think I must have been staring at him oddly as he asked, almost with embarrassment, if what he had said sounded really stupid.

'Oh no!' I began to gush. I very much wanted to tell him how lovely I thought what he had just said was, but something stopped me.

I tried to read again but he had snapped out of

his musing mood and now kept pestering me with stupid questions, and not just about the book. He was lying on his side, facing me, propped up on one elbow.

'Can I ask you something?'

'What now?'

'You do like me, don't you?'

I turned and looked at him for a second or two and before I knew what I was at I said, 'Of course I do.' I still considered him the most infuriating person of my acquaintance, but without realising it I had gone from thinking him a total prat who could sometimes be very kind to thinking him someone who was very kind but could sometimes be a bit of a prat. After all, he had put up very bravely with my family. He looked at me for a few minutes with an inscrutable expression in his usually candid dark eyes.

'Good,' was all he said. Then he rolled over and went to sleep.

I switched the light off and tried to sleep. I lay awake for what seemed like an age, which was unusual for me, but I suppose I must have dozed off at some point as I was awoken with a start during the night by something whacking me in the face – his arm. Then I felt a dead weight fall across my left leg – it was his leg. I glanced over. He had turned over on his front and was sleeping starfish fashion. He was also snoring his head off. I was mightily pissed off but also relieved, as I felt my normal feelings of mild irritation creeping back. I managed to extricate myself from the tangle of arms and legs, took a rug that was draped over the back of the sofa and stomped off to the sofa in the kitchen.

I woke the next morning to find him standing over me with a cup of tea.

'What on earth are you doing here?' he asked. 'Are you that allergic to me?'

I think I might have hesitated just a little before I said 'yes'.

Marcus left shortly after breakfast the next morning, which upset his new best friend just a little. Ronan would only let go of his leg when Marcus promised to come back very soon to play more football.

'Thank you,' he said as I saw him to his car.

'What for?'

'The ego-bashing. You sorted me out something lovely.'

'But I didn't—'

'Relax, I'm only teasing. So when are you heading back to Dublin?'

'Next day or two I imagine. What about you?'

'Not till New Year's Eve. Will you miss me?'

'Good Lord, no!'

'Likewise,' he laughed, getting into the car.

Just at that moment, the oddest thought popped unbidden into my head – that I had somehow managed to fall head over heels in love with Marcus.

Chapter Sixteen

I felt nervous about seeing Marcus again, which I knew was very silly, but you know how it is; the minute you realise that you're in love you become convinced that every inch of you unconsciously declares the fact. By New Year's Eve I was a walking bundle of nerves. I knew I was being ridiculous, but I still couldn't stop my stomach tightening ever so slightly each time I heard a car pull up outside.

'For God's sake, Anna, what's up with you today, you've got a serious number of ants in your pants and it's most *annoying*. If you could sit down for two seconds in a row that would be great, thank you very much. You're making me nervous with all that pacing around. But as you obviously need something to do, you can come with me and help get the supplies in for tonight.'

Somewhere between the decision to have the party and that day, Angela had decided to make it an 'elegant' one. Not for us a few boxes of Pringles and some Tesco dip. Oh no. Angela, doubtless under the pernicious influence of Xavier, had decided that our guests were going to be treated to a gastronomic feast that evening. But given that she intended to prepare said feast herself, the chances of a gastronomic anything were slim. 'I wish I'd never agreed to this,' she whinged as she disconsolately wheeled her trolley around Tesco in Phibsboro.

'So do I.'

An hour later we emerged with some ingredients for Angela to be inventive with and some Tesco party food – 'just in case' I said to reassure a highly offended Angela. When we got home my stomach lurched just the tiniest bit when I heard Marcus call out a hello from upstairs. Then he came bounding down the stairs, gave us each a hug and told us how much he had missed us and how glad he was to be back. So that was that. I had managed to face him without blushing, flushing, stumbling or stuttering.

'So who's going to get this lot ready?' he asked, poking about inside the bags.

'I am!' Angela declared proudly, to which Marcus groaned in response. 'Shut up, Marcus. I'm a perfectly competent cook when I put my mind to it.'

'It's just a pity then that you never put your mind to it,' he replied, grinning at me, and I responded with an even bigger one.

I found myself bemused by this odd feeling of happiness. When he said something funny I thought it was the funniest thing I had ever heard. When I laughed, it seemed like the longest and loudest I had laughed in a long time, my smile felt like the biggest I had ever smiled. Everything that afternoon was a superlative. Later, however, I managed to drag myself away from him so that I could grab the shower before Angela ensconced herself in it. Happy, skippy love was all very well, but it offered no excuse for being smelly.

Just as I was about to jump into the shower I realised that my towels were still sitting where they had been drying on the sitting room radiator. I left the shower running and put on just enough clothes to make me decent and ran downstairs to get one.

I could hear Angela and Marcus having a particularly animated discussion in the kitchen. I paid them no heed and was just about to go back upstairs, but then I heard my own name mentioned by Angela.

'Marcus, I don't want Anna to get hurt.'

'I'll be gentle with her, I promise.'

'I'm serious, Marcus.'

'What makes you think I would hurt her?'

'I know what you're like. I've seen your flirting therapy in action before. Remember the post-Aoife fling with Caroline and the post-Claire fling with Liz? And what about the post-Liz fling with Louise? Need I go on?'

'Jesus, you make me sound like a right Lothario.'

'That's because you are one. And Anna isn't the kind of girl you want to go toying with. I think she might bruise more readily than she lets on.'

'Would you mind not making me out to be such a callous womaniser?'

'But don't you think that all this is a bit soon after Isobel?'

'It's not *that* soon.'

'This is Isobel we're talking about. It'll always be too soon after her.'

There was a pause.

'You're probably right. I should just leave her alone.'

I didn't stay to hear anymore. I quickly and silently hurried back up the stairs and locked myself in the bathroom.

I should have known! God knows I'd been given enough hints about Marcus and his way with the ladies. For goodness sake, Angela had spelled it out for me after the incident with the flowers. But no, stupid Anna chose to ignore the obvious. But the part of us that falls in love always thinks itself wiser than the better half of us. I'm sure I wouldn't have felt so foolish had it not been for that admission of the previous week. I felt a barely controllable urge to literally kick myself for being so bloody stupid.

And then I really did kick myself. This was the second time in my life that I had made an idiot of myself over a man.

I suppose I had better explain myself by relating the sad tale of Brian.

I met Brian shortly after I came to Dublin to go to college. He was in one of my tutorial groups and was a mature student. I thought he was wonderful from the moment I met him. He made me laugh and I was still young enough and stupid enough to be impressed by the fact that he had just published a slim volume of short stories. Brian was an attractive man, tall and dark, funny and clever. But perhaps the most amazing thing about him was the fact that he seemed to find me interesting. I wouldn't say he swept me off my feet exactly; he was too laid back for that kind of thing. But he did sort of overwhelm me off them.

Together we would read the reviews of his book, and the childish eagerness with which he lapped up the critical praise always made me smile. What touched me even more was the fact that my praise seemed to give him even more pleasure than that of the critics. He seemed to genuinely value my opinion, which I was flattered by, and as a result I gradually found myself becoming more interested in his writing than my own futile attempts and Brian began to forget to encourage me to keep at it.

We had never been what you might call a close couple; Brian valued his independence and I told myself and my curious friends that I similarly valued my own. He wasn't a demonstrative man. For him any display of affection was a strictly private affair, and while I wasn't given to lavish public displays, I couldn't help but feel a little sad each time he refused to hold my hand in the street. Even *I* felt that this took independence a bit too far.

I eventually allowed a little doubt to sneak into my mind. I began to suspect, or rather wake up to the fact, that the relationship was a bit one sided. A rational person would have forced themselves to acknowledge that they were a convenience rather than a partner. But I was besotted and so I convinced myself that he cared about me in his own way.

'In his own way.' A classic euphemism for self-delusion.

Then I made *the* mistake.

I had cooked dinner one evening and had possibly poured more wine into myself than into the saucepan. After dinner and yet more wine we settled down for one of our all-too-frequent nights in. These, I had convinced myself, were the result of his need to be with me and no one else. I listened to some music and drank yet more wine while he did some rewriting of chapter ten. I got squiffier and squiffier until, out of the blue, as though I had no control over my brain or my mouth, I let those dreaded words pop out.

'Love you too,' he mumbled, briefly removing the pen from between his teeth, then shoving it back in. He hadn't even looked up.

Of course I was thrilled and decided that the casual way he had tossed love back at me proved that he really meant it.

Two weeks later he told me that he found Dublin too small and he could no longer write there. In short, he was moving to London and by the end of the month he was gone.

And that was that.

I think I must have spent the following few months with my eyebrows raised in a permanent arch of surprise.

From then on I rolled up into a little ball when it came to men. Given that my first real declaration of love had such a detrimental effect, I swore that I would never again be the first to admit it. Famous last words.

Needless to say, I wasn't in a party mood that evening. However, I had to resist the urge to sulk in my room and went downstairs as though nothing was wrong. I decided to allow myself the luxury of not dressing up. The party was, after all, in my own home so I could be scruffy if I wanted to. So I stayed in my jeans and my comfortable boots, changed my top and tied back my hair. Passable was all I would aim for.

When I came downstairs Angela immediately tried to engage me in conversation about outfits.

'Shouldn't you be worrying about what people are going to eat rather than what you're going to wear?'

'Oh, crap, do you think people will settle for Pringles? I really couldn't be arsed.'

'Yes, I think that given the amount of booze we've laid in, people will forgive the lack of luxury nibbles.'

'So what are you going to wear?' she asked me, having just given me a blow-by-blow guide to her own outfit.

'Ta da!' I exclaimed, throwing my arms open wide.

'Anna! You can't go to a party like that!'

'Oh for Christ's sake, Angela, would you ever stop hectoring me about my clothes. Are you *trying* to give me a complex?'

She was shocked by my outburst but quickly apologised for her tactlessness.

'Oh Anna! I'm so sorry, I didn't mean to hurt your feelings. I can be so stupid sometimes. Have I been annoying you all this time and you never said anything? You should have told me to stop.'

'It's all right. I didn't mean to snap at you like that. I'm just not a glamorous kind of girl – never have been, never will be. The sooner we both just accept that, the happier we'll both be.'

'You don't need to be glam, my love,' she said, engulfing me in a hug. 'You're lovely as you are.'

'Can anyone join in?' I heard Marcus ask from the doorway and instinctively I felt myself stiffen.

Angela laughed and immediately freed an arm. I smiled a tight little smile and backed away. I was unable to resist a quick glance in his direction, and though I wasn't certain I thought I saw a slight look of hurt on his face.

Angela had decided that the time had come for us to be formally introduced to Xavier. Up until then our conversations with him hadn't extended beyond 'yes, she's in, I'll just get her for you' or 'no, she's not in, can I take a message' or 'goodbye' as he flew out the door first thing in the morning. And so Angela called both Marcus and I over to her and the deity and did the honours.

'Anna, Marcus, I would like to formally introduce you to Xavier. Xavier, my flatmates and good friends, Marcus and Anna.'

'Hello Xavier, nice to meet you, at last.'

''Allo.' That was all we got out of him for the next five minutes or so.

I studied his face quite intently, realising that he had one of those faces which strikes you afresh with its good looks each time you look at it. He was idiotically handsome, but his looks weren't of the kind that would ever offer any surprises. He would remain conventionally handsome for the rest of his life and would probably continue to turn heads well into his later years. He caught my gaze and obviously misinterpreted it, as he offered me the slightest of smirks in return.

Angela decided to abandon us to get to know

each other a little better, which involved Marcus struggling to ask a number of polite questions before deciding that enough was enough.

'Ah, look, there's John over there looking a bit left out, I'd better go and say hello. Good to meet you Xavier, excuse me, Anna.'

'So, Xavier,' I began once I had finished inwardly cursing Marcus. 'How long have you been in Ireland?'

'Three years.'

'Angela mentioned that you only intended to stay for one.'

'That is right.'

'But you must have really liked it here, as you seem to have forgotten to return from whence you came.'

'Dublin is a dirty city. I don't like it much but the money was too good to refuse.'

I glanced quickly around the room to see if there was anyone I could signal to come to my aid. When I turned back around I caught him staring rudely, but not at my face.

'They don't talk, Xavier.'

He glanced up at me with a hint of amusement and without a trace of embarrassment.

He shrugged his shoulders, then, spotting Angela in the corner, he walked over to her, put both his arms around her and bent down to nuzzle her neck. He then lifted his head momentarily and looked right at me with something like a leer. Then he bent his head again and kissed Angela in what you might call a very friendly manner.

'Is it just me, or is there something a bit weird about the amazing Xavier?'

I jumped, as I hadn't heard Marcus creeping up behind me.

'Sorry, I didn't mean to startle you,' he smiled, resting his hand on my arm.

'Oh, that's okay,' I said, smiling and taking a step away from him. Then I moved off and left him looking puzzled once again.

On the whole the party seemed to go quite well. Most people looked like they were having a good time. I drifted about with no aim other than avoiding Marcus and, alarmingly, fending off the advances of a drunken James.

Needless to say I hadn't actually invited James to the party. Trish and Julie had run into him in the street that afternoon, had let slip about their plans for the evening and James promptly invited himself along. Of course he turned up empty handed, but, being James, he felt no shame in heading straight for the drinks the minute he was in the door.

Being stalked in my own house by James offered enormous comedy value, which I would have relished more had I not been in such a stinker of a mood. James's 'lines' were certainly original if nothing else and I was dying to ask him if he had patented his technique and, more importantly, if it had ever worked. In the sitting room, for instance, he asked if I had an opinion on some tribunal or other. At the top of the stairs he asked me what I thought the implications of revisionism might be on the future of Irish historical research and analysis. In the kitchen he asked me if I thought that football was proving itself to be a cohesive force in an increasingly fragmented society.

'James, you really ought to know better at this point than to ask me questions that require an intelligent answer.'

'Oh Anna, you know I've always suspected that you're more clever and interesting than you give yourself credit for.'

'Really, I'm not. Trust me.'

'Not what, Anna?' came Julie's voice from behind me.

'Ah, Trish, Julie, I was just asking Anna if she considered football a cohesive force in an increasingly fragmented society and if she thought it could help return Ireland to a sense of its community – which I for one believe we have lost.'

'Hmm, yes, that's a tricky one all right James. Trish and I often ponder such issues of an evening.'

'You do?'

'James, could you not just admire the players' legs like every one else?' This from Trish prompted a look of horror from James.

'But . . . I thought you were . . . ah, you know . . . erm . . . .'

'Jesus, James, for someone with such a large vocabulary you're having severe trouble with a three-letter word.'

James began to look a little flustered.

'Patricia, I have no problem with the word "gay". I can say it quite easily, as you can see . . . or should I say as you can *hear*, ha ha. I have no problem, none at all. I have no problem with *gays* at all. In fact, I used to be quite friendly with a boy in fourth year in St Tiernan's who I hear has since turned out to be gay.'

'That's great, James,' Julie responded. 'Hurray for solidarity. Where's the drink?' With that she abandoned me and dragged Trish off with her.

James then turned to me with a very odd smile.

'Now, where were we?' he asked, taking a step closer. I took a simultaneous step backwards.

'You were droning on about football, James,' I said, hoping that rudeness might prompt him to bugger off and leave me alone.

'Droning. Ha ha! That's a good one,' he smirked, taking another step closer.

'Yes, "droning" is indeed a good word and it's an activity which you are very familiar with.'

'I think it's an activity *with which I am very familiar*. Really, Anna, and you an editor,' he chuckled. Once again, he took a step closer and I took a step backwards. I was now edging out into the hall, where I spotted John sitting on the stairs. I mouthed 'help' at him, but he was clearly enjoying the show as he merely grinned at me and did nothing.

'Would you like another drink?' James suddenly asked, eyeing my almost empty bottle.

'Yes! Good idea! A drink!' When he zipped off to get me one I took the opportunity to sit down next to John on the stairs.

'John, protect me!'

'Ah, he seems like a nice enough chap.'

'John, you have no idea. How are you anyway? Did you have a good Christmas?'

'I'm grand . . . .' he said, not sounding altogether convincing.

'What are you doing out here on the stairs anyway? Aren't you enjoying the party?' Just as soon as I asked him the question, Angela came waltzing down the stairs after Xavier. They both looked slightly dishevelled.

'Ah, of course' was all I said as I realised that the party was probably a bit traumatic for him.

'Tell me something honestly, Anna: am I a fool?' he asked with a smile. I wasn't expecting that and was beginning to think that I might have been better off continuing my conversation with James about the cultural contexts of association football. I knew he wanted me to tell him that he wasn't a fool, that if he held on for long enough Angela would one day wake up and see that he, John, was in fact her true Prince Charming. But I doubted if Angela would ever have enough cop-on.

'John, I can't pretend that Angela is likely to dump this idiot any time soon. But if it's any kind of consolation, there are a lot more fools out there than you might imagine.'

'I guess so,' he mumbled sadly as we both caught sight of the pair in a messy-looking lip lock, at which point John decided that he could take no more and took himself off to another corner to sulk in. I was left by myself on the stairs, and out of the corner of my eye I could see both Marcus and James making a bee-line for the spot next to me, but Marcus got their first. He sat down and handed me a beer.

'John said you were running low.'

'I don't think he's enjoying himself much, poor sod.'

'And I don't think he's the only one. Is there something wrong, Anna?' He added after a slight pause, 'You don't quite seem yourself tonight, sweetheart.'

Of all the inappropriate moments to start using terms of endearments, that one took some beating. I couldn't look at him because a part of me felt a bit silly and melty, but I quickly brought myself back down to earth by recalling his chat with Angela.

'Come on, tell me,' he coaxed, 'perhaps I can fix it?' He gently tugged at my ponytail, then let his hand rest on my shoulder.

Of course a little bit of me relished all this, I'm only human, but I summoned all the iron in my blood. I was buggered if I was going to allow myself to be used as a post-Isobel therapeutic doll.

And I was also buggered if I was going to let him see how much this idea affected me.

'There's nothing wrong, Marcus. I'm having a great time,' I said and practically downed my beer in one mighty slug.

'Oh come on, Anna, I know you better than that and you know that I know you better than that. I have come to understand the Anna Malone way; the look that says "I'm not fine but I'll kill you if you even try to suggest otherwise".' Once again he tried to stroke my hair. I yanked my head away tetchily.

'Stop it, Marcus! You don't know me. You might like to think that you do, but you don't. If you did, you would know what was wrong,' I said, realising how irrational it must have sounded.

'Hey! What's all this?' he asked, looking both puzzled and hurt. 'Have I done something to upset you?'

'That's a bit of an understatement,' I muttered and could have kicked myself. I didn't want him to know what I had heard.

'Tell me, please, you know I would never—'

'Oh look, there's James, I should just go and have a word with him—'

'Anna, what the hell is going on inside your head? Sometimes I really don't understand you.'

'No one asked you to try and understand me, Marcus.'

'Jesus Christ, Anna!' he said, sounding more angry than puzzled now.

'Don't talk to me like that!' I snapped and stood up to go. But just as I did, the countdown started. Was it that time already?

'Ten, nine, eight . . . .'

'Anna, I'm sorry, please, I don't understand . . . .'

'. . . seven, six, five, four . . . .'

He stood up. The doorbell rang.

'Who on earth?'

'. . . three, two, one . . . .'

'Happy New Year!'

'Anna?'

I opened the door.

'Hello, Marcus!'

'Isobel!'

Chapter Seventeen

Needless to say, the advent of Isobel had a profound effect on the party.

'What are you doing here, Isobel?' Marcus asked as soon as he had recovered from the shock.

'I've been calling you loads, Marcus.'

'I know.'

'I've left messages.'

'I know.'

'Marcus, we need to talk. We never really did, I mean we never talked *properly* about things.'

'Well, as far as I was concerned there wasn't much to talk about. You cheated on me, I was angry, I left. I don't have anything more to say on the matter.'

'But you never gave me a chance to put things right.'

'There was no way you could have put things right. Apart, of course, from winding back time . . . or . . . let me see . . . oh, I know . . . how about . . . *deciding not to have the affair in the first place!*'

'Marcus, it wasn't an *affair*.'

'You slept with someone else, I don't know what else you could call it.'

'It was an accident.'

'An *accident*. You *accidentally* slept with someone on more than one occasion?'

'Marcus, you're still angry, and you have every right to be, but you—'

'Well, I'm glad that my being angry is okay with you. Of course I'm still angry . . . .' He paused. 'Actually, you know what? I'm not angry, not anymore. I don't have the energy anymore to be angry with someone who just isn't worth the effort.' He accompanied this with a look of contempt that made Isobel wince. Indeed, it made me wince in something like sympathy.

Isobel caught the sympathy wince and it seemed to wake her up to the fact that she and Marcus had an audience. I know I shouldn't have been standing there all that time, but I had become so intrigued by the drama I found myself glued to the spot, watching them, goggle eyed, following their exchanges like a tennis match.

'Excuse me!' Isobel said, turning to me. 'This is a *private* conversation.'

'We have nothing to say to each other that Anna can't hear.'

'Oh, so it's like *that*, is it?'

'No, it's not *like that* . . . not that it would be any of your damned business if it were *like that*.'

'*What* is the spawn of Satan doing in my hall-way?' Angela had just come weaving out of the kitchen and had been stopped dead in her tracks by the sight of the said spawn.

'Out! Get out, get out, get out of my house, *now!*' she roared at Isobel while eyeing her with naked hostility and pointing magisterially towards the door.

'Marcus lives here too, Angela, and you can't stop me talking to him.'

'I can stop you doing anything I want to stop you doing with Marcus in *my* house. *My* house, Isobel, *mine*, *my* rules apply so out you bloody well go.'

'Angela, I can deal with this, thank you,' Marcus said through gritted teeth.

'Clearly you can't or she wouldn't still be standing there, looking at me like that. Stop looking at me like that.'

I decided to tighten my slackened jaw and to intervene before any blood was spilled.

'Angela, come on, we should leave them be.'

'I don't *think* so. If I leave him alone with her for two minutes, she'll have him back in her clutches

235

faster than you can blink. Ow! Stop tugging at me, Anna.'

'This is none of our business, Ang. You're coming with me whether you like it or not.' I yanked her off back into the kitchen with brute force. Marcus threw me a look of gratitude, which I didn't really want.

'Five minutes!' Angela yelled over her shoulder as I dragged her off. 'Five minutes and I want her out. Out! Do you understand? Out!'

Thankfully, she then spotted Xavier looking bored in a corner so she lurched drunkenly towards him and sought to soothe her ruffled feathers by half falling on, half draping herself over him. When drunk, Angela became so floppy you could wear her over your shoulders like a scarf.

And so I was left to mull over what I had just seen and heard.

It's not like that. Marcus's words repeated themselves over and over inside my head. Of course I hadn't any *real* idea what he had meant by 'like that', but given what I had overheard outside the kitchen earlier on, I could guess. I cursed my stupidity for having fallen for him. How? I asked myself. How could I have allowed myself to be blinded by someone like Marcus? He wasn't even my type, for God's sake! My self-chastisement was cut short, however, by loud voices from the hall.

Angela had taken her 'five minute' edict quite seriously and was at that moment trying to man-handle Isobel out of the door.

'Angela, for God's sake leave her alone. She's going now anyway. Aren't you, Isobel?'

'For now, Marcus, but just for now,' she said sadly, and with that she left.

All three of us stood looking at the door for a few minutes, as though we couldn't quite believe what had just happened. Marcus broke the silence.

'Ah shit, I can't let her walk home by herself.' He grabbed his coat from the hook and his keys from the bowl and went out after her.

As far as I was concerned, the party was now well and truly over, so I ran up the stairs into my room, removed all the coats that had gathered on my bed, threw them out into the landing, climbed in, pulled the duvet up over my head and burst into tears.

The next morning Angela knocked on my door at about nine thirty.

'Are you awake? Can I come in?' she asked and without waiting for an answer she came in and plopped herself down at the end of my bed.

'I've brought you some tea,' she said, proffering the cup with an apologetic smile.

'Xavier has left, I told him that I needed to be available for Marcus today. He was none too pleased.'

'I know, I heard.'

'Oh, he'll be fine,' she said, ignoring my sarcasm. 'But will Marcus?' she wondered.

'Poor Marcus,' I mumbled as I took a sip of tea.

Isobel had sort of sunk into the background recently and we all thought that she had finally decided to throw in the towel, that she now understood that Marcus was not merely angry, but unable to forgive.

'So what on earth prompted her to the grand gesture last night?'

'She was trolleyed, Ang.'

'That's an excuse for the behaviour, but not an explanation,' Angela retorted loftily.

Isobel had looked lovely and I was surprised at how Marcus had steadfastly refused to wilt before her eloquent and heartfelt pleading. She told him how she had decided to spend New Year's alone as she didn't think she deserved or wanted a good time, certainly not when she couldn't have one with him. But at about eleven o'clock it all got too much for her. She had been looking at their old photos, especially the ones from their first two years together. Maybe the drink had made her maudlin, she didn't know, but she did know that she had to see him that evening, 'Not to let the year go down on a quarrel,' she'd with a tiny laugh. 'Looks like I was too late, though,' she finished sadly, but then, as if just struck by a wonderful idea, she'd said, 'But I've made it in time for the very beginning of a new one. Don't you think that could be a good omen, Marcus?'

No, he didn't.

'So what are we going to do, Anna?'

'Absolutely *nothing*, Angela.'

'We can't sit back and let him get enmeshed all over again!'

'We can and we will! Besides, aren't you jumping to conclusions a bit here . . . I mean, he hasn't—'

'No, I am not jumping to conclusions!' she interrupted me angrily. 'You have no idea of this woman's power over him. She was positively vampiric with his personality all those years. See all that chirpiness and silliness and ego and charm? Well, she sucks it right out of him, chews it up and spits it back out. She turns him into a Stepford Marcus. Believe me, if she's really determined to have him back, she'll get him back . . . and will stop at nothing.'

'Ha, she sounds like the Terminator.'

'Anna,' Angela squeaked, 'this is no time for laughing. This is all such a disaster,' she moaned as she cradled her head in her hands. 'God, maybe I shouldn't have warned him against . . . oh!' she stopped abruptly.

'Shouldn't have warned him against what, Angela?'

'Nothing, nothing,' she flushed, conscious no doubt of her terrible lying skills. I raised my eyebrows at her.

'Really, it's nothing to do with you,' she said in obvious confusion and I decided to let it go. After all, there was no point in forcing her to admit to something I already knew.

'Well, I think he should talk to her.'

'Are you insane, woman?' she exploded.

'No, Angela, I'm trying to look at this in an adult way. If he really wanted her to leave him alone, then he would tell her that straight. The fact that he just isn't answering her calls shows that he doesn't really know what he wants.'

'Anna,' she began loftily, 'I've known Marcus a lot longer than you have and I know better what's good for him, and believe me, that wench is not good for him.'

'I think he might be the better judge of what's good for him,' I insisted quietly.

And how, you might wonder, did *I* react to the dramatic entrance of Isobel, stage right? Surprisingly well, I must say. I think her return woke me up. Naturally, at first I felt a little disappointment, but then, having already woken up to the insanity of my feelings, I decided that the reappearance of a complicated ex was just the thing to nip them in the bud. And in order to help this process I decided to pursue some DIY aversion therapy: I forced myself to imagine kissing James each time I found my feelings for Marcus wandering off in a non-platonic direction.

Thanks to the whole Marcus/Isobel debacle I experienced another of those rare epiphanic moments in life. I began to think more seriously about what Mother and I had discussed at Christmas and I felt a sort of euphoria over my newfound clarity of vision. I now knew what I had to do and there was no man to obscure the view of the marvellous future I now saw for myself, so I decided that it was time to move on. It killed me to admit it, but Mother was right. I could sit and moan about how I hated Dublin and my job and my life, or I could do something about it. And with that in mind I began to scour the papers for new jobs. That may not seem like a momentous life change, but for me it was a huge step.

Until I found that great new job, though, I still had to go into the old one every morning and I still had to face James, but that was easier than I expected. He showed no signs of embarrassment over his behaviour at the party.

'Hello, Anna. How are you?'

'Fine, thank you, James. And you?'

'Oh grand, you know. Have your crossword?'

'Yep.'

'Me too.'

'Good, good.'

And that was that. All returned to normal on the James front. He never mentioned the party, nor the concert he had almost asked me to. I thanked God for small mercies. However, my euphoria and clarity of vision were blunted and blurred, respectively, by the simple fact that it was January.

One particularly wet and slushy Monday towards the end of that horrible month I was heading into work in a fouler mood than usual. It was one of those Monday mornings that make you want to steal the petty cash and run away to the Bahamas. The sun had been too depressed that morning to be arsed getting up. I went mad in Bewley's and bought two jam doughnuts with my coffee, but as I turned the corner, my excitement at the thought of the two doughnuts was quelled; Tony was waiting on the steps.

'Anna!' he beamed excitedly at me, as though he was surprised to see me. 'Lovely morning, isn't it!'

'Fantastic. What can I do for you, Tony?'

'I just wanted to give you this,' he said, handing me an envelope that was bulging with papers.

'Is this the finished draft at last?'

'Oh no, I've hardly even *started* that!'

'You know you have a deadline, don't you?' I asked with not a little panic.

'Don't you worry, pet. I'll have everything ready. What you have there is some more of my poems. I was hoping you might take a look at them for me. Let me know what you think. I sent you some before, but I don't think you read them. Or at least you never wrote that you had read them.'

'Tony, I'm pretty swamped at the moment, and poetry isn't my area,' I protested, trying to hand them back.

'It won't take long,' he insisted as he pushed my hand back towards myself.

'Honestly, Tony, I'm hopeless with poetry. I can never tell my Wordsworth from my Byron.'

'That's all right. I don't want to know what an expert thinks of them. I want to know what *you* think of them.' As an afterthought he added, 'I'll buy you a pint if you take a look at them,' and chuckled.

'I had better get in and open up the office. Linda will be in soon.'

'Well, I'll be off then,' he said, but made no move to leave. As I closed the front door, he was still smiling at me.

At ten to five that afternoon the phone rang. Unfortunately Linda had decided to work a full day (she called it 'working late'), otherwise I would have ignored so late a call.

'Anna!' Tony's voice came booming down the line at me. 'How are you? I just thought I'd give you a wee call to see if by any chance you'd had a chance to glance over the poems?'

'Well, like I explained to you this morning, Tony, I'm very busy finishing a book right now.'

'Oh.'

Silence.

'Couldn't you take them home with you?'

'I'm not paid enough to take work home with me.'

He roared laughing at this. 'Ah, you're a geg, Anna.'

I had no idea what a 'geg' was, but I knew that I didn't want to be called one by Tony. In fact, I didn't want to be called anything by Tony.

'I have to go now, Tony, because it's time for me to go home.'

'I seem to always get you at the wrong moment, don't I? I'll call in proper office hours next time, promise.'

In order to give him a hint and to get him off the phone, I reminded him of our officially timetabled meeting next week.

'Oh, don't you worry, I have it written down.'

'Goodbye, Tony.'

'Goodbye, Anna.'

I hung up first.

Two days later I received another of the nice artistic postcards Tony had taken to sending me at least once a week. They always seemed to be of romantic tableaux or naked people. Once, for instance, he sent me a card with Klimt's *The Kiss* on it. According to the note on the back of that one he just saw it and thought of me. This time it was a Degas pastel: a red-haired woman stood in a tin basin, bending over in order to sponge her legs. I flipped it over and read the message on the back: *This lady reminds me of someone! I'm sorry I disturbed your work, didn't mean to bother you. Sorry again. Tony. X.*

I told no one about Tony because I couldn't figure out whether or not my nervous reaction to him was either rational or justified. In a way, though, I was grateful for this distraction of sorts, as it helped take my mind off Marcus. I can tell you that it isn't easy to concentrate on being in love with someone when you're preoccupied with the unwanted attentions of a nutcase.

As Tony began to call me more and more frequently and for less and less reason, my thoughts became so completely absorbed by him that I began to wonder if I had actually hallucinated being in love. Perhaps it had merely been a strange, fleeting side effect of wearing a pink cardigan. Who knows? But I also noticed that as I grew more and more perturbed by Tony, Marcus became equally embattled by the tug of love between Isobel and Angela.

Isobel made daily attempts to contact him. When the land line wasn't ringing, his mobile was. If Angela got to the phone first she would tell Isobel that he wasn't in and warn her not to ring again. Undeterred, Isobel would ring Marcus's mobile the minute Angela hung up on her. To my mind, the simplest thing would have been for Marcus to actually talk to her. That way he could tell her to leave him alone, that is, if he wanted her to leave him alone.

Neither of us really knew what Marcus wanted; Angela just assumed she did. Marcus had clammed up.

'I think he was so overwhelmed by the fact that someone like her was going out with him that he spent most of the time in thrall to her. It breaks my heart to see him so unhappy and I could break both Isobel's legs for it.'

245

One Saturday morning not long after that, Marcus came downstairs looking particularly rough and unkempt.

'Good night last night I take it?' Angela asked.

'I met Isobel last night,' he replied with a certain amount of defiance.

'Marcus! I told you not to.'

'Sorry, Mammy. She seems really sorry.'

'Sorry? Of course she's bloody sorry. Marcus, I can't believe you've given her a second chance,' Angela moaned, cradling her head in her hands.

'I didn't say that I have,' he snapped.

'Well, what happened?'

'We talked.'

'You talked. And?'

'And nothing, that's it.'

'God, why did you come down here making your grand bloody announcements when you aren't going to give us anything more to go on?'

'Ang, you ought to know by now that we men don't discuss feelings over breakfast. Sorry. That's all you're going to get out of me.'

'Men don't talk about their feelings because they don't have any,' I quipped in a lame attempt to detract from the fact that Angela was going to choke on her muesli any minute. Marcus laughed the first laugh I had heard from him in a long time, and even at that it was a short-lived, pathetic little burst, nothing like his usual guffaw.

Chapter Eighteen

Tony and I had our first *formal* meeting the following Tuesday, as planned, and he seemed determined to use the time in order to discover as much about me as he possibly could.

Linda liked her editors to take writers out for coffee and a cosy chat during the first meeting. I tried to get out of this one by claiming that the petty cash wouldn't stretch to it, but she suggested (in other words, she ordered) that I pay and re-imburse myself when the cash box received one of its sporadic credits.

'Linda, we've met many times. I feel I know Tony like the back of my hand at this stage,' I said and then shuddered at the very thought of it.

'What you get up to in your own time has nothing to do with me or the company, Anna. As far as I'm concerned this is your first meeting and you know the procedure.' I resigned myself to my fate with a sigh and some very loud disgruntled muttering. I was careful to stress to Tony that the whole jaunt was my boss's idea. However, I hadn't reckoned on the selective brain processing of a psychotic with a crush. What I actually said was, 'Tony, my boss has instructed me to take you out for a coffee.' Judging from the look on his face, I think what he heard was, 'Tony, I would love nothing better than for you to take me out for a coffee so you can ask me millions of personal questions and fantasise about how I might look in expensive black underwear.'

'So,' asked Tony as we settled at a window seat, 'are you married then, Anna?' Tony obviously liked the direct approach.

'No,' I answered automatically, completely forgetting that I had slipped a ring onto my wedding finger that morning in the hope that he would see it and stop himself in his tracks. He glanced at my left hand and I could feel myself going a little pink about the gills. I admit that it was a silly idea. Have you ever noticed, though, that it's the people who drive you to silly lies and ruses who are the very ones to see right through them?

'Why the ring then?'

'I . . . ah . . . my boyfriend gave me that . . . he, um . . . died . . . yes, ah, died . . . last year I think

248

. . . I mean, it *was* last year.' What the hell? He died last year? The man had clearly shot my nerves to pieces. Why didn't I just use Marcus, the ready-made, fully functioning boyfriend again? I had left logic behind with my pyjamas under the duvet. Perhaps I thought he might find a grieving widow a bit off-putting. Oh no, he loved that.

'I'm really sorry to hear that. You must have loved him very much.'

'Emm, yes, I did.'

'How did he die?' To be fair the guy looked genuinely concerned, but he was a psychotic so he may have been faking it. In his head he was probably figuring out the best spot in the Wicklow Mountains to dump my black underwear-clad body. Shit, he had asked me a question, what was it again? Oh yes, how did he die. How *did* he die?

'He em, sort of fell . . . .' I hoped my vagueness would make him think it was too painful for me to talk about.

'Fell? You mean *off* something?' He disturbed me by pushing for the gory details despite his feigned concern.

'He fell into . . . into a . . . river.'

'Oh, where?' It was asked in a 'oh really, you've been to Italy, what part, I go there every year' sort of way. I suspected that he didn't believe me, which was fair enough as I wasn't very convincing.

'The Liffey. He threw himself in. Look, I'd rather not talk about it if you don't mind.'

'Sure, Anna.' If he didn't take the fact of a suicidal boyfriend as a hint, then he really *was* mad. 'Though a nice-looking girl like you shouldn't take too long getting over this guy . . . it's not fair on the rest of us.' As he said that he winked at me!

I just about managed to steer the conversation away from men, marriage and preferred positions and back onto the task in hand, his memoirs.

'Well, I haven't got round to putting the whole thing together just yet. It's all up here, though,' he said, tapping his head. If this was meant to reassure me, it didn't work. Linda was expecting me back in the office by three o'clock, happily working away on the first draft. Linda had a wonderful, nurturing way with authors. She could make them feel special, she understood the pressure of waiting for the muse to visit. In other words, anything that went wrong was bound to be my fault; even the muse's failure to visit Longkesh would, no doubt, be my fault. I tried to explain this in as tactful a way as possible, pointing out that he had signed a contract and his failure to present me with something on paper that afternoon could well result in my death.

'I grew up on the streets, you know.'

'What on earth has that got to do with the price of chips?'

He roared laughing for slightly longer than was warranted, then he fixed me with his steady gaze, as though he had just realised that the question was actually a bit smart assed. I guess he wasn't used to smart-ass comments, or at least smart-ass comments from someone whose face he couldn't smash against the shower wall.

'I didn't get an education. I didn't have the advantages that you and James and that Linda had. Anything I know I learned inside. I read. I read all the time. It kept my head sane. But I'm not good with words. That was why I was hoping you might help.'

What?

'As an editor.'

'Tony, I can't write your book for you. I'm an *editor*, not a ghost writer. Linda isn't going to be happy when I go back. She was expecting me to start work on the first draft this afternoon. She'll blame me for this, you know.'

'You'll get into trouble?'

'Yes.'

'Right then,' he said in the manner of a super-hero who is just off on another job, 'just for you, I'll have something ready for you to work on really, really soon. It's hard for me to write this stuff, you know, but I wouldn't want a nice girl like you getting into trouble over an eejit like *me*.' He said it with a relish that led me to believe that he would very much enjoy me getting into trouble over him. Now I had to deal with a psycho with a crush, a socialist chip on his shoulder and a newfound sense of perverse chivalry. Was this really worth the

€20,000 a year and the faint hope that Linda might die? No, I didn't think so either.

Tony was babbling away at me about life on the mean streets of Derry, drugs and the IRA. I'm sure it was all fascinating and if I had been clever I could have typed it all up and told Linda it was the first draft. But I was lost in my own thoughts and was busy drawing up a shopping list when Tony suddenly announced that I was looking 'dreamy and far away'. I rapidly snapped out of my musing mode and told Tony that his time was up.

'What, you mean you have a bullet with my name on it?' He went off into hysterics at his own joke.

As I predicted, Linda indulged in a nice bout of the blame game that afternoon and I was reminded of what a liability I was in O'Sullivan & Hackett. But did I care? Nope. I had reached the point of no return. I was sure that I was soon to leave the world of O'Sullivan & Hackett, never to return. As she lambasted me, my mind entertained itself with various versions of my resignation . . . some were violent, others merely verbally aggressive. They were all highly enjoyable.

'What are you smiling at? Haven't you heard a word I've just said?'

No, you old bitch, and I don't give a flying . . . .

Chapter Nineteen

Tony seemed to take our little chat to heart, as he worked like a demon over the next few weeks. Unfortunately, he seemed to feel the need to report to me at the end of each day's work. He also sent me postcards once a week. He made several attempts to arrange out-of-hours meetings to discuss his work, but I didn't think anything would be gained by my correcting his grammar over a plate of carbonara and a bottle of Chianti. Eventually, my persistent refusals paid off and he stopped asking me. He then took to sounding sorrowful and wistful on the phone. He would ring on a Friday and ask me what my plans were for the weekend. They inevitably involved Marcus; I was trying to give him a hint. He would give a sad little laugh and say things like 'I hope he treats you right, you're a lovely girl' for the millionth time. I was beginning to believe him. 'You deserve a good guy.'

How did he know what I deserved? He had no idea what I was like. We had met only twice and I had avoided answering all questions that might have led him to anything like in-depth knowledge. I think this is what disturbed me most about Tony. I suspected that he had invented a personality for me and twisted everything I said or did in such a way that it reinforced that invention. God, don't I sound deep?

But we all do this. Think about when you last had a crush on someone you barely knew. You might have thought they looked kind or sad or happy or whatever. You might have ascribed some trait to them that you were in need of at that time, like kindness, and as you didn't know them, you would never be disillusioned. You could think of them as the perfect partner because you would never find out otherwise. That's the charm of the harmless crush. But there's something almost unreal about those people. They don't really figure in your life, or they oughtn't to unless you're a stalker. The minute you speak to them, even if it's just the once, you have to see them as human, not as the answer to your prayers. You have to understand that they have a personality that might not match the one you imagined for them and if you can't get to know what that is, then you have no business continuing to think of them any old way you like.

I think that was how Tony was with me. He had some idea of what he wanted from a woman and due to, let's say, limited access over the past few years, he didn't really know very many. It wasn't me he was interested in; I was merely a vessel into which he poured all his wishes. He had no real interest in getting to know me any better. However, no matter how long and how philosophically I mused, he still scared me a little.

In an unprecedented act of daring I left without making up the ten minutes I owed from that morning. Needless to say, Linda wasn't around to notice. Just as I was about to get on the bus I suddenly remembered that I had foolishly promised to go to a yoga class with Angela. She couldn't give me a sensible reason why she couldn't go on her own, but she pleaded and pestered me so much that I gave in for the sake of peace.

Angela had been quite tense lately, which I had initially attributed to the Marcus situation, but it then dawned on me that she only mentioned Xavier of late in every third sentence, rather than every second. Something was wrong, but because she was being ridiculously (though unconvincingly) chirpy, I decided that it would be best to wait for *her* to raise the subject.

As we made our way along Dame Street towards the Dublin Yoga Centre she talked happily about what a good day she'd had, what lovely weather we were having for the time of year, the state of the sales and such like.

'You know, I really do love my job. I know I complain about it all the time, but underneath it all, I really do like it . . . Ooh, look at her shoes, wonder where she got them . . . Do you know what I would love right now? A holiday! I know I don't *need* one, but wouldn't it be great . . . oh look, Anna, look, over there – that's the kind of coat I've been looking for, no, not the green one, the pink one standing at the bus stop over there. You know, I've been looking forward to this class all day. I used to do yoga years ago, but I'm so rusty now. It's going to be so good. Oh, yes, here we are . . . oh sod it, Anna, let's go shopping!' She threw me such a pathetic, pleading look that I burst out laughing at the sudden disappearance of her enthusiasm for yoga.

'Well, I guess going around the sales with you for the third time this week might just be marginally less painful than trying to tie my legs behind my head.'

Off we went and our first port of call was – guess where – Brown flippin' Thomas. I had been inside that shop more times that week than I had ever been in my whole life. Angela had been keeping an eye on a dress she was hoping would drop to €200. It had been €250 the last time we'd checked . . . two days before.

'You never know with sales, Anna,' she chided me gently when I aired my grievance at having to check once again.

'But you know, I think I'm going to take it anyway, even if it's still two fifty. I mean, what's fifty euro?'

She knew where she was going and headed straight for the rail.

'Here it is!' she squealed delightedly. 'Oh, hang on, that's an eight. Damn. Here . . . no, fourteen . . . and six. Six? Who wears a six, for God's sake . . . and finally . . . .' she checked the label carefully, '*sixteen*!' She wailed, 'Anna, it's *gone*!'

With that she burst into loud, blubbery tears.

'Angela, honey,' I soothed, 'it's just a dress.'

'It's not just a dress, it was *the* dress, the dress of my dreams, and I left it there. I didn't keep a careful eye on it and someone else came along and snaffled it up. It's my own fault. Oh Anna, I'm so stupid!'

'It's not the dress, is it, petal?'

'Noooo,' she wailed.

'Come on, let's get out of here,' I coaxed her while throwing a vicious look at the assistants who were visibly squirming at Angela's performance.

'Can I have a drink please?' she whimpered at me.

'Of course you can.'

I took her off to O'Neills as it was the closest pub I could think of, but by that stage she had recovered enough to whimper that she would prefer the Clarence, so I gritted my teeth and took her there instead. I sat her down with a double vodka, for which I had paid the price of a full bottle. She took a massive swig of it and then blurted out, 'I think he might be seeing someone else.'

'Xavier?' I asked stupidly.

'Who else?' she snapped.

'Well, the vodka seems to be working.'

'Sorry, I didn't mean to snap.'

She then explained to me that a 'friend' of Xavier's had let something slip one night. She asked Angela if she had enjoyed Guilbaud's after all the difficulty Xavier had had in getting the booking. Apparently her reaction to Angela's look of confusion was to giggle nervously and protest that she was sure it was Angela he mentioned. Of course Angela later questioned Xavier, who simply laughed at her and told her not to be so suspicious. He didn't like suspicious women.

'Well, there's one bloody suspicious woman he wouldn't like by the time she was finished with him,' I said.

We were both distracted at this point by a very loud voice booming at Angela from across the bar.

'Angela, how the hell are ye?'

We both looked up to see a tall, slightly overweight man of about thirty-five heading our way.

'Ah, crap, Peter bloody Mahoney . . . Peter! Hi! Nice to see you.'

He leaned over her and placed a rather slobbery kiss on her cheek. His lips were fat and moist and his complexion couldn't be better described than by saying that he had a head like a huge tomato topped with ginger hair swept into an alarmingly bouffant hairdo.

'You're lookin' great, as always, Ang.'

'And you . . . that's a nice suit you're wearing.'

'This thing? Jesus, I've had it for fucking years. It's Armani, though, and he does wear well. Fuck, it's good to see you.'

'And you, Peter,' Angela replied in a polite but clipped tone, which, together with her reddened eyes, would have been enough to prompt most people to remove themselves tactfully. But not this eejit.

'D'ye mind if I join you?' he asked, pulling a chair up.

'Won't your group miss you?'

'That shower of bastards? Hell no! It's only a work thing. Mick got his promotion today so we're out on the raz. Stupid bastard's shitfaced already. Ha ha ha.'

'And so are you.' The words slipped out before I could stop them, but he didn't seem to notice anything other than Angela's breasts.

'Your da tells me that your books could do with a bit of a looking over.' I don't know how he'd done it, but he'd just managed to make accountancy sound sleazy.

'My books are fine, thanks, Peter,' Angela responded in a steely tone. 'How's Marion these days?'

'Oh Jesus, we split up months ago. Mutual decision. Are you seeing anyone yourself at the moment?' he leered at her.

I thought I sensed Angela stiffen ever so slightly, but quick as a flash she answered, 'I am, as it happens.'

'Oh, right.' There was a few minutes of silence while I fidgeted in my chair, he fidgeted with his tie and Angela knocked back the rest of her drink.

'Well, I'd best get back to the lads.'

'Nice to see you, as always, Peter.'

'Yeah, good luck.'

'Who was that charmer?' I asked as soon as he was safely back in his place.

'That, my dear, was Peter Mahoney, my brother's close friend and the man my parents would love me to marry.'

'That? They want you to marry that? But he's so . . . .'

'I know, I know, but he's of good stock and is fairly wealthy, as you might have guessed. He's an asshole, of course. Thinks the sun shines out of his own very large arse. But forget Peter bloody Mahoney. Do you think all that I've told you means that Xavier is two-timing me?'

'Honestly, Angela, I don't know. That girl may simply have been making mischief. You know him better than I do. What do *you* think?' I was in a dilemma. I could so easily have told her that I had disliked Xavier the minute I met him, but it was plain that she still liked him and had really only confided in me so that she might hear someone else deny that he could do anything so dreadful. Like an alcoholic needs to admit to himself that he has a problem, Angela would believe no one but herself, and only when she was ready would she admit that the man was a creep. The fact that he had given her underwear two sizes too big would have been enough to give most people a hint, but not Angela. She wanted so badly to believe that Xavier was perfect, so the only sensible thing for me to do that evening was to sit and listen.

And there was a lot to hear. Once she had *forgotten* that he told her he would be out and rang him and he had been home. Okay, not exactly criminal. Then there was the time she rang his mobile and some girl answered it. Still, not a hanging offence.

'Then why did she scream his name angrily and hang up?' I couldn't think of a plausible excuse for that one.

'Why do I keep going for such tossers? What do you think I should do?' she pleaded. 'Should I dump him?'

'I can't tell you that.'

'Oh please, I don't know what to do. You have to help me.'

261

'C'mon, Ang. I can't tell you that I think you should or shouldn't dump this guy. You still like him and I don't know him well enough. Tell me he's definitely two-timing you and I would have no hesitation in telling you to dump him.'

'So what do I do?'

'Find out whether or not he *is* two-timing you and then get back to me.'

'So exactly how do I do that?'

'Sneak me into his house, hide me in his wardrobe with enough provisions to keep me going for a week, a chamber pot and a camera and I'll get back to you with my findings . . . Jesus, Ang, you're the one going out with him. You figure that bit out.'

Well, it got something approaching a laugh out of her at least. She was just about to start on *my* love life, or rather, my lack of one, when I decided it was time to go home.

As she turned the key in the front door Angela turned to me and announced that she had never had a girl friend like me. I looked slightly askance; I hadn't done anything wonderful. If anything I had been a bit hard on her.

'You just listen and I think you're the least judgmental or biased person I've ever met.' She turned and gave me an enormous hug.

Relations between Marcus and I had inevitably begun to change after the New Year's debacle. He continued to see Isobel now and again, but neither

Angela nor I could find out what was going on between them. Her campaign was relentless – she clearly wasn't going to let him go without a fight. She phoned constantly. For every 'no' Marcus gave her she would ring fifty times till he caved in and reluctantly agreed to meet her to 'talk' again. And it was slowly sucking the life out of him.

The weeks trickled on quietly till they reached my second most hated day of celebration – Valentine's Day. And I wasn't the only one who wasn't particularly looking forward to it that year. Linda was, inexplicably, single again and not very pleased about it. Not even the extra helpings of unctiousness that James was serving up on a daily basis had the power to soothe her. Meanwhile, on the home front Angela had been cast into a pit of despair. Xavier hadn't phoned her in a long time, nor was he returning her increasingly anxious calls. And as for Marcus . . . well, he had disappeared long ago. I had no idea what was going on inside his head, but he certainly wasn't happy. I did miss the old Marcus, the one with the ego and the infectious laugh. He had been replaced by a cranky, moody, narky, humourless guy who seemed not to like either of his flatmates very much. Having said that, it did help me smother the very last remnants of what I had mistaken for love. Now the idea that I had ever thought myself in love with Marcus was quite amusing.

And then there was Tony. That situation was worsening daily. James, being an insensitive humanoid, thought the whole thing vaguely amusing. Initially so did I, but as the weeks passed the cards became more frequent, their pictures more dubious and the quotations from love poetry grew longer. He had also developed a habit of popping into the office in order to drop off bags of sweets and chocolate bars. Don't ask me why he did this. He would proffer them with a flourish and would always say 'sweets for the sweet' and think it original and hilarious in equal measures. I always handed them straight over to James, who would eat anything that he hadn't paid for.

I had discovered that the trick to dealing with Tony was to not listen to a word he said but simply to nod and say 'yes' or 'no' at appropriate moments. I have no idea what I said yes or no to that day. It could have been suggested changes to the manuscript, could have been an offer of marriage. Didn't know, didn't care. Tony seemed happy with whatever I said, though, as he left the office whistling 'All You Need Is Love'.

I awoke on the day of doom with a feeling of nauseous anxiety in my stomach because I knew Tony wouldn't let the day pass unmarked. As I came downstairs the letterbox flipped open. Two brown envelopes and some flyers plopped onto the mat. I had never before experienced relief at not getting any post. I agree that I was perhaps being a little paranoid. After all, Tony didn't know where I lived. Nonetheless, the relief made me quite chirpy.

Angela, however, assumed that, like her, I was bravely masking no-card induced misery.

'Never mind,' she consoled, 'maybe someone has sent one to the office.' I spluttered my flakes back into their bowl. Of course, Tony might have sent one there! I should have thought of that! My nausea returned and stayed in my stomach all the way to work. I walked very slowly that morning, convinced that an evil red envelope awaited me there. As I turned the corner onto our street, my attention was caught by some graffiti on the ground. I walked over a giant red 'I'. I walked slowly on and over a giant red heart. My stomach tightened. Just outside the office door I stood on my own name. From any other man this might have seemed like a stupid but romantic gesture. But not from Tony. I turned and ran back up the street, jumped on a bus back home and rang in sick.

I spent my day off mulling over the whole Tony situation. Was it normal, I wondered, to have to deal with this sort of thing during a typical working day? James didn't and Linda didn't. Angela did, but then, by her own admission, it was her own fault. If you insist on running that kind of establishment, lunatics come with the territory. Maybe it was similarly the case with publishing. But if that was true, then I'd had enough of the territory.

The next morning I ate a hearty breakfast, as I knew I was going to have a battle on my hands before elevenses. I marched into work and the minute Linda made her appearance I asked to see her in her office. She looked taken aback, of course. I followed her into her office and shut the door behind me.

'Anna, what can I do for you?'

'Linda, I'm no longer willing to deal with Tony O'Hanlon.'

'Excuse me?'

'I'm no longer willing to deal with Tony O'Hanlon.'

'Anna, in case you hadn't noticed, I'm the one in charge around here and I say who deals with whom. You can't pick and choose your authors like that.'

'This has nothing to do with picking and choosing, as you put it. The man is a nut case. Don't tell me you didn't notice the pavement yesterday?'

'Oh, that!' she exclaimed. 'I'd almost forgotten about that. It's a pity the rain washed it away. Come now, I thought it was a rather sweet gesture.'

'From any other man it might have been, but not from Tony.'

'And what, may I ask, is wrong with Tony?'

'He's practically *stalking* me, that's what's wrong with him.'

'Anna, calm down and don't be so foolish. I mean, why on earth would he be stalking you? I think perhaps you're overreacting a bit.'

'What about these then?' I smacked down the by now large bundle of postcards on her desk. 'Go on, have a read. How about this nice one of the naked redhead that reminds him of guess who? That's right, me! Or this one of *The Kiss*, oh, and look, here are Rodin's lovers, and here's another pair. And how on earth would you know whether or not Tony is harmless, Linda? You've never dealt with him.'

Her face froze and a cold wind came whistling into the office, bringing a cold front with it.

'Anna, I see that you might find his attention a bit . . . .' she paused and fumbled for a suitable word, 'full on, but there's nothing I can do about that. You just have to learn to handle him. James is too busy right now and personally I think you're taking the whole thing a little too seriously. Try not to be so melodramatic.'

I was beyond boiling point at that stage and so without saying another word I turned around and stomped out of the office. I held my breath while I ran up the small flight of stairs to the toilet, where I doubled over and screamed as quietly as possible into my knees. Then I splashed some water on my face, took a few deep breaths, went back down the stairs and back into Linda's office.

'Linda, I quit.'

Chapter Twenty

Angela became increasingly convinced of Xavier's infidelity. She still had no solid proof but she had the little incidents that, in quantity, can sometimes seem like sufficient substitutes. He phoned even less than before – which amounted to hardly ever. He would make arrangements then cancel them at short notice, offering only the flimsiest of excuses for doing so. Similarly, he would fob her off then ring late on a Saturday night, his plans having suddenly altered. He would be free and expect Angela to drop everything in order to meet him. And she did. Once or twice he reminded Angela of somewhere they had been, some restaurant they had eaten in, some evening they had enjoyed and Angela would realise, with mortification, that he was confusing her with someone else. She spotted him in town one weekend when he was supposed to be in France. But she still hadn't dumped him. I couldn't understand why this girl who could have had any guy she wanted insisted on turning herself into a doormat for this loser.

It was on one of those by now inevitable cancelled Friday evenings that things finally came to a head. I was sitting in front of the television numbing my brain with *Coronation Street* and alcohol, feeling sorry for myself because I still had no life. Marcus was out having yet more 'talks' with Isobel and Angela was upstairs beautifying herself for her evening with Xavier. The phone rang. It was him. I knew what was coming – another cancellation. Angela came in and threw herself on the sofa beside me. She was clutching a glass full of ice and a full bottle of vodka in one hand and a packet of cigarettes in the other. Things were bad.

'That's it, I've had it. He is *dumped*,' she mumbled through the cigarette she was lighting. 'That's the fifth arrangement in a row that he's cancelled.'

'Ang, you can do so much better than him.'

'Oh don't bloody start, Anna. You never liked him, you hated him from the off so I bet you're feeling dead smug now, aren't you?'

I was taken aback by this vicious little attack. As sympathetic as I was, I wasn't prepared to sit back and allow myself to be lambasted because she was pissed off with Xavier.

'Angela, if you're going to take your ill humour out on someone, then take it out on him, not me. You needn't think that my sympathy extends to allowing myself to be used as some sort of whipping boy. You know I'm always ready to give you a shoulder to cry on, but if you're going to be like this you can piss off.'

'Sorry. That was unfair. It's just that I really like him.'

'Why, for God's sake? He's an asshole. I'm sorry, but I have to be blunt. He hasn't treated you too well, not as well as you deserve.'

'That's just it, though, I don't deserve any better.' I glanced at the vodka bottle. There wasn't much gone out of it yet so it wasn't that talking. She meant it.

'Angela, what are you talking about? Look at you, you're gorgeous, your best mate loves you to bits and even my stony heart is beginning to warm towards you ever so slightly.'

'I'm one of life's losers. I don't deserve someone as successful and handsome and charming as he is.' I wondered if we were actually talking about the same person. I was worried by her tone, though. She seemed to really mean all this. I had always thought of her as fairly confident. I didn't think it was possible to look like her and not be. 'Look at me, Anna. Look at my life. I've wasted so many years pissing about, managing, or rather, *mis*managing, that sorry excuse for a shop. I couldn't even manage to buy my own house, my parents had to lend me money, and they only did it for the sake of their pride. If their daughter will insist on screwing up her life, then at least she should do it in the privacy of her own home. What am I doing with my life? I don't even believe in the shit that I sell.' She took a massive slug of vodka straight from the bottle. The more she talked, the more depressed she got and nothing I said made her feel better. I knew it wouldn't help, but I had to offer the lame platitudes, the assurance of support that wouldn't make any difference that night but that had to be said so she knew that at least I cared. I hoped that at some point the next day, or even the next week, she would think about what I said and maybe take some of it to heart. But she was so entrenched in her black mood that no amount of soothing could coax her out of it. She was convinced that she had failed in life. She looked at those around her and saw success of one kind or another and compared it with her own lack of it. She even included me in this. If only she knew (but that was not the night for revelations). She couldn't see that her independence, in life and in work, was so much more admirable than my plodding. I let her talk, not knowing if it was doing her any good or if it was only darkening her mood.

We eventually returned to the subject of Xavier and she fluctuated between thinking him the greatest shit ever to have walked the earth and all that she

271

deserved and his being the most amazing man ever to have walked the earth and far too good for her.

'Maybe I should settle for someone like Peter, he's more my level.'

'Angela, no one could be so bad that *Peter* is all they deserve.'

'No, I really think that someone like him is exactly what I deserve. In fact, I'm going to ring him and ask him out.' Before I could stop her she ran to the kitchen, picked up the phone book and started hunting for his number.

'Aha, here he is.' She started dialling.

'Angela, stop it.' She wasn't listening, so I tried to grab the phone from her. She ducked and dived out of my reach. I managed to grab her but she wriggled out of my grasp.

'You can relax,' she said, 'I've only got his answering machine.' But just as I backed away from her she started to leave a message.

'Hi Peter, it's Angela,' she crooned drunkenly. 'I was just wondering if I could take you up on that offer of . . . em . . . *looking over my books*. Maybe you might give me call sometime . . . bye.' Well, the way she said all that ensured that no male would seriously think that it was a lesson in accounting that she was after. I looked at her in horror and she returned my look with one of defiance and triumph, as though she had just beaten an evil genius in a plot to destroy the world. It was a Pyrrhic victory at best.

'Angela, have you completely lost your marbles?'

'Possibly. It's hard to keep an eye on the little critters when you're this pissed,' she giggled.

There was only one way to stop the madness and that was to appeal to her better nature.

'Angela, I swear, if you go ahead with this I'll go into work next week and shag James on my own desk. On my granny's grave, I swear I will.'

'Fine, you do that. You never know, you might find you like it.'

'Angela—'

'Oh don't be such a mammy. I know what I'm doing,' she said as she stuck another fag in her mouth and tried to light the wrong end.

'Angela! Get back here now!'

'Nighty night,' she called out as she headed up the stairs and into her room.

That Monday morning I felt a frisson of revulsion as James wished me good morning and sat down at his desk.

James, of course, had been particularly unfazed by my sudden resignation. But Linda had gone into a tailspin of panic. At first she chose not to believe that I was being serious and called me into her office the next day.

'Anna.'

'Linda.'

'Sit down. Anna, I'm willing to overlook your little tantrum and put it down to PMT or something, but you can't actually be serious about resigning?'

'I am perfectly serious.'

'But you know how few jobs there are in this area.'

'I do and I have no intention of looking for another one.'

'You can't just leave, you know. It's a bad time for the company.'

'I've given you the required notice.'

'Anna! This is disgraceful.'

'There's nothing disgraceful about it and you know it.'

'You needn't think that this is going to get you out of working with Tony,' she said, slightly menacingly.

'I am not working with Tony.' I must say I was very pleased with my own zen-like calm throughout this whole exchange.

'Well, I'm afraid that is just not possible. As I explained to you on Friday, James is too busy at the moment.'

'If that's the case, then how come he spends most of his day reading *History Ireland* at the moment? Linda, the long and the short of it is this: I reported a case of harassment in the workplace and you appear to be refusing to fix that situation. That's not good, now is it?'

'Are you threatening to take this elsewhere?'

'I'm doing nothing of the sort, I'm merely showing you how the situation really is.'

You can imagine how well we got on after that. Linda couldn't wait to see the back of me, particularly as *she* now had to deal with Tony. Of course he was as good as gold with her, but I think she was torn between a sense of 'I told you so' and confusion as to why he wasn't stalking *her*.

Of course I had lied when I told Linda that I had no intention of looking for another publishing job. I had thought long and hard about it and I realised that it wasn't the job per se that I didn't like, it was O'Sullivan & Hackett that I didn't like. I had thought equally long and hard about where I was going to look for a new job and I found that I still longed for an escape from Dublin. I couldn't think of anything worth staying for. Angela? I had certainly grown very fond of her and she of me, but it wasn't enough. Marcus? I had long since buried that episode.

Then one day, while blatantly slacking and browsing through *The Bookseller,* I saw it – a dream of a job. A London publishing house of some renown was looking for a junior editor. I knew they would never dream of publishing books about nymphomaniac nuns, they published good books, books that people wanted to read. I felt a little fizzle of something I used to recognise as enthusiasm go pop inside my stomach.

Of course I knew I didn't stand a chance of getting it. There would be hundreds applying for it. Enthusiasm was slowly being choked to death by my good friend pessimism. Just when it was in the final death throes, Linda stomped into the room. Her beady eyes zoomed in on the open magazine and she whipped it off my desk before I could stop her. I had made the mistake of circling the ad in red pen. She took one look at it and offered something between a squeal and a titter. She looked at me pityingly.

'I don't think so, Anna.' She dropped the magazine and swished out of the office, chuckling to herself.

I never thought I would see the day when I would have something to thank Linda for, but strange though it may seem, it was her reaction that prompted me to immediately start typing up a new CV and an application letter that would leave them no choice but to give me the job. I didn't know if resentment and anger could get me a job, but I was sure as hell going to try.

It was around this time that I began to experience an unaccountable urge to visit Mother. Perhaps I was unconsciously looking for advice from her, as my two flatmates were understandably a little wrapped up in themselves at that point. But the thought of seeking advice from her made me wince. I couldn't admit that I needed her, especially not to her. However, the Friday after I had begun to experience this disturbing sensation, she rang.

'Hello, Ma.'

'Anna! It's lovely to hear from you, how are you?' She sounded weird; she didn't usually gush at me like that.

'Are you all right, Mother?' I asked tentatively.

'Of course I am, lovey. So what are you up to tonight?'

Ah, this was more like it!

'Nothing, staying in.'

'Oh well, never mind, things will pick up for you soon, wait and see. Trust me, I'm a mammy,' she laughed. What the hell was going on? Where was the nagging? The retribution? The anguish? The disappointment? The torment? Where was my mother?

'Are you sure you're all right? You don't sound like yourself.'

'I think I actually sound more like myself than I have done in years.'

She was talking in riddles again.

'Actually, dear, I was hoping you might be able to come to Armagh some time in the not-too-distant future. I've asked the boys as well, there's something I need to talk to you all about.'

Oh dear God, she was ill! My stomach tightened and I felt an urge to throw up.

'Mother?' I began in an uneven voice.

'Now there's nothing to panic about, Anna, don't be silly, I'll explain all when I see you.'

'Why can't you just tell me now?'

'Well, it's not the kind of thing you can tell someone over the phone.'

'I'll get the first bus up tomorrow.'

'But I wanted to tell you all together.'

'I'm not waiting for bloody Jason to crawl out from underneath whatever rock he's hiding under at the moment.'

'Anna, that's no way to talk about your brother . . . but it's a fair enough point, I suppose,' she added with one of her best martyred sighs. 'Well, if you would *like* to come tomorrow, that would be lovely . . . and we'll make a nice cake for you.'

After I had hung up I wondered what the hell she was doing making cakes when she was clearly about to announce that she was fatally ill. *'Hello dear, I'm dying, but do have some of this delicious poppy seed cake. It'll cheer you up no end.'*

And who was 'we'?

The following morning I arrived in Armagh after a bus journey made even more torturous by the driver's relentless playing of country and western music. My ears were still ringing when the taxi pulled up outside Mother's house. The door was opened by Patrick, carrying Ronan in his arms. He greeted me with the casual friendliness of someone who was used to being there.

'Anna, lovely to see you again. How was the journey?'

I don't know if I was more surprised by how 'at home' he looked or by how calm and peaceful Ronan seemed. He was munching on a raw carrot, which threw me even further as the Ronan I knew had an aversion to everything that was good for him. The little fecker even greeted me with a smile and insisted that 'Uncle' Patrick hand him into my arms for the purpose of giving me a hug and a slobbery kiss. I put him down, took him by the hand and led him out into the garden where my mother was pottering about in her greenhouse. Her greeting was, as ever, casual to the point of being a little cool.

'Hello. Journey all right?' I asked her why Ronan was there. 'Ronan is staying with us for a couple of weeks. Geraldine and Paul are in Spain. The change in him is quite astounding, don't you think?' I was just about to agree with her when I realised that she had just said 'us', Ronan was staying with an 'us'.

'Who's "us"?' I blurted out, making no apologies for my bluntness.

'Sorry, lovey, what did you say?' she asked, feigning stupidity, as she was bright pink.

'You said he was staying with "us". Who did you mean?'

'Why, Patrick and I, of course,' she said, attempting casual, failing miserably.

'Is he . . . are you and he . . . ?'

'Yes,' she sighed, like a teenager exasperated by her mother's naïveté, 'we're living together and you needn't look so shocked, I've been on my own long enough. I can't go on mourning your father forever.' She sounded extremely defensive.

'I didn't say you should. I'm just, oh, surprised is all.'

'Why? I sometimes think that your age group is more prudish than mine. You'd think I was geriatric.' She paused and took a deep breath. 'Patrick and I are very much in love.'

'Mother, I'm going to get straight to the point. What is the matter?'

'Why do you keep asking me that?'

'Because last night you gave me the impression that you wanted to gather us all to break some terrible, terrible news.'

'I really don't know where you get your pessimism from, but it's certainly not from my side of the family.'

'Mother!'

'What?'

'Spit it out.'

'Patrick and I are getting married!'

My jaw dropped.

'You're getting married,' I repeated stupidly.

'Yes.'

'Properly married?'

'No, pretendy married. Of course properly married, you silly girl.'

'To Patrick?'

She merely sighed in response. 'Let's get you some tea and cake.' She gently guided me back into the kitchen, where the man himself was helping Ronan to a bowl of cornflakes. 'Well, Patrick, as you can probably guess from the state of her, I've told her the good news.'

'Would you like some tea, Anna?' he asked in a very nervous way. I nodded dumbly in reply. After I took a sip of my tea I remembered my manners and congratulated them.

'It might take a little while to sink in and I hope it isn't all too rushed for you,' Patrick said.

'It's just a surprise, that's all.' I must say, the change in Ronan is staggering. How did you do it?' I asked, for some reason deciding that it would be a good idea to change the subject.

'We sent him into cold turkey one weekend he was staying here,' Mother explained. 'We banned Smarties and Coke and introduced him to a new word – "no". It's worked wonders. He's still no angel, but he's definitely better than he was.'

'You like saying "we", don't you Ma?' I smiled.

'I just haven't been able to in a long while,' she smiled back and reached across the table for Patrick's hand.

As if to rescue me from any embarrassment, Ronan came running up to me with a smile on his face and a football in his hands. He demanded rather than asked that I play with him.

'Is Marcus coming?' he asked.

'No, Ronan, he isn't.'

'But you're no good without *him*.'

Patrick made dinner that night and I must admit that it did feel odd to realise that someone who was, to me at least, a perfect stranger knew better than I did where everything was. He knew exactly where each pot lived, whereas I would have had to ask. It may seem like a small thing, but it made me feel ashamed. How seldom did I come home that I barely knew where to find a cup in my mother's house?

I watched them closely during dinner. They had all the natural, instinctive choreography of a real couple. They insisted I sit while they washed up and cleared away. They moved around each other with perfect co-ordination, handing each other plates, dishcloths, knives, forks, glasses with a wordless choreography. They exchanged half sentences, half smiles. I felt almost envious, but I noticed how happy she was and I realised for the first time in my life what a rarity this was. I don't mean to suggest that she was miserable. She wasn't, but she wasn't always happy either. She had raised four children by herself and had put up with loneliness till she had finally seen the last of us fly the nest. I wondered if perhaps her frequent impatience and her intolerance were at least in part born of a sense of what she had sacrificed in order to do the right thing. Did a tiny part of her resent what she had been forced to give up for so many years? She must have felt something like the relief of Easter chocolate after Lent.

After dinner Patrick was corralled by Ronan for a marathon storytelling session. Apparently no one else's version of *The Three Bears* was quite good enough and Patrick was under a nightly obligation

282

to recite it, but it had to be exactly the same as the night before, otherwise screaming would ensue.

'You won't try and change the words like last night, will you?' Ronan asked him anxiously as Patrick led him away by the hand.

My mother and I were left by ourselves for the first time that day.

'You don't mind, do you?'

'What?'

'You don't think it's weird, you know, Patrick and I?'

'I wish I knew him a bit better, but no, I don't think it's *weird*.'

'Well, you could have known him better if you had visited a bit more often.'

She was right, so I had no right to argue.

'Yeah, I know.'

'Good God! No argument. Are you feeling all right? But enough about me for the moment, I'm not used to this much attention,' she said with a martyred sigh, and I smiled to see a glimpse of the old Mother. 'How have you been?'

I then filled her in on how in a fit of pique I had thrown in my job and hadn't yet managed to line up another.

'Good for you!' she almost squealed with jubilation.

'But I'll soon be jobless, homeless and penniless.'

'Never mind. You've taken a step in the right direction.'

'I have?'
'Absolutely! I have every faith in you.'
'It's just as well one of us does.'

Chapter Twenty-one

My last day at O'Sullivan & Hackett eventually rolled around and the only hint of emotion about the whole thing came, ironically, from James.

'I thought you had ages to go yet. Ah well.'

Linda had soon got over her panic and came to look forward to my departure as much as I did. On this, my last day, her joy was barely contained. She handed me the last of my wages with a gigantic smirk.

'James and I clubbed together to get you something as a mark of appreciation for all your hard work here. Go ahead and open it,' she said, handing me a second envelope with a flourishing wave of her hand. I had a foolish idea that perhaps she had discovered some nice personality in the bread bin that morning and had relented and decided to give me a decent send-off. But when I opened the envelope I discovered nothing more than a horrible card and a €15 book token.

'Are you serious, Linda?' I asked, holding the token as though it was a pair of unwashed socks. I just looked at her and the malicious smile she had plastered over her face froze and turned glacial.

'That's a little ungracious now Anna, isn't it?'

'Oh, I don't think so. You know, I just don't get you, Linda. Whatever else you may think of me, I've always worked hard, never missed a single one of your crazy deadlines and have taken more shit from you than any employee should be expected to take without recourse to legal action.'

'How dare you speak to me like that? I don't need your pity, Anna,' she said, almost spitting with rage. James looked shifty and anxious.

'Not much point in hanging around, is there, after all I have the rest of my life to be getting on with. Nice working with you James, well, sort of. Here, you have this,' I said, dropping the token onto his desk. 'Buy yourself something nice with a sub-title.' I grabbed my coat and bag and left the office with what I hoped was an admirable nonchalance.

When the last of my triumph finally melted away, I stopped in the middle of Grafton Street and suf-fered a mild panic attack. I wondered what I was going to do. I had tried and failed to get a job in time and though the last of my wages would at least pay the next month's rent, I had to get some kind of job and soon if I was planning on eating anything more substantial than grass and air. I had warned Angela about my impending homelessness and she had been remarkably unfazed by it. I thought she might have got a bit anxious about her rent and so on, but all she'd said was, 'Never mind, you'll get another one soon.'

I didn't share her optimism, however.

I decided to make my way to the shop for some tea and sympathy. When I got there Angela was standing in the window, artistically displaying a large pile of books entitled *Live Each Day Dr Wright's Calm Way*. She waved eagerly when she saw me and knocked over the said pile as she scrambled out of the window.

'Ah, shite, it's taken hours to get that friggin' window right. How are you, my love? Is it all over?'

'Yep, all over. And now I'm jobless and moneyless and potentially homeless,' I moaned as I sat down on a free chair next to a man who was poring over a book about how to change your life through reiki. He was the only customer, but the minute I sat down he upped and left.

'Was it something I said?'

'Oh, don't mind him. He comes in every day but only stays if the shop is absolutely silent. I think he confuses the place with the Central Library.'

'What am I going to do, Angela?' I wailed.

'Well, I was thinking about your dilemma and I've thought of a brilliant arrangement which could be mutually beneficial.'

'Do tell.'

'Well . . . .' she began with an ominous caution, 'you know how Aoife is about to have a baby . . . .'

'Yes.'

'Well, I need someone to fill in . . . .'

'Angela, don't ask me that, anything but that!'

'But it would be fun, you and I working together!' she enthused.

'And living together, we would kill each other!'

'No we wouldn't! Besides, what else are you going to do? I'd just take your rent out of your wages and it would all be much easier than you going on the dole.'

'Hang on, I bet you're not registered, are you?'

She looked shifty. 'Ah, c'mon, Anna, you know it's a good idea!'

'I don't really have much choice, do I?'

'Not really!' she beamed happily.

'Ah, crap. When do I start?'

'Now!'

Angela then explained the intricacies of the till ('not something you'll have to use all that frequently' she explained drearily) and the shelving system (A–Z by category, simple).

'It's all really straightforward, there's no great mystery to this place . . . apart from how it's still open, that is.'

By the next day I was ready to admit that this was not the job for me.

'I'm just not cut out to deal with the public, Angela,' I opined after a customer complained to the management because I had forgotten to put their book in a bag. That, after all, was what I was being paid to do, was it not? Another one got a bit miffy because I couldn't stop myself laughing when a shifty-looking cove came in and asked if I could order a copy of *One Is Fun*. Let's just say that it had nothing to do with cooking for the single person.

'The thing is, Anna,' explained Angela, 'you can't laugh at a customer, no matter what they ask for. No one likes their preferences sneered at by a shop assistant.' I began to apologise when she burst out laughing. '*One is Fun*? The freak.'

'But Angela,' I said in mock surprise, 'what about what you just said to me about good customer service?'

'Oh, shut up.' She was doubled over with laughter at that stage. 'Now you see why I'm starting to feel why I've had enough of this lark. For example,' she said, slamming a book down on the counter in front of me, 'look at this.'

It was a well-read copy of Dorling Kindersley's *Illustrated Karma Sutra*.

'Every day the same people come in and look through this. They think I don't notice. Another regular comes in and treats the place like his personal library. He started with auras and is making his way through to whatever he finds in Z. Comes in and reads for an hour each day. Very polite, thanks me on the way out. He's as far as Raelism now, so not too long till we part for ever . . . thank God.'

'By the way, I almost forgot!' Angela suddenly exclaimed later that morning. 'I snatched up all the post this morning not realising that there was something for you. Now where did I put it?' she wondered as she rooted around in the hundreds of receipts and old pieces of paper that lay at the bottom of her bag. 'Is this . . . oh God, I thought I had paid that! Oh here it is, sorry, it's got a bit dog eared now!' She handed me an envelope with the logo of the publishing house offering the dream job that I had no chance of getting. I set it aside to read later, assuming it was just another rejection letter. I was getting well used to the drill at that stage.

Later that afternoon, while Angela nipped out to get us some coffee, I remembered the letter. I opened it and began to read, the words coming automatically to me.

Thank you for applying for the position of junior editor with the company that shall remain nameless. The standard of applicants was very high . . . I knew what was coming next. *We are pleased to inform you that you have been shortlisted for interview . . . .*

Hang on, I thought, *there's definitely something wrong here*. I stupidly flipped the letter over. I don't know what I expected to see there – perhaps a handwritten P.S.

Sorry, our mistake! You didn't get an interview. Oh well, too bad. Best of luck with your career and all that. Oh, and thank you for your interest in the large publishing company which shall remain nameless.

But there was no P.S. By some miracle they had decided to offer me an interview. It was the best, yet most surprising, piece of news I had had in a long time.

Chapter Twenty-two

It had been a couple of weeks since Angela's drunken phone call to the lovely Peter. Xavier still hadn't made any real effort to get in touch. He had sent the odd text and had left the odd message on the machine, but most normal people would have recognised the final death throes of a relationship in pain. Even Angela was running out of excuses as to why he might not call. But I was wrong in thinking that the Peter fiasco had been forgotten about.

One Saturday evening as we were closing up the shop Angela appeared from the staff loo looking spruced up and lovely.

'Off out?' I asked innocently.

'Em, yes, I'm meeting an . . . an old school friend for drinks and a bite to eat.'

'Thought you quote unquote "grew out of all your schoolfriends".'

'Oh, well, Sh, Shar, Siobhan is different. She's terribly nice. Would you mind finishing up here?' Before I had a chance to say yes or no she was away.

The next morning I made my way downstairs for brekie, full of joy at the thought of having a day off, but my serenity was shattered by the sight of Peter Mahoney in our kitchen, unshaven, unkempt, undressed! Well, the last bit is untrue. He was (almost) fully dressed. I stared at him open mouthed and was dismayed to notice that he had that look about him that some men get when they've got, if you see what I mean. In other words, I knew I wouldn't need to confirm with Angela whether or not anything had happened.

'You're out of milk,' he said, picking up his jacket from a chair and heading towards the front door. 'Tell Angela I had to leave, I'll call her.' And off he went. I was still in a state of shock when Marcus came down.

'Morning,' he offered, opening the fridge door then closing it again. 'We're out of milk.'

'That's what *he* said.'

'Who? Have you been putting drugs on your cornflakes again?'

'Peter. Peter just told me that we were out of milk.'

293

'You've lost me, I'm afraid. I'll go get some.'

'Some what?'

'Milk.'

'Fine. You might want to put a few more clothes on first.'

By the time he had come back with the milk I had gathered my wits sufficiently to tell him that Angela had spent the night with a man who was possibly an even bigger idiot than Xavier. I told him about Peter and the Clarence jamboree, but he cut right across me with, 'Peter Mahoney? That wanker? What the hell was she thinking of?'

Marcus, it transpired, had known and despised Peter at college.

'He's an asshole. Drove daddy's Beemer to college. Brought his pals out to restaurants while the rest of us got excited if we actually had a tin of tuna to share between fifteen. Thought the sun shone out of his own arse. Played rugby, all the rugby groupies fell in love with his wallet. I'm going to have to have a word with Angela. Is she insane?'

'Don't.' I put a restraining hand on his arm. I suspected that Angela was feeling just about as low as she could and a lecture from Marcus was the last thing she needed. I made a mug of seriously strong tea and took it upstairs. I knocked on her door. A small voice told me to piss off, but I tentatively opened the door regardless. She looked at me briefly then rolled over, pulling the duvet over her head.

'Please, Anna, go away,' she moaned. 'I don't think I can handle the "what were you thinking of lecture" just yet.' I went over and sat on the bed, setting the tea on the table beside her.

'Wasn't planning on giving you one. Drink that, it'll make you feel better.' I don't really know what I thought tea would do for her, but it sounded like the right thing to say.

'It's going to take a hell of a lot more than a cup of tea to make me feel better. You haven't spiked it, have you?' she asked hopefully. She sat up in bed and the look she gave me was almost enough to break my heart. Never had I seen so perfect an expression of regret in anyone's face. I put my arm around her and she rested her head on my shoulder and cried her heart out.

When she had finished she told me what had happened.

'I'm really sorry, you're going to have to shag James now, aren't you?'

'Perhaps Granny won't hold me to such a rashly made promise.'

'I planned it all quite cold bloodedly. I went out yesterday evening with every intention of sleeping with Peter,' she shuddered as she said it. 'I decided that the best way to get my own back on Xavier was to do to him what I think he's doing to me. Of course, it didn't occur to me to make sure first that he really is doing the dirty, or to pick my correspondent a little more carefully. God, it was awful. Peter really is the bad . . . .' she paused, 'company you would imagine.' I was tempted to point out that this fact was evident as I had slept undisturbed, but I restrained myself.

'He duly flashed his cash, ordered champagne cocktails, talked about his car as though it was his baby and I grew bored and drunk in equal measure. I knew what I was doing was really stupid, but I just kept doing it regardless. I think I wanted to make myself feel even lower . . . if that's possible.'

'Are things really that bad, Ang?' I asked, stroking her hair.

'Worse. Everything I said the other night still holds, it wasn't just the vodka. I'm tired of drifting around in this daze I've fallen into. I think all those years ago I started up that shop just to get up the familial nose, but now I'm sick of it, it's a dead weight around my neck. If I was happy I could put up with it, I could put up with anything, but I'm not.'

'It's not a life sentence, Ang. If you really want a change you can have one.'

With that she indulged in another bout of healthy tears. There really is nothing like a good, snottery roar to set the soul back on course.

'Why doesn't Xavier ring any more?' she wailed and once again dissolved into tears.

The weird thing was that Xavier *did* ring a couple of nights later. It was if he had some sort of antennae and somehow knew that Angela had been busy elsewhere, so to speak, and he didn't like it. I could easily imagine him being the kind of man who jealously guarded any woman he was even vaguely interested in. He was also sure of his chances with her, even now. That Friday night, while I was cooking, Angela pottered about the kitchen humming a tuneless little ditty in an unconvincingly casual fashion.

'Top tune, Angela. What is it? A composition of your own?' I asked.

'What are you talking about? I'm not humming, I never hum.'

'Actually, you were and I've known you long enough to know that, thankfully, you only hum or whistle when something is troubling you.'

'Nothing's up, really. Well, I am . . . em . . . going out with . . . er . . . *someone* this evening.' She began to waffle on in a nervy, shifty way which made my ramblings seem coherent in comparison.

'Who with?' asked Marcus, who had just arrived home.

'With whom,' I automatically corrected him.

'With whom are you going out?' We both really knew what the answer was going to be and two pairs of eyes searched her face in accusing fashion. She reddened painfully.

'It's that shite Xavier, isn't it?' I demanded. Marcus hadn't waited for confirmation, he had already started to fume.

'Anna, remember that you're my employee and must show me respect at all times.'

'Stop evading. It *is* him, isn't it?' She hung her head in assent and shame.

'What can I say? He was so apologetic for his behaviour over the past while, he was under such pressure at work and when I didn't ring he realised how much he missed me and would I give him the opportunity to make it up? So I said yes, I'm afraid.'

'Fool,' said Marcus flatly.

'God, no chance of any ego boosting from either of you two anyway. Anna, do you think I'm mad?'

'Yes.'

'Sometimes you two are such a pair of cosy, colluding . . . ugh,' was all she managed.

We ignored her for the rest of the night. When she was ready to leave she stuck her head around the sitting room door, looking for some last-minute absolution for the crime she was about to commit. We sat, stony faced, staring at the television, ignoring her pleading face.

'Oh fine, be like that then, but at least one of us in this house is going to have a good time tonight . . . and . . . and . . . well, at least I'm honest with myself about who I lust after.' And with that she slammed the door behind her, leaving the pair of us to contemplate her parting shot. Neither of us asked the other what they thought she might have meant by it.

At some point that night I was woken up by a preternatural, blood-curdling scream. Normally a heavy sleeper, as you know, that fact will give you some idea of just how loud it was. I sat bolt upright in the bed, waiting for another to prove that I had not merely dreamed it. There it was again! Louder and followed by a slow, agonised moan – Angela had brought Xavier home. I fumbled in my bed-side locker for earplugs but found none. I groped around under the bed for a while and managed to excavate a single, particularly fuzzy one but decided that I wasn't prepared to risk permanent ear damage. As it was a Friday I was irritated by the side show, but not overly so. I decided to go downstairs, make some tea and see what televisual shite was being served up at four thirty in the morning.

I managed to while away quite a few hours and I didn't notice the time before the front door opened and a very drunk Marcus came weaving in. He threw himself onto the sofa.

'Aiming for your lap. Just missed, unlucky me. What are you laughing at? And what's a nice girl like you doing in a sitting room like this at this time of night?'

Just as he finished his question, a loud groan was heard from upstairs.

'Ah, I see! But who's up there right now? I'm confused.'

'Are we talking specifics here or do you just mean in a general sense?'

'Sense . . . not really capable of any right now. But if you think I'm bad . . . budge up would you, stop hogging, oh hang on, I'll just stick my feet on your knees if you don't mind . . . what was I saying? Oh yeah, think *I'm* in a state, you should see John. Had to pour him into a taxi. Fuckin' mess.'

'I imagine that could apply to either of you.'

'I have to say I think I gave him great advice. Told him to forget all about Angela. She may be funny and intelligent and kind hearted and gorgeous but that she wasn't that great and he'd find someone else if he actually made a bit of an effort and she can be a bit hot headed and snappish, better off without, I said . . . what?' I was groaning.

'Oh top advice, very sensitive!'

'It's sensible advice, think I'll take some of it myself. So what are we watching then?'

'*I* am watching the television, while *you* would appear to be watching something in the middle distance. Tea?'

'Yes.' Manners and niceties tend to disappear in the wee small hours.

'Something must be done,' he almost wailed as I shoved a cup of tea at him.

'Well, we can hardly go up and ask them politely to keep the noise down.'

'I don't mean *that*,' he growled. 'I mean the fact that she's still running after that dickhead.'

'Are you jealous, Marcus?' In reply he merely turned his head and looked at me as though I was insane.

'Fond though I am of Ang, going out with her would be my idea of hell.'

'That sounds like someone protesting too much.'

'Look, I'm not quite capable of rational and coherent speech at this time of night, but I can tell you that going out with Angela would be like going out with one of my sisters.'

'Okay, I get the message.'

'Why, would you be bothered if I *was* interested in her?' I was too tired to know if he said this with his usual flippant smarminess or if he was asking me seriously. I was saved the bother of having to either contemplate or answer this by a crashing noise from upstairs.

'We have to split them up.'

'Yes indeedee, preferably before I get into bed.'

'I think we should re-educate her!' I declared after a few moments of intense thinking. 'Couldn't we try to set her up with John, a blind date or something? We could have him around more often and as he grew to know Angela better he might start to speak and as she got to know him better, she'll like him, I know she will.'

In reply Marcus simply declared that he had to go to bed. 'Think I should get some sleep.' He swung his legs around and onto the ground, balancing himself by making strange aeroplane gestures with his arms. He clumped up the stairs and his boots hitting the floor made a very loud crashing sound above my head. When at last I thought it was safe to make my own way up to bed I heard a faint squeak from Marcus's room.

'Anna, help . . . .'

I opened his door. He was sleeping in his usual way, as though the duvet was an evil force to be grappled with. I think he thought he was offering me a charmingly boyish smile.

'You couldn't get us some water, could you?'

'Do I look like a bloody servant?' I grumbled as I headed towards the kitchen. When I returned with his glass of water he had fallen asleep. Worryingly, 'This Year's Love' was playing quietly in the backround. David Gray is unhealthy and his CDs should be stickered with some sort of warning. In fact, I would go so far as to say that they ought to be banned, prompting as they do a vague sense that the world is shite. I took the control from his hand to turn it off. And then, as if it had developed a will of its own, my hand stretched out and stroked his hair away from his forehead. It must have disturbed his sleep, as he performed a strange sideways somersault in order to turn over. I left then, just in case my hand led me into any further trouble.

Chapter Twenty-three

'I can't believe she's off out again with that pillock,' Marcus mumbled at me as he dried the dishes that I had been washing.

'He speaks!' I cheered, waving my sudsy hands in the air.

'Oy, mind where you throw those suds! Have I really been that bad?' he asked worriedly.

'Just a little quieter than usual. Can I ask how things . . . ?'

'Let's go for a drink!'

'Oh, but I had planned a nice night in with my old friend, television.'

'Oh, come on. I'm thirsty. And besides, I feel like we haven't had a good chat in ages.'

'That's because we haven't.'

'Well, now's our chance to put things right!'

'Okay then.'

Marcus decided that he needed to stretch his legs so we walked into town. By O'Connell Street his legs decided that they had been stretched enough, so we opted for a couple of pints in Conways.

When he came back from the bar and set my glass down he suddenly declared, 'You're a girl!'

'Thanks for the reminder.'

'What I mean is, as you're a girl, you could have one of those womanly chats with Angela and advise her to dump Xavier.'

'First of all, I have no idea what "one of those womanly chats" is, and secondly, I can't tell her to dump him. It's not my place.'

'Sometimes a little interference isn't such a bad thing.'

'I would never interfere with someone else's happiness,' I said somewhat loftily.'

'Even if it means sacrificing your own?'

I decided to change the subject before we started to sound like characters from a bad novel. We somehow managed to get onto the subject of the lottery and Marcus was in the middle of telling me what he would do if he won when I glanced over at the door and saw Tony walk through it. I think my heart really did go *thud* in an unpleasant way. I grabbed Marcus's arm in fright.

'I know I'm irresistible, but there's no need to hang on quite so tight.' Then he saw the look on my face and asked me what on earth was wrong. I didn't have time to explain to him about Tony before he spotted me from the door, smiled, waved and began to make his way towards us.

'Hello you,' Tony beamed fondly down at me. 'And you are?' he said, smiling at Marcus.

'My name is Marcus. And who are you?' Marcus was entitled to be a bit nettled by Tony's rudeness, but I didn't want Tony to turn nasty.

'Hope you're good to her. She's a lovely girl. Make sure he treats you well, Anna, or he'll have me to answer to,' he said laughingly as he headed towards the bar.

'You're going to have to start paying me equity rates for all my performances as your boyfriend . . . or perhaps I was playing bodyguard tonight, eh?' He asked me to explain to him exactly what was going on with my 'friend'.

I told him all about Tony, from the letters to the meetings, the constant invitations, the personal questions, the postcards and the grafitti. He was shocked and not a little upset that I hadn't confided in him before this and even more shocked when I told him about Linda's reaction to the whole thing. In fact, I think if Linda had walked in at that point he may well have strangled her. Marcus was nothing if not loyal. Halfway through his chivalrous rant, I excused myself and went to the loo. I glanced around the pub on my way, and as I couldn't see Tony, I assumed that he had left.

When I re-emerged from the toilets a hand slammed against the wall, just in front of my face, preventing me from passing.

'I hope he's good enough for you.' Tony was smiling; I wasn't. His action pushed me beyond scared and towards anger.

'Yes, Tony, he's more than good enough for me. I think the world of him. I'm so in love, I'm positively dizzy with it. Now could you please stop all this?'

'Stop all what, Anna? I only ever thought that we could be friends, you know?'

'Tony, we are not and never will be friends, okay?'

'Well, you made that perfectly clear when you got Linda to take over. But I don't understand why we can't be friends. Is it because I've done time? Or maybe you don't like my background? Maybe I'm not good enough? Is that it? You know, I thought you were different, I thought you liked me, I thought, "maybe she's just a bit nervous around me, but I can change that". I thought you were different,' he said again, just a little sadly. 'That's why I painted the street.' His mood had gone from angry to manic and then to this, all in a few sentences. He still hadn't let his arm drop. I didn't know what to do. Now was the moment to catch him off guard and move past him, but I couldn't leave things like this. I had to put a full stop at the end of the sentence, no pun intended.

'Tony, I'm not different, I'm not special. I don't know why you would think that I was. You don't know me.' Oh dear, wrong thing to say.

'Well, how would I know you, you haven't given me the chance to get to know you and you don't seem prepared to give me that chance, now do you?' He was getting angry again and his other hand slammed against the wall on my other side. I couldn't move and I was now too nervous to be angry.

'Just give me a chance, Anna, I'm not a bad guy. Why do you keep acting like I am?'

'I think you should let Anna go now, Tony.' Marcus's voice came from behind him. Marcus may not have been a tall guy but he certainly wasn't what you might call petite, but Tony was a knucklehead and wasn't someone you would want to make an enemy of. Surprisingly, Tony let his hands fall.

'Sorry, no offence meant, friend,' he said, stepping far enough away from me that I could start to breathe again.

'It's not me you should be apologising to.' I was very grateful to Marcus, but he was going a step too far. He shouldn't to have antagonised Tony like that.

'Anna knows I don't mean any harm, don't you, Anna?' They both turned to me, waiting for an answer, but all I wanted was to escape the rutting stag routine, so to the surprise of both I swept past them out into the bar, grabbed my coat and left. Halfway down the street, however, I was assailed by an image of Marcus having the shit kicked out of him by Tony, so I turned and legged it back to the pub as fast as I could, where I collided with Marcus at the door.

'I might have known you'd storm off like that. You're probably going to give me a lecture on how you're perfectly capable of looking after yourself.' I stopped dead in the street and turned to look at him. He was regarding me with a mixture of amusement and concern.

'Seriously, Anna, are you all right?'

'I just want to go home, please.' I don't know if it was what I said or the way that I said it, but before I knew what was happening, Marcus had grabbed me into a great big bear hug. As I lay my head against him, I felt a momentary flash of perfect contentment. I couldn't think of anywhere else I would rather have been. At just that moment I understood that I hadn't stopped being in love with him. I had simply tricked myself into believing that what was most sensible was also true.

'I think we're very stupid,' was all he said as he gently pulled away. Then we turned and walked slowly home in silence. Perhaps we each wanted to say something, but neither of us did.

I never saw Tony again.

The next morning I felt something like relief when Angela told me that Marcus had made one of his jaunts up to Donegal for the weekend.

'Though I didn't think he had planned to go up for a while yet,' she said.

'Did he say *why* he was going?'

'He said something about having some things to sort out . . . I didn't really ask, to be honest with you . . . by the way, did I tell you what Xavier said to me the other night?'

By this stage Angela wasn't even remotely interested in anything that didn't begin with an 'X'.

Needless to say, I didn't enjoy my weekend and by Sunday I felt the same way that I had on New Year's Eve. However, Marcus rang Angela to tell her that he wouldn't be back till Monday morning, so I put my anxiety on hold for one more day.

Chapter Twenty-four

I needn't have worried, though. Monday brought with it a surprise that forced my nerves to take a back seat for a while.

Angela had spent most of the weekend with Xavier, so I had only my own company to share my cornflakes with that morning. I confess that I was a bit leisurely with my brekie that morning, enjoying a second cup of tea when I really should have been heading for the bus, but I knew that after a weekend with Xavier, there was no way that Angela was going to be in much before ten, and what she didn't know wouldn't hurt her.

I sauntered down Dame Street at nine twenty-five, armed with a coffee and a doughnut – some habits die hard. The man who only came into the shop when it was absolutely silent was standing outside and he looked at me accusingly as I unlocked the shutters.

'We don't officially open till nine thirty, you know!' I said, pre-empting any complaint he was about to make. He jumped slightly, then turned on his heels and stomped off down the street muttering something about superior service at Hodges Figgis. When I got in I opened the safe, turned on the till and then stuck one of my own CDs in the player. I had categorically refused to listen to whale song or bird song or a recording of wind whistling through the trees on a balmy summer evening.

By eleven thirty there was still no sign of Angela – mind you, there was no sign of any customers either – but I was annoyed on principle. At eleven forty-five, the first customer of the day appeared. I disliked her on sight because she had a fortune on her back as well as a papoose, in which there sat a baby who was equally expensively clad.

'You see how the books are arranged A to Z?'

'Yes?'

'Where would I find books on cooking?'

'We don't sell any.'

'Why not?'

'It's a specialist bookshop. We only sell books on new age cr . . . philosophies.'

'Oh, all right,' said the customer, looking confused. She headed for the door, then thought better of it, turned to me and asked, 'But if you did, where would they be?'

'But we don't.' I felt my tolerance levels ebb to an all-time low.

'I know, but just pretend you did, that's not so hard, is it?' she asked, growing tetchy as well as insistent.

'Why would I want to do that?' I knew the dangers of engaging with lunatic customers, but barrelled on regardless.

'If you worked in a normal bookshop you would need to know.'

'But I don't work in a normal bookshop, do I?'

'Does your boss know about your attitude?'

'C, all right? The cookery books would be under C.'

'And where would you put macrobiotic cooking?'

'Under P, for piss off and stop annoying me.'

I had found that cheek and naked aggression worked a treat in these circumstances. Most customers were so flummoxed by such outbursts they couldn't think quickly enough of a suitable retort.

At twelve fifteen, Angela chose to bestow her presence on her empire and her serf.

'Nice to see you, Angela! Hope you had a restful morning—'

Before I could whinge any more she cut across me and burst out, 'Xavier asked me to marry him.' Well, as you can imagine, that announcement stopped me mid-tirade. I looked at her, goggle eyed and slack jawed. 'Oh Anna, I'm so happy I could burst!'

I continued to stare dumbly at her. I couldn't think of anything to say that wouldn't either offend her or force me into hypocrisy.

'I wasn't expecting this,' she burbled, 'he really does love me. You got it *so* wrong. He proposed over dinner . . . oh, I can't possibly work today, you don't mind looking after the shop, do you? I knew I wouldn't be in any state to do anything. I have to meet him in an hour, he's taken the day off work, isn't that amazing, I mean, he's so busy and everything. Anyway, I'd better go, I just came in to tell you. I'm so bloody happy I could just explode!' She threw her arms around me and almost strangled me with her grip. Before I had a chance to even think about what to say in response she had flown out of the door.

'Excuse me, do you have anything on chakras?' I was brought back to reality by the second customer of the day.

'Over there somewhere,' I said, pointing distractedly at some shelf or other. I got rid of him as quickly as possible, put the closed sign on the door and dialled Marcus's work number. When I was put through to his extension I was greeted by munching sounds in my ear.

'Marcus here.'

'Angela's going to marry Xavier,' I said, getting straight to the point. I heard a choking noise, followed by something that sounded like 'uck'.

'Are you sure?'

'Of course I'm sure, she just came in to announce it and then left. I guess I could have hallucinated it all, but I don't think so.'

'What are we going to do?' he asked.

'Nothing. What can we do?'

'But he's all wrong for her. He's all wrong for anyone. She deserves so much better.'

'I just don't get what she sees in him.'

'Money and good looks maybe?' he asked with a slight sigh.

'God, no one really marries for that,' I said with certainty.

I thought I heard a slight laugh in Marcus's voice when he said, 'For someone who insists that she's a hard-boiled cynic, you can be really naïve sometimes.' I began to protest and take umbrage. 'It's not a fault, it's nice.' And how did I react to that? I think I flushed like a love-struck teenager.

'Anna, you still there?'

'Yes, yes I am. But seriously, Marcus, no one marries for money. You wouldn't . . . *would* you?'

'Ah, so you actually think that there's some good buried deep down in the depths of my nature?'

'No.'

'Oh, right, well thanks for being so upfront.'

'No, what I mean is, I don't think it's buried.' I'm sure my face must have been on fire. 'But we're not discussing you, it's Angela I'm worried about,' I said, changing the subject.

'I guess there's nothing we can do.' I could

almost hear him shrug his shoulders. He paused for a few minutes and I heard a slight intake of breath. 'Anna, could I—'

'Sorry, gotta go, there's an irate customer trying to beat the door down. I'll see you later.' I quickly hung up and reopened the shop.

It was the Dorling Kindersley *Illustrated Karma Sutra* man. I watched him as he pretended to saunter casually over to the shelf. He paused briefly at the shelf beside it, either prolonging the pleasure of anticipation or trying to fool me into not spotting that this book was the sole purpose of his visit. He moved a little to the left, ah, there it was, on the shelf, waiting for him to open it. He ran his index finger along the edge of the shelf till it reached the right place. He took a quick glance to the right and left, just to make sure that no one was looking at him. He was safe, he was the only customer in the shop. He took it down in a quick movement, then disappeared behind the shelves with it.

There was silence in the shop save for the very occasional faint crackle of a turning page. Something inside me flipped, but now, looking back, I'm ashamed of my cruelty and intolerance. I marched out from behind the counter, fuelled by hunger and the consequent need to close the shop for lunch. Something else fuelled my outburst, but I refused to acknowledge it. I stomped behind the shelves.

'Are you ever going to buy that bloody book or what?'

He looked up at me and I thought he was going to burst into tears. He looked so guilty and had gone scarlet. Probably on all those undisturbed days of flicking he had convinced himself that because no one had said anything to him, then nothing was really happening, just like a child thinks that you can't see him when he hides behind his hands. I had embarrassed him needlessly. He wasn't doing anything wrong, and if that was his tipple, so to speak, who was I to sneer or think him sad? I only had to look at my own pathetic life to realise that the sheen of sophistication that some of us slick over ourselves is a sham. Underneath it all, we're all the same. His panting after a Dorling Kindersley model was no different really from my own after Marcus. He was lonely, I was lonely. The only difference between us was how each of us coped with that. Perhaps his way was the more honest of the two. I convinced myself that he was sad because I didn't want to see just how alike all humans really are.

'I'm so sorry,' he muttered. He got up from the chair, and the book dropped from his lap with a thud to the floor. It fell on its spine and the pages, already delicate from overuse, fell away. He dashed out of the shop and I felt my subsiding irritation turn to remorse. I felt terrible. What I had done was needlessly nasty, and just then I couldn't have disliked myself more if I had tried.

'I'm sorry,' I said to the door as it slammed shut. Too late. The damage had been done.

Chapter Twenty-five

Angela burst in on top of us that evening like a bloody ray of sunshine. We were eating when she marched in and slammed her left hand down on the table. We both looked at her blankly.

'Sorry, is there something we should be noticing, Angela?' I asked.

'Jesus, you can't miss it.' And you couldn't. On her wedding finger she wore three of the largest rocks I had ever seen in my life. One of these would have been plenty by most people's standards. If love could really be measured in rocks, then Xavier had just given her the equivalent of the Taj Mahal. I smothered all my misgivings and admired it as fulsomely as I could.

'What do you think, Mr Silent?'

''Salright, eating, can only concentrate on one thing at a time.' He was making his disapproval too obvious, so I kicked him under the table. 'Well, you know men, we're not good at that kind of thing. It's a big ring. It's lovely.' This wasn't much of an improvement.

'Well, Xavier *is* good at that kind of thing. He picked it out. He has such good taste.' She was practically swooning.

'Clearly, he's marrying you, isn't he?' *Well done, Marcus*, I thought. That went some way towards repairing her visibly hurt feelings over our disgraceful lack of enthusiasm.

'It seems to have been a . . . whirlwind romance,' I babbled politely. I still couldn't figure out why he had gone so suddenly from hardly ever calling to proposing.

'Oh God, yes,' she answered breathlessly. 'The last few weeks have been unbelievable.'

'So we heard,' said Marcus. I choked on my bread.

'He's just so perfect. He's funny, charming, intelligent, way more intelligent than either of you two.'

'Cheers,' we both said at once.

'No, no, he's just so well read and knows things about everything from wine to how to change a tyre.'

'Sounds a bit like James.'

'You have him all wrong. Okay, he didn't ring that often at first, but when we were apart he said he realised that I was the one for him . . . do you know how he proposed? He actually went down on one knee when dessert came. The ring was sitting on top of my strawberries. How romantic is that?' she demanded.

Averagely so, I thought to myself. What does one do when one sees a good friend getting herself tied into knots of ecstacy and pledging her troth to a guy you suspect to be the greatest toad ever to have crawled out of the pond? *Nothing*, you do *nothing*. No matter what you do, you can't win. If she loves him, then nothing you say will make a difference. She's going to go right ahead and throw her life away. Your misgivings and warnings will then most likely be attributed to jealousy. You may even be accused of lusting after him yourself. So, should you ever find yourself in such a situation, carefully examine your motives before launching into the fray. As my dear old granny used to say, marriages are made in heaven and no mortal has any business coming between two foolish people who decide to unite themselves forever. So call it hypocrisy if you like, but I put all my forebodings on hold and did my best to pretend that I was pleased for her. Then she asked me something which completely threw me for a loop.

'Anna, would you do me the very great honour of being my bridesmaid? I'd ask you, Marcus, being my oldest friend and all, but I can't see you in salmon pink tafetta. Would you, Anna? Please say yes.'

There was a pleading look on her face and I suspected that there was more to her asking than just wanting someone to carry the flowers. Did she, perhaps, have some doubts of her own? Perhaps my agreeing to be a bridesmaid would be a vindication of sorts?

'Okay, but on one condition.'

'What?' she squealed as she threw her arms around me and squeezed like she was trying to burst me.

'Make me wear salmon pink taffeta and I'll show up in my underwear.'

'Whahey, salmon pink taffeta it should be then!'

'Shut up, Marcus, or I'll make you a page boy. Don't worry, Anna, I promise you'll be consulted all the way.'

She rambled on for another half hour or so, then went out again as she and Xavier were heading out to Killiney to break the wonderful news to the Merediths. He actually called in for her this time and I was curious to see Xavier newly transformed by love. I was, of course, disappointed. There was certainly plenty of lust there, but his manner towards her was proprietorial and slightly patronising, just as it had been the night of the party. As usual he was barely polite to us. He said hello when he came in and goodbye when he left and that was all.

'You're a girl, tell me, would you think him good looking?'

'Oh, he's that all right.'

'Can't say I see it.'

'Well you wouldn't, presumably. But he's tall, he's very dark, he's classically handsome—'

'All right, all right, I get it, you fancy him too.'

'Hang on, I didn't say *that*. There's a huge difference between recognising that someone's good looking and finding them attractive.'

'There is?'

'Course there is.' I felt I was heading for dodgy territory, but then realised that I was lured by the potential opportunity to tell him that I thought he was the most attractive man I had ever met without actually telling him.

'You're going to have to explain that one. As far as I'm concerned, you think someone's good looking because you fancy them and vice versa . . . I think,' he said, wrinkling his face in confusion. I paused as I had to think of how best to explain what I meant.

'Well, it's like the *Mona Lisa*—' I began.

'She's pig ugly.'

'Could I finish? The *Mona Lisa* is a great painting, it's stunningly beautiful, everyone can recognise that, but would you want to take it home and hang it on your wall?'

'No, because I would be arrested,' he said. I sighed. 'Sorry, continue . . . .'

'Well, you look at it, but it doesn't really do anything for you. It's famous, beautiful, et cetera, et

..., but you're quite happy to walk past it. You might have a poster on your wall, or a framed postcard or something which you love, it has some sentimental value, but you wouldn't trade it for the *Mona Lisa*.'

'Yes I would. Seriously, though, your beautiful, eloquent little speech made no sense whatsoever,' he laughed. Just as well I hadn't tried a genuine declaration of love and admiration or he would have been rolling around on the floor in hysterics at this stage.

'Ah, I'm sorry, I'm not taking the piss. Think I kind of know what you're trying to say. So you really think there's more to it than looks?'

'Of course, don't you?'

'The answer to that would depend on who I'm fancying at the time.'

'Now *I'm* lost.'

'Anna, I—'

I don't know what he was about to say because his mobile rang. He picked it up in irritation, looked to see who was dialling and rejected the call with an impatient roll of his eyes. He took the phone upstairs, from where I could hear the muffled sound of his voice. He came back down the stairs a few minutes later and told me very brusquely that he had to go out. And off he went. I have no idea what time he came back at, but it wasn't before midnight. I suspected Isobel was about to emerge from the shadows once again.

Chapter Twenty-six

I had cleverly managed to sneak over to London for my interview and back in one day by telling Angela that I had to make an emergency call to my mother in Armagh. Of course she was suspicious, but I told her it was a delicate medical emergency and made a disgusted, wrinkly face in the hope that she wouldn't ask any more questions.

The interview went surprisingly well. I got the impression that they quite liked me and they even laughed at one or two of my lame jokes. Apparently, though, the most hysterical thing about me was the way I spoke. They seemed to find no end of amusement in repeating everything I said in dodgy 'Oirish' accents. However, this was the chance of a lifetime and I wasn't going to blow it by getting on my Irish high horse. I grinned (literally) and bore it. If I had bought and worn the giant leprechaun suit on sale at O'Carroll's at the airport, they probably would have given me the job on the spot.

I waited eagerly all the next week for a phone call or a letter, but nothing came. I shouldn't have been surprised.

Meanwhile, the wedding preparations were quickly shifted into top gear thanks to the involvement of Angela's mother. The minute Angela and Xavier made their announcement, Mrs Meredith went into organisational hyperdrive.

'It was quite frightening, Anna. No sooner had the word "engaged" popped out of my mouth than she was scanning the Golden Pages for venues, bridal shops and the like.'

Naturally, she was to be included in all dress shopping expeditions. As, unfortunately, was I. When I was introduced to Sheila Meredith as Angela's 'flatmate and one and only bridesmaid', she looked me up and down appraisingly and then said, 'You're quite short, aren't you? It might look a bit odd, what with Angela being so tall. She could make you look dumpy. We'll have to be careful when choosing a dress for you.'

'Mother!'

'Oh, I'm sure Anna understands that it's not the bridesmaid's day, it's important that everything reflects as well as possible on the bride. Can you walk in heels, Anna? Just about? Good, that will help. They'll make your legs look longer.'

We were sitting in some bridal shop or other, don't ask which one, they all look the same. Vivaldi and Charlotte Church were on a loop and they tinkled and warbled respectively in the background while a ridiculously deferential member of staff waited on Mrs Meredith's every whim. Angela sulked in the corner. I was amazed by what Mrs M. got away with. She commanded poor Angela into a series of hideous white dresses, each one ghastlier than the last. Mrs M.'s taste seemed to tend towards the puffy and flouncy. What she picked out would have been charming if you were after a Bo Peep outfit for a fancy dress. Angela's face grew redder by the second and she continually threw pleading looks my way.

We had a number of such sessions, but sometimes, if I had been a very good girl, I was allowed to try something on myself, but Mrs M. soon put an end to this, pointing out that the bridesmaid dress would be chosen *after* we found a dress for Angela. I could see that if we weren't careful she would call the whole thing off simply because she couldn't take the agony of dress hunting anymore.

'Anna, think of being in a hot changing room at the end of a hard day's shopping and trying to fit into jeans that are about two sizes too small. Then multiply the frustration and discomfort by ten.'

'Angela, love, I'm beginning to lose patience with you. How many dresses must you try on? You've seen so many wonderful dresses, I think there must be something wrong with you, or maybe you don't really want to get married . . . .'

Angela bore up better than I would have underneath such a burden of maternal disapproval and impatience. One day it got too much for her, though. She had been forced into a particularly hideous confection with a huge hooped skirt and an ill-fitting décolletage. The assistant had insisted that her opinion of the dress would change if she just tried on the veil and see how good the whole thing looked. She was sticking pins into poor Angela like she was a voodoo doll while the latter looked out dejectedly from about ten yards of tulle and lace, perhaps wondering if having said 'yes' had been worth all this. She'd had her piece of heaven, now she was being punished by a brief stint in hell.

'Angela, Angela, what do you think?' snapped Mrs M., clearly irritated by Angela's now-frequently drifting mind.

'What?'

'Pardon, Angela, pardon. The dress. It is lovely, isn't it?' She and the assistant seemed to have struck up a rapport as they looked at each other approvingly and clucked together in a mother hen-ish way. I must say I would have found this highly irritating, as the assistant was at least five years younger than us.

'I don't want a white dress.' I sat up in my seat. Angela spoke quietly, but her tone was the unmistakably deadly and even one of someone about to lose their temper. Her face had gone from red to ashen grey.

'What's that? Speak clearly.'

'I said, I don't want a white dress.' She spoke with a little more clarity and any sensible person hearing her would have evacuated the shop and taken all breakable items with them. I got out of my seat and made my way over to her.

'What do you mean, you don't want white? Every bride wants white. It's the only colour. What do you want, yellow? Red? Green?' Her laughter increased with each colour. 'How about black? At least then we would have no problem co-ordinating the bridesmaid. We wouldn't even have to buy her a dress.' At which she went off into hysterics and was joined by the sneaky, snivelling assistant.

'I don't want white.' Rage was depriving her of her ability to make up any new sentences.

'Now you're just being silly. Be a good girl and try that ivory silk on. Of course you must have white or cream. Give me one good reason why you wouldn't wear white, hmm?'

'Because I'm not a bloody virgin. I've shagged Xavier's brains out on a nightly basis for the last umpteen weeks. He isn't getting any surprises.'

Well, that told her anyway.

'No surprises? Well, thank you, nor is anyone else now.'

As you can imagine, there was a breach between the two of them followed by many angry and teary phone calls. Now call me old fashioned, but I would have imagined that it was Xavier's job to wipe up this mess. The bridegroom doesn't have to endure the dress hunting hell, so the least he can do is be there to help shoulder the inevitable emotional fallout. Not Xavier. *I* seemed to get most of it. Even Marcus was forced to seek shelter in my room one night.

'She's rambling. I really think she's losing it. Something about dresses and meringues. Please come and help.'

'Where's her bloody fiancé?'

'Actually, he's enjoying his wine and paper in the sitting room.'

'I'm going down there and I'm going to order him to perform his duty.' Before I could get out of the room, Marcus grabbed me and held me back.

'Hold on there, Fido. I think that would make things far worse. All this over a dress. Promise me something – if you ever get married, you won't . . . .'

'Won't what?' He was smiling at me in a most inscrutable way.

'Take your mother shopping for your dress,' he laughed.

'You can let go now, I've calmed down.'

'Not sure if I want to.' For the tiniest fraction of a second there was nothing inscrutable about the way he looked at me, but Angela chose that perfect moment to come crashing into the room. I felt I was living in a really bad novel. Marcus let go his hold of me as Angela flung herself onto my bed and offered us the latest bulletin on her mother's ghastliness. I was irritated, yes, but she was working herself up into an ever-increasing pitch of hysterics, all over a dress, while her useless fiancé sat downstairs, oblivious to the mayhem around him. It was time to take matters in hand. Marcus was right. I couldn't have words with Xavier behind Angela's back. I took Angela by the hand and led her downstairs. We were followed by Marcus, his curiosity getting the better of both tact and manners. I led her into the sitting room.

'Xavier,' I began in the sweetest voice I could manage. 'Your fiancée is having quite a hard time at the moment. Her mother is mad and is doing her best to spoil what will prove, I am sure, to be the happiest day of both your lives. Give her comfort and solace please before she drives Marcus and I insane. Thank you.'

I gave Angela a push towards the supine lump on the sofa and shut the door behind them. Shortly after that the door opened again and the pair of them dashed upstairs. I suppose there are different kinds of comfort.

Chapter Twenty-seven

In order to celebrate Angela's engagement and some unusually fine late spring weather, the Merediths decided to throw a bash. Now there's nothing I like better than a good old knees-up, so you can imagine my disappointment when Angela handed me an invitation which stipulated semi-formal dress.

'Does that mean I can wear my jeans so long as I wear a decent pair of shoes?' I asked Angela hopefully.

'Don't be so facetious. Of course it doesn't. I'll help you shop for something if you like.'

'Ah, no, you're okay. Not sure if I want to go dress shopping with you *ever, ever* again. No offence.'

The wedding dress problem had been resolved. Angela and her mother had made their peace, but Angela made her promise that if she was to continue to help in the dress hunt she was to keep her mouth shut and only speak when spoken to. Okay, Angela didn't quite put it that way, but after a lot of tears on both sides, Mrs M. agreed to keep interference to a minimum. In the end Angela chose a charmingly simple little number and, guess what, it was off white. So everyone was happy – Angela because she got to choose the dress herself, her mother because she felt vindicated. After a battle of wills I managed to convince Mrs M. that the sight of my legs in the short dress she had picked out would prove far too distracting for the congregation. I still had unhappy memories of my disastrous meal with Tom. In the end I got a lovely floor-length, bias-cut velvet number in a dark rose colour, which, of course, pleased Mother no end when I told her about it.

'I always told you that pink was your colour!' she cooed at me.

'Not a conventional bridesmaid's dress, though, is it?' Mrs M. muttered darkly, but I was happy and Angela was happy so that was that.

By comparison the shop had become an oasis of calm. I was growing used to the boring routine of the place. My inner dullard was putting its feet up and relaxing. This was by no means the exciting new career I had hoped for, but it required no thought and it was easy and I was always one to take the easy option. I knew I would soon tire of looking for something better and I would end up drifting once again.

One morning in the shop, after I had tidied up all three books that were out of place, the phone rang for the millionth time that day. Only Angela or Marcus ever rang. I don't think the place was even in the phone book. Angela, for obvious reasons, had more or less vanished. She said she was taking her 'annual leave'. In fairness, she did raise my salary temporarily from a pittance to just below the national minimum wage, though that wasn't payment enough for the torment she was putting me through with her non-stop telephone calls. I had no idea how many tiers a wedding cake should have and I didn't know if it would be more tasteful if the little bride and groom were left off the top. I had already told Angela that it was Xavier's job to decide between invitations with gold writing and invitations with silver.

I stomped over to the desk and picked up the phone.

'Would you just let me get on with the job? *What* do you want now?'

'Em, is that Anna?'

Christ, it was one of the interviewers from the company that shall remain nameless.

'Oh God, yes, sorry,' I whimpered.

'You're probably wondering why it took us such a long time to get back to you, but our head of HR was ill and then you know it was a very close call between you and another candidate . . . .' *Here we go*, I thought, *We're very sorry . . . thank you for your interest in the company which shall remain nameless and we wish you every success with your career.*

'. . . and it was such a hard decision to make . . . .' I didn't really need to hear the rest. '. . . and we're delighted to offer you the job.'

'Well, thanks for calling anyway,' I said glumly.

'We'd like to *offer* you the job.'

'Shit, no! Really? God, sorry, for the swearing I mean, I don't usually.'

'Never mind,' she said a little stiffly and I didn't blame her. She must have thought I was an absolute half-wit.

'I'm really thrilled.' I think the sincerity in my voice must have mollified her, because she laughed and said, 'I'm reely trilled.'

I laughed my very best 'I'm a cheeky little leprechaun' laugh. There would be time to set them straight about all this nonsense once I had passed my probationary period.

I couldn't believe my luck.

'Luck has nothing to do with it,' said Mother when I phoned her to tell her the news. 'When will you be leaving? Have you told Angela? Will you be able to come back for the wedding? Will you make it back for *my* wedding?'

'Of course I will, I'll sort everything out, it'll be fine.'

'Angela will miss you.'

'Oh, she'll be fine. Besides, she's got Xavier now.'

'And she's not the only one who'll miss you.'

'They have phones in England, Mother, I'll phone you.' In response she laughed a dry little laugh.

'Actually, I wasn't thinking of me.'

'Wha?'

'Sorry, or pardon if you must, but not "wha". And I was referring to your friend, Marcus.'

'Marcus? I don't think it'll make much difference to him.'

'Wouldn't be too sure about that. Just go easy when you tell him.'

'Mother, you're making no sense.'

'You always say that, but you know I usually do.'

And with that little enigma she left me. I thought that perhaps Marcus might miss me, but not in the way I wanted him to miss me. Whether or not Marcus and I could ever be right for each other would never be an issue because he would be too wrapped up in Isobel, one way or another, for some time to come.

When I told Angela the news that evening she burst into tears, sobbing that she was going to lose the best flatmate she had ever had, apart from Marcus, of course. This was all very touching, but also, as I pointed out to her, a bit foolish, as we wouldn't have been living together after she married Xavier. She perked up no end then and expressed complete happiness at my news.

'Though we won't be able to see each other that often.'

'Nonsense, you can always come and visit me. Imagine all those shops in London.'

'Ooooh, hadn't thought of that.'

Not long after that the front door opened and a very dejected-looking Marcus came into the kitchen.

'Marcus, you'll never guess what!' Angela exclaimed excitedly.

'I told Isobel that I never wanted to see her again.' I felt something inside me flip. I think it was my stomach. I felt slightly breathless.

'Is it for good this time or are you just having another little holiday from each other?' Angela asked with uncharacteristic flippancy.

'Oh, it's very definitely for good this time,' he replied.

'What's so different this time?'

'There's someone else.'

'Again?' she asked as she fumbled in her bag for the phone that was ringing. 'Sorry, it's Xavier, I'd better take it. We'll talk later.' She ran upstairs to closet herself in her room.

So Isobel had two-timed him again? Clearly the girl was deranged. I felt sorry for him, of course, but I'm afraid more selfish feelings prevailed. She'd hurt him a second time. The first time around was bad enough, but now that she had struck twice he would never get her out of his system. Okay, it might have been hatred and bile pumping through his veins, but a bitter rebounding is no better than the lovelorn variety. She may as well have tattooed her name all over him.

'Aren't you going to ask who it is?' he asked tentatively.

'It's none of my business.' To be honest I didn't really care who she had shagged. He obviously did, though, and a bit too much.

'But it *is* your business,' he said gently with a slight smile.

'How so?'

'*You're* the someone else.'

'How can I be . . . is she gay . . . she doesn't know me . . . oh!'

'Oh!' he imitated with a laugh as he took a step closer.

'But I don't understand . . . .'

'Are you deliberately being stupid? Or do you need absolutely everything spelled out for you?'

'Pretty much.'

'Right then!' He shot out of the room and before I had time to wonder where he had disappeared to he returned with a piece of paper and a pen in his hands. He wrote something on the paper then handed it to me. On it was written *I'm in love with you.*

'God knows why,' he sighed, 'but there you go, I've spelled it out for you.' I smiled despite myself. This was a disaster.

'This is a disaster!'

'What?'

'I'm leaving.'

'Well, I didn't think you'd take it *that* badly. What do you mean you're leaving?'

'I'm leaving Dublin.' I looked up to see his face fall.

'Where are you going?'

'London.'

'Ah, crap.'

I told him why I was leaving.

'You didn't even tell me that you had an interview. I thought that we were at least friends,' he added sadly.

'I wasn't expecting this reaction,' was all I could manage.

'Exactly what kind of reaction were you expecting? Cheers? A party? Indifference?'

'I thought you'd be pleased for me.'

'Anna, I *am* pleased for you, but I'm not exactly pleased for me. I can't believe that I've been so stupid, that it took me so bloody long to do what I should have done months ago.'

'Which was?'

'Tell Isobel that I had met the most fantastic girl I had ever met, or would ever meet, that I had fallen head over heels in love with her and that just being in the same room as her made me the happiest I've been in a long time.'

'My God, you . . . you really think? I don't know what to say.'

'Well, you've taken long enough to read the note, so feel free to tell me that the feeling is entirely mutual, et cetera, et cetera.' He smiled at me, but it was a slightly nervous one.

'But the conversation, in the kitchen.'

'What conversation?'

I flushed as I admitted to having eavesdropped. 'I heard you and Angela talking in the kitchen on New Year's Eve. She told you to leave me alone, that you were just using me as post-break-up amusement.'

'Well, if you're going to eavesdrop, my dear, you should at least stick around till the end.'

'What do you mean? Angela told you that you would never be over Isobel and that she didn't want to see me get hurt and you said that she was probably right.'

'I then went on to tell her that if she *was* right, then how come I couldn't stop thinking about you, about how thinking about you always makes me smile, that I could be myself around you, that you took me as I came, oh, and last but by no means least, that I fancied you something rotten.'

'I don't know what to say.'

'Yes you do. Go on, say it,' he said gently. 'Please.'

I looked at him nervously, not quite wanting to meet his eye.

'Please,' he repeated as he took a step closer and took my face in both his hands. But still I didn't speak.

338

'Please,' he said once more and he lightly and fleetingly brushed my lips with his own.

'I'm in love with you.'

Then he leaned forward and . . . oh, you know the rest, you don't need me to spell it out for you. Oh, all right, you can have the abridged version – kissing . . . birdsong . . . sunshine . . . fireworks . . . twenty-four-piece orchestra, blah-de-blah.

'But it can't change anything,' I said when the birds had stopped trilling.

He looked as though I had just kicked him in the stomach.

'So I'm not enough, is that what you're saying? I think about you twenty-four hours a day. I spent the last couple of months in misery because I thought you thought me a prize idiot. And now you're saying, "Marcus, I'm in love with you, but sorry, I can't ever see you again."'

'No, that's *not* what I'm saying. My going doesn't mean—'

'It means you're putting an ocean between us.' I thought that he was being irrational and I could feel tears of frustration well up in my eyes.

'Oh, great, cry and make me feel like a bastard. Just answer me one question: why are you leaving?'

'Because I have to.'

'That doesn't really answer my question.'

'Marcus, my life is rubbish. I mean, I don't have a life, I have no job, or at least no real job. I have nothing to stay for . . . .' The words were out before

I could stop them.'

'Well, when you put it like that.'

'Marcus, I didn't mean—'

'Sometimes the things we don't mean to say are the most revealing, don't you think?' Without giving me a chance to say anything he pulled me to him, kissed me, then turned, walked out of the room, out of the house and probably out of my life. Part of me was angry at his little Rhett Butler act. I sank into a chair and buried my head in my hands. All my life I had made sensible decisions. Now I wondered if making the sensible decision had been the most foolish thing I had ever done.

Angela came tripping down the stairs and into the room and smiled beatifically at me, but even the bluntest pencil in the box could have spotted that something was wrong.

'Hey, what's wrong, chicken?' she asked as she sat down beside me and put a comforting arm around my shoulders. 'Where's Marcus? Have you two had a row or something?'

'You could say that. Marcus and I just had an interesting little chat.'

'Go on.'

'Well, it seems that he's in love with me as much as I'm in love with him.'

Angela's expression of both shock and puzzlement momentarily relieved my misery and made me laugh out loud.

'What are you gibbering about?'

'I'm in love with him and he's—'

'Yes, yes, I gather that. But when did this . . . have you . . . how are you going . . . I don't understand!'

'It's quite simple really, dear. We've both been secretly hankering after one another for a while but chose the worst possible time to reveal how we felt.'

'What on earth are you going to do?'

'What can I do?'

'Where has he gone?'

'Dunno, he just left . . . in a huff, I think.'

'You can't go to London now.'

'What do you mean I can't go to London? I have to go to London.'

'But you *can't*,' she wailed. 'This is too unbelievably bad.'

'I don't see why you're so upset anyway. After all, you did warn him off me, remember?'

'What? Oh! How did you know about that?'

'I heard some of it from next door.'

'Oh Anna, I didn't realise he was that serious! If I had . . . but I didn't imagine that you could like him like that . . . is this my fault?' she asked as a look of guilt began to cloud her lovely face.

'No, of course it isn't, silly. It isn't anyone's fault. It's just a case of very, very bad timing.'

Chapter Twenty-eight

Marcus stayed with John that night, and the next night, and the one that followed that. I hadn't seen or heard from him in three days. On the evening of the fourth day, which was a Saturday, I came home from a shift in the shop to find an envelope addressed to me sitting on the kitchen table. It was from Marcus. I opened it eagerly and read the following:

Dear Anna,

I thought it might be best if I made myself scarce for a little while. John has offered me his sofa and I've taken it, just till things can go back to normal. I'll see you at the party, if not before.

Take care of yourself,
  Marcus

Needless to say, I didn't see him before the party and for the next couple of weeks I felt like Marcus and I had bypassed the relationship and had headed straight to the break-up. Trust Anna Malone to do things arse over tip.

Angela offered comfort when she could, but her mother had corralled her for the party preparations and any time she had left over was, naturally, spent with Xavier. Xavier continued to be aloof and virtually non-contactable. He continued to say when and where they met and seemed all but indifferent to the chaos created by Mrs Meredith and her hordes of caterers.

After a good deal of trauma, the night of the big party did eventually arrive.

Was I nervous? Of course I was nervous! I was petrified. My only communication with Marcus had been that note. I had no idea how he would react to me, indeed, I had no idea how I would react to him. I took the DART to the Rockefellers and judging from the number of cars in the driveway I was probably the only poor person to have used nasty public transport that evening.

I rang the bell and the door was answered by a youngish woman who looked startlingly like Angela, only with none of the latter's charm or open manner. When I told her who I was, she greeted me with what my granny would have called a 'tenant's nod'. I thought her rather rude. Inside, the place was thronging with uncles, aunts, nieces, nephews, cousins, neighbours, friends. In a normal house you would have had to stack them on top of each other to fit them all in, but this house was huge, so everyone fit in with a fair degree of comfort.

The house was eloquent about its owners. Here was wealth, but not of the nouveau variety. This was old money. The place was crammed with antiques, but these weren't acquired in an antique shop and displayed as 'key pieces'. Every chair, every table, every picture looked perfectly at home and comfortable in its spot because it had probably been there for as long as it could remember. The house was grand and impressive, but it was not welcoming. Mrs Meredith offered me a cursory greeting and Mr Meredith offered me a brief how do before heading off in search of worthier company.

There was no sign of Marcus yet, but I didn't know if I was glad of the respite or whether it simply offered more time for my nerves to work themselves up into an even higher pitch. I could see Angela in the other room, but she was doing her hostess bit so I decided to leave her to do her duty. I grabbed myself a glass of champagne and amused myself by scanning the photos and pictures of relatives and worthy ancestors which covered the vast wall space.

Just as I was inspecting a print of some Judge Meredith or other, a voice from behind me declared that 'he was a kindly man in his own way, but he did hang people.' I turned around to see an elderly gentleman with a kind face. A Meredith? I wasn't sure, he looked too pleasant.

'Who are you?'

'My name is Anna, I'm a friend of Angela's.'

'Who's Angela?'

'Angela Meredith.'

'I'm Gerard Meredith. Which one is she then?'

'That one,' I said, pointing to her.

'Ah, Angela, of course. Lovely girl, so much nicer than her bloody sisters and brothers. She's the daughter I never had,' he said with a sigh. 'Let's find a seat.'

'Do you know anyone here?' he asked as we sat down. 'No? Well then, I'll give you a guided tour. See that one?' he asked, pointing at the girl who let me in, 'that's Elizabeth, the eldest girl. She's a doctor, a registrar now in fact, well on her way to becoming a consultant. The man standing next to her *is* a consultant and also her husband, so that's quite useful for her. Michael over there,' he said, pointing his finger quite angrily at a tall and very good-looking man, 'is a total bollocks . . . pardon my French. He's also a barrister, his wife's a vet. And finally, that one, yes the skinny one, is Niamh, a psychiatrist. So you can see what Angela is up against. The poor girl being only a shopkeeper and all that. She's not quite the black sheep, she's the grey one. *I* am the black sheep, the devil incarnate sheep if you will. However, being heathens, they of course will be the ones to suffer the everlasting torments of hell.' Then he laughed and I couldn't decide whether he was nice but mad or just mad.

'I'm sure you're wondering what the hell I'm talking about.' Before I had time to answer, he launched into an explanation. 'You see, they,' he said with a magisterial wave of his arm around the room, 'are all heathen Prods. I converted to the one true church back in nineteen forty. In fact, I went off to Buckfast to become a monk. *I had a spot of bother with my nerves,*' he whispered. 'I think you young people call it stress now, just before I was due to take my vows. Anyway, Abbot Grey sent me off to, em, *recover*, to Sligo in fact, for a holiday. Dreary place, I've always hated it. Anyway, fortunately for me, unfortunately for the abbey, I met a girl there, Kate. She was lovely and I was smitten. I spent a month of joy in that hole with the lovliest girl I had ever met . . . she had a bit of a temper sometimes, though. Needless to say, I ended up slightly confused. I was, after all, supposed to be heading back to take vows. So I left Sligo and tried to get back to what had been till then a normal life. But something about it all didn't suit me any more. I was wandering around in a haze. I think I left half of myself in Sligo and Abbott Grey was an astute man, he knew something was up. He took me aside one day and asked me if I was sure about my vocation to the monastic life and all of a sudden I *was* sure, sure that I didn't have one. So I left, went back to Sligo, asked Kate to marry me and she said yes and there you go. Never looked back. What was the point of telling you all this? I can't remember. Where's Kate?' Elizabeth was walking past just as he said this. She stopped, bent down and explained in a clear, slow and clinical way that Kate was dead. She died last year. Then she walked off. It was as though someone had just asked her the time. Poor Gerard's face fell; he looked as though someone had just kicked him in the stomach.

'Oh,' he said sadly, 'what *will* I do without her? Ah, Kate,' he sighed. Then he suddenly perked up again.

'Oh look!' he cried. 'It's young Marcus! Do you know him? He's a great friend of Angela's. I always had a hope that she might marry him, instead of that great lump she's saddled herself with. But there's no accounting for taste, is there? Do you have a young man? No? I'm surprised, a nice-looking girl like you.' He paused and then exclaimed excitedly, 'I know, I'll introduce you to Marcus!'

He waved at and called out to Marcus, who, seeing me, flushed and hesitated but then made his way towards us.

'Mr Meredith, how are you? Good to see you again. Anna, how are you?' he added in a slightly more subdued manner.

'How are you, Marcus?'

'Ah, you two already know each other! Excellent! Oh, excuse me, here comes my beloved grand-niece, so if you don't mind I am just going to . . . .' And with that he slipped away into the crowd.

'How have you been?' I asked.

'Crap. And you?'

'I missed you.'

'And I missed you. Hence the feeling crap,' he smiled faintly.

We quickly fell into an uneasy silence.

'John's been invited, you know,' I announced.

'I know.'

'But of course you know, sorry, I'm not thinking.'

'I think it might help him bury that ridiculous crush of his once and for all,' he said with an uncharacteristic bitterness.

'Do you think it'll work?' I asked tentatively.

'I doubt it. You don't get over something like that, or at least you oughtn't to.' He paused, then continued, 'But he realises that he has to get on with the rest of his life and he can't do that if he continues to hanker after what he can't have.' He looked at me sadly. Two more minutes of that look and I would have feared for my resolution, but Mrs Meredith chose that perfect moment to leap on Marcus from behind.

'Marcus, I didn't see you arrive. How lovely to see you again!' She went to air kiss him, but whether by accident or by design, the kisses landed firmly on his cheeks. He had one lovely big lipstick mark on each cheek. She was bleary eyed already, but not so bleary eyed that she didn't give me a good, disapproving once-over.

'Black would appear to be your signature colour, Anna. But of course you do look nice.' I had already noticed the number of young lovelies floating around in enchanting, flimsy, pale chiffon and was beginning to feel like an Italian widow. Angela, who had just joined us, bristled at her mother's tactlessness.

'Anna looks lovely, as always. Doesn't she, Marcus?'

'Yes,' he offered a little flatly.

Mrs M. then (literally) whisked Marcus off to the drinks. She linked arms with him and asked him amicable and bland questions about his family and work. I was left with Angela, who was joined by Xavier, who greeted me with his usual indifference. I was forced to endure some boring conversation with him while Angela stared stupidly and dumbly at her Prince Charming, hanging on his every boring word. I wish I could recount the conversation, but I honestly can't remember it. In fact, I can't actually remember anything the man ever said. All this time I've been making up dialogue for him. I struggled for such a long time and wasted too many precious pages of my notebook trying to make him seem more three dimensional. After several attempts, I accepted that the problem, just this once, wasn't my ability, but the fact that Xavier was as dull and flat as any human can be. Apart, perhaps, from Tom.

The place was stuffed full of middle-aged women with big hair and Escada outfits and as I passed through the throng of beautiful and appropriately dressed girls I felt desperately funereal in 'that black dress', which I had been forced to wear through lack of options. I had attempted to relieve the austerity by wearing my pink cardi, but now I just felt hot and looked a mess.

I made my way through the hall, through the enormous drawing room and out the doors to the garden. Angela had been lucky with the weather. The day had been unseasonably hot and sunny and was turning itself into a lovely, still and balmy evening. A flight of steps led from the drawing room down into the garden. These had been strewn with tiny nightlights and a very slight breeze from passing dresses caused them to waver and sparkle in the dusk. The trees had all been strung with white lights and the charm of it had lured many of the guests out onto the lawn.

Marcus sat on a bench at the end of the garden talking with Gerard, who saw me and beckoned me over with a wave of his hand.

'There's that girl again. She's a ringer for Kate!' he said to Marcus as I approached.

Then Mrs M. appeared out of nowhere again and descended like a Valkyrie on poor Gerard. She insisted that he come indoors as the dew would be bad for his rheumatism. Gerard told her politely where she could go, but she replied that she wasn't going anywhere without him. He reluctantly gave in, telling her that he was only doing so because he needed another drink and Marcus and I needed to get acquainted, obviously having forgotten the fact that Marcus and I already knew each other. Gerard's disappearance left Marcus and I nursing another silence, which he decided to break by getting me another drink. He snatched my nearly full glass from my hand and charged back into the house. I sighed at his unsubtle attempts to avoid me, but I couldn't really blame him.

While he was gone I spotted an unusually cheerful-looking John at the top of the steps. I waved to him and he beamed back at me and made his way down the garden. We made our usual polite enquiries of each other and just as I was wondering at his lack of dejection, he raised his arm and waved to someone. I followed his gaze and saw a very dark and very pretty woman of about my own age approaching us. He introduced her as Maria, a colleague of Marcus's. Apparently they had met one evening when John had joined one of their Friday night post-work sessions. Of course I was happy that John had found someone to take his mind off Angela, but secretly the deeply buried romantic in me was a tiny bit disappointed. Apparently there was no such thing as ever-lasting love.

Marcus returned with my drink and seemed ludicrously happy to see the other two and I found myself growing silent as they grew animated and decided to take myself back inside for another aimless wander. As I was helping myself to yet another glass of wine I heard a booming voice behind me.

'Hoi, it's Angela's flatmate, isn't it?' I recognised the awful voice and the braying laugh. I turned around to find Peter Mahoney smiling, or rather leering, drunkenly at me.

'I almost didn't recognise you in that dress. Has anyone ever told you that you have fuckin' great legs?' As if this wasn't a bad enough start he continued to rattle on under the assumption that I remembered who he was, which I found rude. When he eventually paused for breath I asked him his name. Yeah, I know I knew who he was, but I didn't want him to know that he was memorable in any way. I hoped that he might be insulted by my failure to notice him. No such luck.

'I'm Peter, a . . . erm . . . *friend* of Angela's.' He emphasised the word 'friend' with a suggestive smirk. 'Fantastic fuckin' news about her and that bollocks Xavier, isn't it? She's a great girl,' he chortled. His speech was ever so slightly slurred and his florid complexion was practically alight. I agreed with him about the engagement and began to politely excuse myself when he suddenly demanded what I did for a living, but before I could answer, he launched into a spiel about what he did. Wish I could tell you what that was, but I dozed off. I was thinking about how I could make my exit before he gave me any more details about the engine of his brand-new car when he asked me if I would like to go outside and take a look. I sighed and agreed as I couldn't think of any excuse why I wouldn't want to that wouldn't involve insults and swear words. Most men would have taken my indifference as a put-off, but Peter, alas, did not.

'Here she is,' he beamed proudly, running his hand along the bonnet of something small and red. It had the correct number of wheels and a windscreen and a steering wheel. In so far as it had all its component parts in all the right places, it was a lovely car. Some think all babies look the same: I feel the same way about cars.

'Oh, look,' I said in as bored a voice as I could manage, 'it has a little picture of a horse on the front. How sweet.' His response was a patronising laugh and a sudden invasion of my private space. Abandoning all semblance of manners, I turned and walked back into the house. I lurked at the top of the garden steps. A band had been hired for the evening. They had been playing all the usual wedding numbers and a handful of brave people were dancing on the lawn. A few of the women had abandoned their foolish, pointy, high-heeled mules and were dancing barefoot on the grass. It all looked terribly picturesque and romantic.

'Not dancing?' A voice boomed into my right ear. Peter again. 'Could I tempt you?' he asked in a way that suggested he was assuming the answer.

'No thanks, I have two left feet.'

'Oh, come on, you can't be that bad surely?' He proceeded to dance around me in what I can only imagine he thought to be a provocative manner. This was mortifying. Each time I tried to leg it down the steps he leapt in front me to block my way.

'Not so fast, not going to let a fine thing like *you* sneak off on me again!' I felt as if I was trapped in a *Carry On* movie. I looked up in exasperation and saw Marcus coming up the garden.

'That's a lovely foxtrot you have there, Peter, where did you learn to do that?'

'Marcus, how are you?' asked a suddenly static and visibly cringing Peter.

'Where did you get to?' Marcus asked as he took my hand and led me down the steps. My rational side was irritated by this little display of manly forcefulness. Who did he think he was? For all he knew I might have fancied Peter.

'Thanks very much, Mr Manly. I was enjoying that.' I was trying to sound stroppy but started laughing.

'I thought that if you ended up with Peter Mahoney then all my faith in women is dead and I'm off to join a monastery.'

'Oh please, give me *some* credit.'

John and Maria were among the brave pilgrims leading the dancing. The band wasn't the worst and as they played on more and more people left their inhibitions at the bottom of their glasses and so the number of bad dancers increased. Even Xavier joined in. Peter had forgotten me already and was now leaping seductively around some luscious, dark-haired beauty. She, oddly enough, seemed not to mind his attentions.

'So why aren't you dancing, Anna?'

'Like I said to Peter, I have two left feet.'

'You can't be that bad?'

'That's what he said.'

Now if there's one thing I cannot stand, it's the pressure to dance at these occasions. I really cannot dance, but so often people take my protestations for modesty. I've found through years of trial that the quickest way to disabuse someone of this is to demonstrate. Two minutes of my 'free-form' dancing later and Marcus was begging me to sit down.

'Told you I was an embarrassment,' I said with the triumph of vindication.

Don't ask me how long we sat there. I completely lost track of time. I know I sound soft in the head, but the balmy weather, the dancing lights and all those laughing, floaty girls went to my head. Marcus was sitting so close to me I felt dizzy. All the earlier strain between us seemed, inexplicably, to have vanished. He was his old smiling, laughing self. When I knew him first his laugh grated on my nerves. It's a loud, wholehearted belly laugh. It can be embarrassing in public places. Now I found myself delighting in it. It made me smile; it was truly infectious. He threw his head back and laughed at something I had just said and I must have had one such foolish grin on my face, for as he tilted his head back, he looked at me and held my gaze and for the tiniest moment I could hear the obvious making a valiant effort to make itself heard. But I looked away quickly and shook my head as though to rid it of unwanted suspicions. I couldn't afford to start thinking that way now. It was too late. I was leaving.

I'm not sure if he noticed anything. I looked at our glasses and said something about being thirsty again.

'Allow me,' he said.

I got up, partly to stretch my legs, partly to find the bathroom. Sorry, but nature intrudes even on the most romantic of evenings. The band had started to play 'Cry Me a River', which I thought was unsuitable given the occasion. Maria and John were still dancing; she was now leaning on his shoulder. Silly Angela. I found myself thinking of what Jane Austen said about women loving longest, even when all hope is gone. How true, Janey, how true.

I spotted Marcus, with two glasses in his hand and an exasperated expression on his face. He had been nabbed once again by Mrs M. Angela grabbed me and asked me if I was having a good time.

'Oh, yes, thanks.' I could hear vagueness even in my own voice.

'Are you okay?' she asked, looking at me in a searching, bewildered way. My hands flew to my face and I asked her if I had a spot on it or something. She was looking at me strangely.

'You just look, oh, I don't know, different somehow. Oh, ignore me, I'm just drunk and very happy.' I excused myself as I was about to burst.

'Oh, don't use the main one, there's a bit of a queue. Use the one in my parents' room. First on the right as you go up the stairs. Don't tell anyone else about it, they aren't too keen on letting the hoi polloi into their room. And if you see Xavier in your travels, could you tell him I'm looking for him?'

I went upstairs and slid quietly past the angry horde waiting outside the main bathroom. I managed to slip into the bedroom without anyone noticing and shut the door quietly. I noticed that a light was shining from under the bathroom door and I thought I heard a scuffling noise. I knocked gently on the door and waited for a reply. None came, so I opened the door to be confronted by the sight of Xavier leaping away from a very pretty, very young and very dishevelled girl. His consternation was obvious, but surprisingly short lived.

'Anna, you won't tell Angela. This is nothing,' he said as he ran a tidying hand through his hair. He regarded me with a cool look.

'Nothing, Xavier? You're insulting both your fiancée and her,' I nodded my head in the direction of Hazy Jane, who was now standing in front of the mirror, trying to rearrange herself. I don't think she had much idea of what was going on. She kept muttering 'shit' to herself over and over again.

'Really,' he shrugged, 'it would be foolish to tell her. Believe me, it was nothing.' There was a slightly threatening undertone that I didn't care for.

'So if it really is nothing, why would you be afraid to tell her?'

'I'm not *afraid*,' he sneered. 'Could you leave please?' he asked the girl. She began to stumble past me, but I stopped her.

'Fix yourself up before you go downstairs.' I readjusted the strap of her dress to give her a hint. 'And a free piece of advice – try not to go for marrieds next time.'

'I'm not married *yet*,' Xavier snapped at me.

'So that's it? You think it's okay so long as you aren't actually married?'

'No, I think what someone doesn't know can do no harm,' he said in a slow, patronising tone.

'You know, I always thought you were a perfect bastard.'

'With the emphasis on perfect, I hope,' he said, smiling at his little joke. Then he suddenly grabbed my arm. 'If I say this is nothing, then I expect you to believe that, and I would not advise you saying anything to Angela. You should just accept that, Anna.'

'Take your hand off me *now*. I'm not afraid of you, and if you dare lay another finger on me I'll make sure not only that you don't marry Angela, but that you won't make anyone a good husband. Understand?'

He let go his grip and smirked at me, clearly unimpressed by my bravado.

'Tell me something, Xavier, just why are you marrying Angela? I have to admit that I'm curious. You never *did* come across as a man in love, you know.'

'She loves me and everyone must settle down at some stage,' he said as though I had just asked a question with a very obvious answer. 'You're quite feisty. I like that,' he smiled and lightly tipped me under the chin before he swept past me, denying me the chance to tell him where to go.

This was the longest conversation I had ever had with the bollocks, and of course I wondered what the hell I should do. Should I tell? Not tell? Could I let Angela drift along under the illusion that he was Prince Charming? She would, of her own accord, wake up one day to the fact that he was a toad, but was it fair to let her go through with things when one short, sharp blow there and then would put her out of her misery? I went back downstairs in a daze. I had to find Marcus to find out what he thought.

He was waiting for me on the bench.

'Thought you had disappeared,' he smiled. He reached across and tucked a stray strand of hair behind my ears.

'Anna, why—' 'I've just caught Xavier getting off with another woman in Mr and Mrs Meredith's en suite,' I blurted out. It took a few seconds for him to register what I was saying.

'What?' I couldn't quite tell from his tone whether that was short for 'what a bastard' or 'what are you talking about?'.

'What on earth am I supposed to do? I always knew he was scum and Angela confessed to me ages ago that she thought he might be cheating on her. What do we do?' I looked at him as though he was instantly going to come up with a solution.

'I don't know,' he sighed. 'Poor Angela.'

As we were shaking our heads, so to speak, we were distracted by the fact that a lot of people had stopped dancing and that there seemed to be some sort of commotion coming from the house. Then we saw Angela running down the garden, looking dreadfully upset. She had found out! She came up to us.

'It's Gerard,' she said breathlessly, 'something has happened. Something's wrong.' We dashed into the house to find Gerard collapsed, surrounded by anxious faces. Someone had already called an ambulance. Angela was in a state so I held her, telling her that everything would be fine. Platitudinous, I know, but I couldn't think of what else to say. As more people began to realise that something was wrong, the room began to fill with the curious. The band stopped playing. Marcus, with the help of Angela's brothers, cleared everyone out.

'Where's Xavier?' she asked in a whisper. He was standing at the back of the room looking as though all the chaos around him was an inconvenience rather than a potential tragedy. He stepped forward and took her outstretched, shaking hand. The ambulance arrived and took Gerard and Mr and Mrs Meredith. Angela had wanted to go but there was no room.

'Get me to the hospital please,' she asked Xavier.

'How?' he asked stupidly. 'I have no car.'

'A taxi,' she snapped.

'I will call you one, but I don't think there is much point in my going, there would just be too many people around, and besides, I wouldn't be any use to anyone, I hate hospitals.'

Angela gave him a withering look.

'You would be there for *me*. But don't bother if it would all be too much for you.'

'I will phone you tomorrow,' said Xavier as he closed the taxi door on three glaring faces – Angela's, Marcus's and mine.

Gerard didn't last the night.

Xavier did call the next day, but when he was told what had happened, he assumed that she would want to be left alone for a while. What was the man thinking? Angela was in a bad state before he called, but a million times worse afterwards – she had been very attached to Gerard. Xavier rang every day to see if she was all right, but he didn't come to the house until the day of the funeral. She feebly began to explain that Xavier wasn't good in intense, emotional circumstances, but I don't think she managed to convince even herself. By that stage it was too late.

He arrived at the door that morning with a huge white bouquet. The three of us were in the hall waiting for a taxi when the doorbell rang. Angela opened the door.

'I hope I am not too late,' he said with the charming smile that Angela used to ramble on about.

'I'm afraid you are, Xavier, much too late.' She took the flowers from his arms and flung them over his head out into the street and then slammed the door in his face. And that was the end of Xavier. I heard the whole saga in the days that followed.

Angela had a stunningly low opinion of herself. Sh'd been flattered by Xavier's attentions. Of course there was a mutual physical attraction, we all knew about that, but essentially she was flattered that someone so handsome, charming and sophisticated would even notice her. My eyebrows shot up to the ceiling when I heard him described as 'charming'.

'Ang, to everyone else he just seemed like a total pillock.'

'No, really, he could be very charming. Well, he was to me anyway,' she added a little wistfully and I could sense that she was starting to look at things with the all-forgiving sight of regret.

'Do you know what Gerard and I had been talking about just before he had his attack?' I shook my head. 'He was telling me that he didn't like Xavier and that I could do much better for myself.'

'I think he was absolutely right,' I said as I stroked her hair and let her have a good cry.

Chapter Twenty-nine

Naturally things were at sixes and sevens in our house for some time. Being a mother hen to Angela took all my time and energy, so thankfully I didn't have much opportunity to brood on what had happened (or rather hadn't happened) between Marcus and I. Plus it was far too late to start thinking like that now.

I had made a short trip to Armagh one weekend, leaving Angela in the capable hands of Marcus. I had started to grow used to the status quo again. Working in Angela's shop had the charm of novelty, but I forced myself to imagine dealing with the lunatics for years to come and I had to admit that the charm would probably wear off after a year or two. I forced myself not to think about the 'what ifs' of the Marcus situation. When I thought about it logically, I was still really in the rut that I thought I had escaped when I moved in – all I had done was swap one rut for another. At least, that's what my mother told me. I knew she was right, but it galled me to accept advice from her. I never had before. Why start now?

'Because you know I'm right. You can't possibly even think of not going! Suppose you stay. What then? Do you think you'd be happy playing shop-keeper? Of course you wouldn't, you'd get bored and we all know what happens when you get bored, Anna, hmm?'

'We do?'

'You get ill tempered and cranky.'

'I do?'

'Oh yes, quite vicious at times. You were always like that, even as a wee thing. I remember the time—'

'Hang on, hang on! Back up there a bit! Vicious?' Incredulity made my voice shoot up several octaves.

'Yes, you do. Look, surely you must have noticed that the number of our, em, contretemps has decreased drastically since you decided to leave work?'

'Have they?'

'I used to mark our rows in my diary the way you might mark your period. Mind you, if I'd had as many periods as we've had rows—'

'All right, all right, I get the message!'

'There!' she exclaimed triumphantly.

'Wha?'

'"What", dear, "what". But listen to yourself, you're getting all tetchy again. Bored in the shop by any chance? Look, there's no need to get paranoid. All I'm saying is that I can see the seeds of a lot of unhappiness. Don't make my mistake. I resented how my life turned out for so long and I never saw how it might have affected you lot.' Before I had a chance to say anything she began busying herself with pots and pans in a very noisy way. I was stunned. I knew that this was an apology from her, and I had to reciprocate. I went up to her and put my arms around her and just said 'thanks'.

'Now, let's have some cake!'

'Ah, Mother, you and your cakes.'

'Anna,' she began kindly after we had scoffed half a carrot cake and swilled down more tea than was good for us, 'I know the timing of all this change is not the best, but changing your life and your plans for someone is not something to be done lightly . . . especially when you don't know him well enough to know if he's worth it.'

I hadn't thought of things like that, but the minute she said it, I knew she was right. I had to go, regardless of what I *thought* I felt about Marcus.

I returned to Dublin to discover that Angela had had some rather surprising news.

'I always knew he was fond of me, but I never guessed just how much!' she said to me.

Gerard and Kate couldn't have children. They had tried and failed and eventually reached the consolatory conclusion that they had each other and that would have to be enough. As a result, however, they lavished all their pent-up parental love on their nieces and nephews.

Gerard was convinced that from a very young age Angela was the image of Kate – which was, of course, impossible as the two weren't related in any way. Nevertheless, Gerard, and indeed Kate, developed an affection for Angela that far out-stripped what they felt for any of the other nieces and nephews.

'I must have been an incredibly cute sprog, I suppose,' Angela said as she tried to explain their regard.

Much to the Merediths' disapproval and without Angela's knowledge, they opened a bank account in her name. They added to it, and added to it, and even when Kate died, Gerard continued to add to it.

The day before my return, Angela had found out not only about the account, but also that she was now a woman of considerable means, which meant that she could 'close that buggerin' shop. Seriously, though, I may actually do something sensible with it. I may even go back to college, who knows? Though I think I'll start with a little jaunt into BTs,' she smirked.

As my departure drew ever closer, Angela grew increasingly emotional about it.

'I think you're my best mate really,' she announced. 'I'm really pleased for you, but I can't pretend that I won't miss you and I hate you for leaving me!' She paused to consider something, then said gently, 'But I think someone else is going to miss you more.'

'Please, Ang, don't say any more.' I really didn't want to hear what I thought she was going to say.

'He's going to be heartbroken,' was all she said.

Chapter Thirty

Perhaps you're wondering by now what I've done with Marcus, as he hasn't made an appearance in a page or two.

Marcus and I waited at the hospital that night of the party until Angela was ready to come home. She had lost Gerard and already knew that she had lost Xavier, for what he was worth. She was heartbroken and fatigued. Together she and I went upstairs to her room and she stood and dumbly watched as I hauled clothes, books, magazines, make-up and a hairdryer off her bed. She climbed into it gratefully and asked me to sit with her for a bit, which I did. I remembered how when I was little and I couldn't sleep, my father would sometimes come up and gently stroke my forehead, over and over, until the rhythmic movements soothed me into sleep, so I stroked Angela's forehead over and over, until at last I saw sleep creep up on her and carry her off.

When I was sure that her sleep was deep enough, I crept out of the room and downstairs. I had been up there quite a while and so I had assumed that Marcus would just go to bed. But when I came downstairs, I saw that the kitchen light was on.

'How is she?' he asked as I gently closed the door behind me.

'Asleep at last.'

'Good.' Without another word, he reached for my hand and pulled me towards him and put his arms around me. 'Don't go to London.'

'Marcus,' I said, pulling away from him so that I could look at him, 'Marcus, I can't not go. You know that.'

'I know that it's that stubborn bloody independence of yours that attracted me in the first place. Never thought I'd end up suffering as a result of it. Promise me something, though.'

'If I can.'

'That you'll take my notebook with you.'

'I think I can promise you that.'

I don't need to tell you that I didn't sleep terribly well that night. At about four thirty I was still awake. I got up and did something unexpected and out of character. I knocked on Marcus's door. There was no reply, so I opened the door, stepped into the room and quietly closed the door behind me. I crossed the floor to the bed and climbed in. I put my arm around him and shortly after that I drifted off.

We both thought it would be best if he stayed with John till I had gone. We decided to say our good-byes the next day and leave it at that.

'I'll come to the airport,' he offered tentatively.

'No, don't. I don't think I could handle that.'

'So this is it, then, isn't it?' he asked as we loitered on the top step outside the house. For the briefest of moments I considered asking him to come with me, but I quickly realised that I couldn't expect him to do what I wasn't willing to do myself, so I kept quiet.

'Well, goodbye, Anna. I don't think I'll forget you in a long time.'

'Me neither.'

'What, you mean you won't forget yourself in a long time?'

'You know what I mean,' I said with a half-hearted laugh.

'Maybe you should take . . . .' he began as he patted his jacket pockets. 'Aha, this is what I want,' he said as he pulled an old receipt from the left one. 'Now a pen . . . pen . . . ah, here we go. Here, hold these,' he said, handing me his keys. He leaned the receipt against the palm of his hand and wrote on it.

'Keep this safe, just in case. It's easy to get lost in London,' he said as he handed me the receipt. On it he had written: *My name is Anna Malone. If found, please return to Marcus Shaw.*

'Goodbye, Anna.' He ran down the steps, got into his car and drove off.

Chapter Thirty-one

The morning of my departure arrived. I had asked Angela not to see me off as I knew that an emotional farewell at seven o'clock would be more than I could handle. However, she didn't listen and so I left the house wet with her slobbery tears. We swore to keep in contact and I'm happy to report that we have.

As I sat in the airport waiting to board, I drank one horrible cup of coffee after another till my head felt funny and my hands began to shake. I think it must have been the caffeine rush that prompted the irrational hope that maybe, just maybe, a car was pulling up outside and that he was getting out of it. The call came for my flight; I got up and moved towards the departure gates. Maybe, just maybe, he was running in the doors right now, frantically checking the departures board for my flight. I handed over my boarding card and went through to the gate. Maybe, just maybe, he was behind me, wrestling with security, begging them to let him through, that the woman he loved was about to leave and he couldn't let her go. I walked slowly towards the metal detector. I hesitated before going through and involuntarily turned around . . . oh don't be so stupid! Of course he wasn't there. Such things don't happen in real life. And even if he had made a last-minute appearance, could he have changed my mind?

Well, I'll never know.

As I walked out over the tarmac towards the plane it started to pour. I laughed out loud as I wondered if my old friends the gods were trying to tell me something. I couldn't have handled a sunny day anyway.

The first few weeks in London were awful. The few after those were less awful and the following few were less awful again. In other words, I found myself slowly starting to adjust to my new life, and gradually the homesickness and the misery wore away. After a nervous start, work turned out all right. I found my feet after a while and started to enjoy myself. My work colleagues were, for the most part, nice people, and as my confidence began to emerge, my urge to resign decreased.

What hadn't – indeed, what still hasn't – worn off is the novelty of having an in tray that isn't full of crap.

And as for thoughts of Marcus? Well, there was someone at work who I got on really well with. We hung around a lot together and had been out a few times. He was everything Marcus wasn't – reserved, quiet, subtle, intelligent. I was fairly sure that he was ready for something more than just friendship.

But the question was, was I?

One particularly dreary November afternoon as I made my way home from work, my eye was caught by a display in a bookshop window. I had passed it before I suddenly realised what had struck me. I turned back and looked again into the window. There, in the middle of the three-for-two offers, was a book by one Tom Brogan. Of course I had to go in for a closer look. I studied the review on the front of the jacket.

'A challenging and exciting work from one of Ireland's most talented new authors,' said The Irish Times. *'Tom Brogan is a writer of limitless potential, his sensual prose is a joy,' said* The Guardian.

Well, I never! And I thought he was a bit of an intellectual charlatan! I bought the book – God knows why, I practically knew the damn thing off by heart.

That night I had a phone call from Angela.

'You're going to have a bill the size of today and tomorrow if you keep phoning me all the time.'

'Oh, what else are inheritances for?' She was in great form and for a reason. Remember John and Maria? Well, apparently that ended quite shortly after Angela's split with Xavier.

'Typical, fickle man,' I muttered darkly.

'He's not fickle!' she cried, leaping unusually quickly to his defence.

Apparently she'd been moaning one evening that there were no decent men left in the world and that she had given up on them all, blah-de-blah. John exploded in frustration and (almost) shouted at her that if she would only open her bloody eyes she would see that there was one right under her nose.

'I thought he might have meant Marcus and I was a bit embarrassed, given . . . well, you know. Then he turns and roars at me, "not him, *me*"! Well, I was floored. It was a revelation. Apparently he had this crush on me for years and years.'

'It's a miracle, Ang finally wakes up!'

'You mean you knew?' she was astounded.

'It was obvious for all to see, you idiot.'

Anyway, Angela decided she had nothing to lose and was now coming to realise that there was at least one decent guy in the world. There then followed a twenty-minute eulogy on the many perfections of John.

'So I take it you like him then?'

'Just a little.' I could hear the grin on her face.

'You know who's pretty miserable,' she announced without any warning.

'So when are you going to come and visit? Bring John if you like.'

'Anna!'

'What?'

'Stop changing the subject. Marcus has disappeared and has been replaced by some miserable, moaning git that even his two best friends can barely tolerate.'

'Ang, you do this to me every time you call. It's been months now. It's time to stop harassing me.'

'Do you still miss him?'

Did I miss him? What a stupid question. Not a day went by that I didn't think of the fecker every two minutes. I was like the walking wounded. I felt like someone had cut a huge chunk out of me. It was like having a persistent headache; no matter how many painkillers I took, it still wouldn't disappear.

'Of course I miss him, Ang,' I sighed, 'but it's been such a long time, I don't know if . . . and . . . there's someone here . . . .'

'What do you mean?' she sounded edgy.

'I mean there's a guy at work—'

'Oh shite!' she said and slammed the phone down.

One day a few weeks later I went to bed early as I was coming down with some sort of horrid dose.

The next day I could barely keep my head up. When my head went crashing down on the desk in front of me I decided to give in, go home and stay in bed for about ten years. By the third day, however, I began to feel human again and ventured as far as the sofa. I indulged in some daytime television, sitting a manuscript on my lap in order to salve my conscience. After I had learned how to cook the perfect soufflé and discovered the joys of *Judge Judy*, I fell asleep but was woken about three hours later by the doorbell. I plodded out to the door, noting in the mirror that I was looking pale, but not necessarily interesting. I opened the door and barely had time to register who it was before I was grabbed into a suffocating embrace.

'Marcus, I can't breathe.'

He let me pull back a little, but not much.

'I'm not too late, am I?'

I looked at him dumbly. I wondered if I had accidentally overdosed on Benelyn and was in fact hallucinating.

'I've just spent the last couple of months wandering around like a miserable lost soul without you, trying very, very hard to forget about you. And now you just turn up out of the blue for a visit? What are you trying to do to me?' Bloody hell, I could feel myself starting to cry.

'Don't cry,' he said ever so gently and wiped the tears away. The smile he wore was so self-assured, I wanted to thump him.

'What do you expect me to do? You can't just turn up here for a nice little visit, turn everything upside down and then head back home again. It's not fair. You can't do this. God, what timing, Marcus! You leave it just long enough so that I think that maybe, just *maybe* I'm starting to feel all right again and then, like you have some sort of antennae, you pick this up and decide to come swanning over here and—'

'I'm going to leave Dublin!'

'—and you think you can smile your smile at me and . . . you wha?'

'"What", Anna, "what."'

'Have you been talking to my mother?'

He didn't reply, he just smiled.

'Would you stop bloody smiling at me.'

'Anna, it seems I can't do without you. I've no idea why, perhaps it's your grace and charm, who knows. I knew you had to leave Dublin, but after you were finally gone I felt so pissed off that you really *didn't* think I was enough to stay for. I hate to admit this,' he said with a slightly sheepish look, 'but until Angela rang me and told me you had really gone, I, em, kind of, ahm, relied on you changing your mind.'

'You arrogant—'

'And I was very happy being pissed off with you,' he continued hurriedly, cutting right across me, which of course did nothing other than fuel my annoyance. 'But once the novelty of that wore off, I just missed you. Badly. All the time. Non-stop.

379

Constantly. Twenty-four hours a day. Seven days a week. Four weeks a month—'

'Okay, okay, I get the message,' I said quietly.

'So then I got to thinking.'

'Oh dear, did it hurt very much?'

'I got to thinking that maybe I could come over here. If you'd have me.'

'You'd give everything up? Just like that?'

'Just like that,' he smiled. 'But this guy? Am I too late? Would he be on for a duel?'

'There isn't anyone else,' I sighed, and as I said it I realised that it was true. Marcus was a pain in the ass, but I couldn't do without him in the same way that he couldn't do without me.

'I knew really that you'd never meet anyone quite like me again!' There was the cheesy, cocky smile back again, plastered all over his silly face. I'm surprised he didn't leave then as I stopped snivelling and began to laugh. Anyone less tolerant might have thought me mentally unstable.

So there you are. Reunited. I've almost run out of space in my notebook, but there's nothing more to write. You may be asking, 'but did they live happily ever after'? Could someone as arrogant, smarmy, unflappable and infernally good humoured as he is and someone as quick-tempered, grumpy and smart assed as I am live happily ever after? Well, if he doesn't stop singing 'White bloody Christmas' at me every day, I can assure you that it will all end in tears.